Yanina Gotsulsky

MARK SARVAS is the author of the novel *Harry, Revised*, which was published in more than a dozen countries around the world. His book reviews and criticism have appeared in *The New York Times Book Review*, *The Threepenny Review*, *Bookforum*, and many other publications. He is a member of the National Book Critics Circle and PEN America, and teaches novel writing at the UCLA Extension Writers' Program. A reformed blogger (*The Elegant Variation*), he lives in Santa Monica, California.

ALSO BY MARK SARVAS

Harry, Revised

Additional Praise for

Memento Park

"A gripping mystery novel about art that is also a powerful meditation on fathers and sons, and the need to face up to the falsehoods spawned by the horror of the past."
—Salman Rushdie, author of *The Golden House*

"A psychologically rich portrait of familial discord."
—Michael Margas, *Newsday*

"Sarvas is an expert at depicting the dualities of the immigrant experience . . . [He] develops each setting with admirably unique language . . . As its protagonist puzzles over his identity, his relationships, and the painter Ervin Kálmán's troubled past, *Memento Park* assembles these pieces into a satisfying whole."
—Ingrid Vega, *Zyzzyva*

"Mark Sarvas's second novel leaps well beyond his first one into a spectacular realm of imagination and daring. *Memento Park* has everything in precisely the right proportions: pace, plot, suspense, intricate characters, and meditations on the loneliness of a secular Jewish life that are heartfelt . . . In short, Sarvas has somehow managed to nail down in this novel what it means to truly come to terms with a difficult past."
—Elaine Margolin, *The Jerusalem Post*

"A thrilling, ceaselessly intelligent investigation into the crime known as history."   —Joseph O'Neill,
author of *Netherland*

"Sarvas's rich and engaging second novel is worth the decade's wait since his first . . . Sarvas couples a suspenseful mystery with nuanced meditations on father-son bonds, the intricacies of identity, the aftershocks of history's horrors, and the ways people and artworks can—perhaps even must—be endlessly reinterpreted."
—*Publishers Weekly* (starred review)

"Because of its scope and deft handling of aspects of identity in matters of love, family, religion, and loss, this literary work is highly recommended to the broadest audience." —*Library Journal* (starred review)

"Sarvas delivers a lively, thoughtful, psychologically compelling novel about the ties that bind, and the ties that fail to." —*Kirkus Reviews*

"In Mark Sarvas's elegant, poignant, and intellectually arresting novel, the attempts to reclaim a painting seized by the Nazis opens up into a moving story about a father's desire to bury his past and a son's to claim it. Propelled by the intrigue of mystery and suffused with a knowing humor, the novel explores the vagaries of historical memory, the ways in which identity is equal parts inheritance and invention, and the delusions of ownership. *Memento Park*'s reach is wide and its concerns profound."
—Marisa Silver, author of
Little Nothing and *Mary Coin*

Memento Park

Memento Park

MARK SARVAS

Picador   Farrar, Straus and Giroux   New York

MEMENTO PARK. Copyright © 2018 by Mark Sarvas. All rights reserved. Printed in the United States of America. For information, address Picador, 175 Fifth Avenue, New York, N.Y. 10010.

picadorusa.com • instagram.com/picador
twitter.com/picadorusa • facebook.com/picadorusa

Picador® is a U.S. registered trademark and is used by Macmillan Publishing Group, LLC, under license from Pan Books Limited.

For book club information, please visit facebook.com/picadorbookclub or email marketing@picadorusa.com.

Designed by Abby Kagan

The Library of Congress has cataloged the Farrar, Straus and Giroux edition as follows:

Names: Sarvas, Mark, author.
Title: Memento Park / Mark Sarvas.
Description: First edition. | New York : Farrar, Straus and Giroux, 2018.
Identifiers: LCCN 2017038321 | ISBN 9780374206376 (hardcover) | ISBN 9780374713416 (ebook)
Subjects: LCSH: Fathers and sons—Fiction. | Family secrets—Fiction. | Domestic fiction. | GSAFD: Mystery fiction.
Classification: LCC PS3619.A758 M46 2018 | DDC 813'.6—dc23
LC record available at https://lccn.loc.gov/2017038321

Picador Paperback ISBN 978-1-250-31035-4

Our books may be purchased in bulk for promotional, educational, or business use. Please contact your local bookseller or the Macmillan Corporate and Premium Sales Department at 1-800-221-7945, extension 5442, or by email at MacmillanSpecialMarkets@macmillan.com.

First published by Farrar, Straus and Giroux

First Picador Edition: March 2019

10 9 8 7 6 5 4 3 2 1

FOR THE FATHERS:

Szarvas, Mihaly (1927–2009)

Szarvas, Dezső (1899–1973)

Geszti, Jozsef (1904–1977)

It seems that things are more like me now,
that I can see farther into paintings.
I feel closer to what language can't reach.
—RAINER MARIA RILKE, *"Moving Forward"*

The first problem in finding a lost father is to
lose him, decisively.
—DONALD BARTHELME, *"A Manual for Sons"*

Memento Park

CLASSIFICATION: Paintings
ACCESSION NUMBER: 56.838

Budapest Street Scene
1925
Ervin Kálmán, Hungarian, 1883–1944
Oil on canvas mounted on cardboard
57 × 63 cm
Whereabouts unknown

Part One

I STAND BEFORE THE PAINTING, which is small and, frankly, ugly. I can admit that at last, can finally see it, since it no longer represents serendipitous millions or retrieved history or much of anything more than a garish trio of midnight revelers on the *Andrássy út*. It's about two feet square and is full of sound. Receding echoes of the last war mingle with the next war's approaching thunder, ahead of which the jittery brushstrokes struggle to remain. The work is hobbled by interwar deprivation: brittle cardboard in lieu of canvas, the cheap paints cracked with age. The world reducing itself to ash around him, and still he painted. Making do. Now, in its nocturnal solitude, clinging to the baize wall of the empty auction house, the painting looks smaller and uglier still. These doomed Hungarian partiers, faces strangely like crows—or is it ravens? Why do I always think of ravens?—bounded by thick black lines, impasto sludge gurgling within. How could I have failed to notice its shabbiness until now?

I'm here, alone at night, at the indulgence of the venerable auction house of Hathaway and Sons. To say goodbye, I told them. To spend one last evening communing with these shades, my request tinged with the unspoken threat of taking my ill-gotten gain to one of their rivals. I am aware of my presence in this room, of the figure I must appear to cut, my fealty always to my unseen audience. My ostentatious gravity. This weakness for the grand gesture must come from my father, a cardplayer. Lately, I find myself wondering if he was any good at it. Cards, that is. My mother left him about five years ago, so perhaps by the old adage, he was. I only have his word on that, though I've come to see how little that means.

The street outside is quiet now, punctuated by the occasional late-night bus whishing along the damp blacktop. In a dozen hours or so, this gilded room will begin to fill with murmuring buyers straining for this elusive masterpiece. The doors will open promptly at ten, and Monsieur Leclos, my glistening French auctioneer, assures me it will be standing room only. Kálmáns are few and far between, and the appearance of a new one on the market, especially one as celebrated as the sixth and final *Budapest Street Scene*, will turn out the deep pockets. The painting, he assures me, will sell well beyond its estimate, renowned as he is for wringing every last bid from the room.

And so, tomorrow *Budapest Street Scene* will no longer be mine. Though I suppose, technically, it stopped being mine as of seven o'clock this evening, when I advised Rachel, my very capable attorney and erstwhile traveling companion, to call Rabbi Wolfe and convey to her my final instructions. Actually, it was, I see now, never really mine at all, though that scarcely seems to matter now. At least these final hours will be mine. Ours.

What a strange journey this has been. Do you ever think back to our afternoon in Budapest, Rachel, that sweltering day among the statues, so close to the end of all this? Were you thinking about it as you hung up the phone, secretly proud of my decision, as I'm sure you were, as I wanted you to be? With so much to think about, I am surprised how often my memory returns to that mad moment, the sun blazing on our perspiring bodies, your sweat-soaked thighs sliding feverishly against my—

I'm sorry. I've been inaccurate. I am not alone tonight. A solitary security guard shambles about the place, fiddling with keys on a retractable chain. Thin hair, thick middle, ill-fitting black polyester trousers and shirt, the latter with the name of his security firm—VIGIL, if you can believe it—stenciled across his heart. Though at first glance, I read it as Virgil. He regards me suspiciously, not, I think, because he recognizes me, although that's certainly possible, but because my behavior is probably beyond his imagining. What can there be to look at for so long in a single painting, he must wonder. Surely, he can only conceive some sinister purpose, that I'm casing the joint, trying to figure out how to make my getaway with the painting. The thought had occurred to me. But what I'd rather do, what I still might do before this long night is over, is tell him that it's possible to spend an entire lifetime looking at something, and even then, to fail to behold it in any meaningful way.

For example, if he were to come and stand beside me, absently yanking on his keys, I might point out that one of the revelers appears to bear a slight resemblance to himself. I would ask him to try to imagine himself on a street like that one, so different from the ones he knows, this city with its wide, palm-lined boulevards. I would ask him to try to feel the jostling pressure of the crowd, to hear the guttural music of the language, to inhale the smells of sizzling lard, garlic, and paprika. I would ask him to try to imagine being oblivious to approaching doom.

I suspect he would nod politely and place his chair where he could keep a constant eye on me. You're onto me, aren't you, Virgil? Perhaps I've sold you short—your eyes, though tired behind thin, wire-rimmed glasses, show flashes of empathy.

There are no such flashes in the dead, shark eyes of your canvas doppelgänger. The face is largely featureless, but the eyes stand out from the inverted triangle, repositories of an eternal nothingness, and I find myself wondering yet again how I could have failed for so long to see this painting for what it is, a rotted memory, an epitaph to everything that I imagined I knew.

MY NAME, THE NAME I USE, IS MATT SANTOS. The name I was born with is Mathias Santos. The name I might well have been born with is Mátyás Szantos. I am none of these people and I am all of them. I was born the year America elected president a B-movie actor who promised them a "shining city on a hill"; born to a refugee fleeing an old country in ruins who believed in such visions.

I am an actor, and although you probably don't know my name, chances are you would recognize my face. My IMDb listing is littered with roles like "Second Engineer" and "Reporter #3," and though the work might seem trivial to you, I've established a reputation among the people who fill these thousands of roles as a reliable, drama-free journeyman who can be counted upon to arrive on time, find a reasonably original way to deliver my lines (though not so original that I risk eclipsing the star), and to behave with moderation at the craft services table and with the female production assistants. When the part calls for a brainy expositor with just a dash of edge, I have been on the casting directors' short lists for several years. I've been in a dozen films you are sure to know, have stood in the glow of the women whose exploits you follow in gossip magazines (careful never to get in their sight lines), have donned costumes from three of the last four centuries and one yet to come, and even enjoyed a brief moment of attention for playing a character with a proper name on a television series that was a low-rated critical darling for the only season of its existence. I've dabbled in Shakespeare, Beckett, all the stations of the cross you visit to assert your thespian bona fides, but in truth, I am not much of an actor and never have been. What I have is the convincing appearance of a certain ragged intelligence. Whether I actually possess it or not, I look the part: dark-eyed intensity, slight of stature but firm in the conviction of my wits, the man who gets the last word in the heated argument about which deadly tunnel the hero must crawl through or what the nuclear terrorist's next move is likely to be. That intensity has kept me working for more than a decade.

It is an absurd way for an adult to make a living, and I am often embarrassed by it, my embarrassment compounded by the fact that my name never quite comes to the lips of those who squint and cock their heads my way with that look of almost-recognition. I remember watching my first televised role, a one-line walk-on in a popular New York police drama, with my parents in our Queens living room. My assignment was to let the star know that his next interview had arrived. My character was required to stick his head around a corner and say, "We've got Hughes in interview three." The star looked my way with appropriate gravity, contemplating the difficult exchange awaiting him, and murmured "Thanks" with a heat that validated his weekly millions. He rose to face poor, bereft Hughes and faded to a commercial.

I turned to my parents expectantly. My mother was effusive, hugged me proudly, but my father cleared his throat, unsure what to say. "Vhere vas the rest of you?" It was the best he could manage. I stared at him, deflated. "Your face, they only showed us your face. Vhere vas the rest of you?" Despite forty years in America, his *w*'s and *v*'s remained stubbornly interchangeable.

I tried to explain the mechanics of the shot, the director's intention (which had less to do with art and more with wanting to shoot as few setups as possible), but finally gave up.

"It's a line," I said. "My first speaking part. On network TV."

"How much did they pay you?" His favorite question; I would hear it often.

I cited a figure that was more than he made in a week. My mother gasped. I was nineteen, and by the end of that year, I would be living on my own in Los Angeles.

THE LONG TRAIL to my private audience with *Budapest Street Scene* began, as such journeys often do, with a phone call. It came while Tracy and I were decorating our Christmas tree. My family always kept Christmas trees, and I've maintained the tradition, something not uncommon among Jews of my parents' generation and nationality, as Rabbi Wolfe later explained to me in a friendly moment before our battle was joined. The trees of my childhood were my mother's doing. She said she preferred the riot of color to the quiet monochrome of the menorah, but my mother is prone to mischief, and perhaps the tree was another of her quiet provocations. After all, this is the same woman who chose to name her Jewish son after the author of one of the Gospels, although, as she would have it, she simply liked the way it sounded. So it is possible that, in my mother's case, a tree is, in fact, merely a cigar.

Either way, decorating a Christmas tree did not, for me, contain the slightest religious reverberation. Nor for Tracy, the daughter of Catholic hippies, whose sole remnant of her up-bringing was an obsessive opposition to the death penalty; al-though she delighted in the yuletide ritual. For me, hanging ornaments was what one did around the middle of December, and I was nothing if not dutiful in doing what was expected, with all the flourishes that such moments are supposed to include. Cocoa in mismatched mugs, a Bach cello suite issuing from hidden speakers, a fire popping and hissing in the grate. It was cold, or what passes for cold in this city, and we were wearing comfortably oversized sweaters. I know how things are supposed to look, and I've always been good at mimicry. And so my fiancée, with her face that launched a thousand direct-mail catalogs, and I tended to our simulacrum of holiday cheer. Gusts of wind occasionally thudded at the picture window.

I confess an embarrassing weakness for tinsels and ribbons and lights and glittering balls and garlands, my mother's riot still churning within me. Whereas Tracy favors simple color schemes, no more than *tricolore*, like her salads: tasteful, small ornaments, a single string of tiny lights and nothing more. Every year, I relinquish control of the operation, and every year I concede that her vision is more elegant than my own, even as I lament the loss of a certain brio.

The ringing of the phone surprised us both. Our lives are conducted via cell phone, the landline reduced to an ironic, retro accessory. Answering it is my assignment—I'm the one who insists on keeping it, Tracy is content to let voice mail intervene—but since I was occupied twisting our solo strand of lights at a key juncture, she picked up. She listened with a frown, and then handed the phone to me.

"For you. A woman. Some kind of accent." Tracy once had a hint of a jealous streak, though it had all but disappeared of late. It's a shame, it was one of the many things I found charming about her. Along with, of course, her stunning, Nordic good looks, so high a contrast to my own brutish Eastern European features. Tall, lithe, icily blonde, Tracy is every Jewish boy's shiksa fantasy writ large. Given the distribution of physical beauty in our relationship, the thought that she would ever have reason to be jealous has always struck me as risible. I took the phone from her hand.

"Hello?"

"Good evening. Is this Matt Santos?" Yes, an accent. Australian.

"Speaking."

"My name is Joanne Mockley, and I am calling from the Australian consulate."

I paused. "Yes?"

"Mr. Santos, I wonder if you might be able to come down and meet with us tomorrow. We have come across some information regarding your family that you might find of interest."

"My family? My family is Hungarian. I think there's some kind of mistake."

"Your grandfather was Bela Szantos? And your father is Gabor?"

"Yes, that's right."

"There's no mistake."

The look on my face must have betrayed my confusion because Tracy paused in her labors to look at me with curiosity. I shrugged.

"Look, I need to know what this is about. Am I in some kind of trouble?"

The woman spoke uneasily. "No, Mr. Santos. But it's rather complicated and to try to explain now would lead to many more questions. It's regarding some property that belonged to your family in Hungary during the war."

"The war? Which war?"

She cleared her throat.

"The Second World War. I realize this is all very unexpected, but if you'd come down tomorrow at ten a.m., I should be able to explain."

I scribbled an address downtown and hung up the phone.

"What was that about?" Was there impatience in her tone? A hint, maybe. I can't remember.

"I honestly have no idea." I relayed the entire conversation to her, and we spent twenty fruitless minutes guessing. Perhaps some real estate? That seemed unlikely; my grandfather's apartment had been sold by my father after the Soviet Union collapsed. An unclaimed bank account? Also unlikely. My mother had done a thorough job with her father-in-law's estate when he died, while my father had been busy doing what? Playing cards? Recovering from one of his heart attacks? I could only remember he was nowhere in evidence. No, surely it was just some kind of bureaucratic formality, a last echo of the Cold War. We soon realized we were getting nowhere, and so we finished decorating the tree.

Tracy kissed me on the cheek and absented herself to prepare for bed, a royal procession of creams and ablutions, and I dropped into an armchair and fiddled with the cold, coagulating remains of my cocoa. The more I thought about it, the more questions I had. Why had they contacted me, and not my father? What property could they possibly have been talking about? I knew that my father was seven when the Germans invaded Hungary. I knew his mother, one of Europe's six million, had been killed before his father managed to spirit them away to London, by means never revealed or discussed. They certainly never spoke of riches left behind.

Then I remembered my last call to my father, that odd

exchange. It had probably been about a month prior, which was generally the longest I could go without calling before some half-hearted sense of filial obligation sparked a brief and strained phone call. I would inquire after his health. He would inquire after my career and love life, but only politely, never betraying much interest in either. In the early calls after his divorce, he would ask if I had spoken to my mother, but my response—a terse *What do you care*—was enough to eliminate that from our limited repertoire. Then the inevitable closing: Not "Goodbye," certainly not "I love you," but rather his admonition to "pushpushpush," a rapid-fire exhortation, thick with implication that I must surely be slacking. I would set down the receiver, the nerve at the base of my neck just above my collarbone twitching.

I don't know why his recalcitrance bothered me as much as it did, as we never had a great deal to say to each other, even when I was a child. Serious conversations were my mother's domain. My father was devoted to task management—arranging for, providing for, handling things—and our interactions were limited to expressions of need (mine) followed by a best attempt (his) to fulfill those needs. I have no doubt that he took his responsibilities as a provider seriously, indeed, but I have come to see that list of necessities as damningly practical. What would he have done, what neural gasket would he have blown if, when he asked whether I needed anything—pocket money for school or a new pair of sneakers—my ten-year-old self had replied that I needed him to tell me something about himself that I didn't know? He would have suspected some malign angle because he himself was a pursuer of angles.

The few times he did tell me stories, they centered, bizarrely, on his sexual exploits as a young man. He loved to recount, in inexplicable detail and with particular emphasis on blow jobs, losing his virginity at thirteen to his father's young book-keeper. My grandfather ran a barely solvent commercial paint-ing business in postwar Hungary. He'd wanted, of course, to be an artist before the war and legend has it he was a gifted copy-ist. He'd sit for hours in the National Museum, making pains-taking studies of old masters. A small canvas of his hung for years in my bedroom as a child, an Arcadian landscape après Poussin as I recall, gamboling sheep and thin reeds upon the surface of a still pond. I don't know what became of it.

But in classic Santos fashion, when he ventured beyond the safe limits of imitation, he failed. After all, second-raters run in the family. His banal landscapes were out of fashion before the paint dried, as kitschy as the gypsy music he favored, and so upon returning to Hungary from England, he opened the shop. Those few lean years of bohemian struggle had instilled in both father and son a terror of want and a subsequent prac-ticality that my father would never forget. I'm sure that's why my grandfather chose to return to Budapest a few years after the war ended. The idea of commencing a second, English-speaking life must have felt beyond him. My father would have to wait for the 1956 revolution for his own chance to quit Hungary.

But in those youthful days, he worked hard learning the family business, mastering the trade that he would bring to America. Years later, he would pause when we passed drying paint and sniff for a long moment or two, then shake his head and walk on. At first I assumed he was reflecting on the declin-ing quality of paint, but I later wondered if he was trying to reach back through the years and smell *her* again, this unnamed bookkeeper. The coupling was frantic and rushed, unroman-tic, in a supply closet, the pair of them high on paint fumes. My grandfather was reliably absent in those days, pursuing his own paramours—another family trait, I am dismayed to discover—so my father had the run of the shop. He learned, it seems, a good deal more than the family business.

This and other stories, told many times before, had entered the family lore, so when we did speak on the phone, there was almost nothing left to say. Which was why that last phone call surprised me. When we came to the juncture to bid each other an eager farewell, my father inquired whether I had documented my key financial information in case something should happen to me, so that Tracy would be taken care of. He was concerned, given we were not yet married, and Tracy would have no legal rights, though what fate he expected to befall me he did not elaborate. Still, I was strangely moved. He'd always liked Tracy, approved of my choice of her in a way that he seldom approved of anything I did. She, in return, was fond of him, laughing at his dreadful puns and generally appearing to agree with his low estimation of my gifts, this done for his benefit, she assured me. I lied to him, as I had many times before, and told him that Tracy was my designated beneficiary in all financial matters. Now I wondered about the timing of his request, wondered if something the Australians were going to tell me had already come across his radar. I thought of calling him to ask, but it was midnight in New York. Such a breach of unstated protocol might well set off the poor bastard's notoriously unstable ticker. I wanted to know, but I didn't want to know that badly.

OF THE THREE CENTRAL FIGURES in the painting, the one I find most arresting is the man on the far left, the one who resembles my vigilant guardian. It's the women we're supposed to notice, one done up garishly in red, the other in electric blue, her head perched atop a high collar. They anchor the painting's visual elements, center everything, but it's the dandyish young man with them who draws my eye. His back is turned to us and the ladies, but he's looking over his shoulder in their direction, giving them, and us, it seems, a second thought. There's something about his apartness, his irresolution, that I cannot shake off.

Deeper in the background indistinct members of the Hungarian bourgeoisie hurry to the cafés, the opera, the parties that await them. The figures are a blur of activity, and although good cheer abounds, there's something sinister about the picture. Perhaps it's the fourth figure, a small, hunched man in the lower right, decked out in top hat and tails but, if you ask me, up to no good as he regards the ladies from afar. His facial expression is an indecipherable smudge, but I'd wager on a leer. The gray stone facades of the *Andrássy út* are only suggested as deep shadows, but they frame the action, proscenium-like, and there's something almost malignant about the way they close in on the subjects and the viewer.

I have stared at this painting for months, thought about it

incessantly. I've read everything I could find on the work, on the artist, Ervin Kálmán, who blew his brains out just hours ahead of the Nazis' arrival in Budapest. I've read monographs, biographies, you name it. That's my specialty, after all, throwing myself into my research, since one never knows where the useful note that brings a role to life will be found. I've imagined lives for each of the painting's figures, this one a cabaret dancer or a jazz singer, that one a daughter of a well-to-do merchant. I've also imagined them dead, gone, everyone on the street wiped out within a decade. There's nothing specifically Jewish about the painting or its subject, but Kálmán was a Jew, and anyway I don't need facts to justify my imaginings. But the thing I imagine most often is that the dandyish young man, the one looking back, is my father. Impossible, I know. My father was not yet born when the painting was painted, but the leap isn't hard for me to make. It's easy to imagine him already beginning to make his move, taking that first step from the cataclysm that would sweep away the others.

My silent Virgil glances my way, chewing his pungent tuna sandwich, sour like urine. Have I spoken out loud? Hard to say. Tracy advised me that I'd developed a habit of muttering all sorts of things. Names, for example. Who is Rachel, she asked me when my mind drifted as we passed Olympic Boulevard Synagogue. She scrutinized me like a poker player as I steadily explained that Rachel was Jacob's wife. Genesis, I think. Those half-truths again. Apparently, at that moment, I'd muttered her name, in a tone Tracy characterized as pleading. Thankfully, she did not think to ask how I had come by what must have seemed to her a piece of Jewish arcana, but I could feel her questioning eyes upon me for the rest of the drive. What else have I been saying out loud?

MY MEMORY OF ANYTHING to do with my family's religion is limited to two episodes. In the first, I was taken to synagogue by my father's father on one of his rare visits to New York. I was a reluctant if dutiful sidekick, eight years old, awkward in my navy blazer and stiff gray slacks, the extent of my formal wear. My father made a show of not attending, though my mother suggested this was an opportunity for some special time with my grandfather. But his extreme age—I remember thick black and gray hairs curling from his ears—and foreign tongue separated us as we trudged the eight blocks to the neighborhood temple. When we arrived, my grandfather took his half-smoked cigar from between his teeth and set it out of view on the lip of the synagogue's foundation stone. I gestured curiously, and he explained in broken English and gestured that the cigar was still good and he would be reunited with it after the service.

Inside, the first thing I noticed was the absence of women. Had I missed a sign coming in, instructing all women not to proceed further? Were they all outside, waiting in their cars? They had to be somewhere, and I spent much time fretting about them, only gradually becoming aware of the possibility that, absent women, some strange power was about to be exercised. My grandfather handed me a kippah, and when I looked at it uncomprehendingly, he scowled and slapped it atop my head. Until he shoved my hand away, I could not stop fussing with it, wondering whether it would slip off and what punishment would befall me if it did.

Sitting on the cold polished bench, I went first for the prayer book, fascinated by the mysterious language that filled its pages. It resembled the Civil War cipher I had memorized for passing notes in class. I tried to connect the symbols on the page to the musical sounds coming out of the rabbi's mouth, but couldn't. I turned my attention to the simple but striking stained glass above the ark, within which a worn Torah slept. My grandfather placed his hand on my knee to stop me from tapping my foot when the cantor sang.

Toward the end of the service, the rabbi pointed at me and indicated I should join him. My first thought was that my kippah had slipped off, but it was secure, pressed into place, it seemed, by Yahweh's long finger. Dear old *Béla-bácsi* looked down at me and, with the kindest look I would ever see from him, bade me to join the rabbi. I walked up nervously, the eyes of the congregation upon me. The rabbi leaned down and whispered in my ear. "Would you like to try some wine?" This was new and exciting, and I understood at last what these men were doing here, hiding from their women. I nodded eagerly. "I'll bet," he said, and handed me a tarnished silver goblet. He indicated I should wait as he recited a prayer, and then, following his signal, I sipped the wine. It was sweet, like cough syrup, but I loved it, loved the simultaneous sense of transgression and initiation. I took another sip. "Not too much now." He smiled and took the cup from me. I returned to my grandfather, my head buzzing, whether from the wine or something else, I'm not sure. I clutched his hand until the service was finished, and we stepped outside, to recover his cigar, where it smoldered untouched. We walked the eight blocks home in the cold Queens darkness, and he died the following year. I would not set foot in another synagogue for nearly twenty-five years, until I slid into the back row of a Chicago temple to have a look at my antagonist Rabbi Wolfe, giving her last sermon before chemotherapy took her from the pulpit.

My second childhood brush with religion came three years

after that, when . . . No. Later, Virgil. There's too much death in this tale already.

I MET MS. MOCKLEY the following morning at the Australian consulate. As I was escorted into her small, drab office, she held out her hand. She was stout and ruddy with limp straw hair. Her palm was dry and flaky.

"Mr. Santos. Joanne Mockley. Thank you for coming."

I nodded, friendly but wary. A slim, buff file lay on the desk before her.

"Please sit down. Would you like some coffee? Tea?"

"Nothing, thank you."

She nodded briskly as though she appreciated my thrift and directness of purpose.

"Well, I will get right to it." She slid the file before me and began to speak. Of the many scenarios Tracy and I played out the night before, nothing could have prepared me for Ms. Mockley's next words:

"Have you heard of the Arrow Cross, Mr. Santos?"

I hate leading questions such as these; they always seem intended to either diminish the responder or to establish a false kinship between those in the know. "Of course," I said. "Hungarian Fascist party. Sort of a homegrown Gestapo."

She nodded, continuing unnecessarily. "Precisely. When the Germans invaded Hungary in 1944, the Arrow Cross went above and beyond the call when it came to rounding up and killing Hungarian Jews."

"As I said, I know. What does this have to do with me?"

A good deal, as it turned out. After the war, Ms. Mockley went on to inform me, some former members of the Arrow Cross made Australia their home. Among their numbers was one Ferenc Halasz, who had lived out the remaining years of his life in relative peace and comfort in a Melbourne suburb called St. Kilda, until he was discovered and outed by an enterprising researcher from the Wiesenthal Center. The remaining years of his life froze into a stalemate as the Australians tried and failed to return him to Hungary, which was less than eager to receive him. He filed legal brief upon legal brief, and managed to run the clock out in his favor, dying in his sleep at ninety-one. As he had no heirs or family, his body was discovered by his landlady, who could scarcely contain her relief at being rid of him. His effects had been cataloged by the authorities, which was the reason for this meeting. Ms. Mockley indicated, via a curt tilt of her head, that I should open the file.

The file contained an eight-by-ten color photograph of the *Budapest Street Scene*, and as soon as I saw it, I felt the tickle of a distant memory. There was something familiar about it, though I was unable to place it. The file also contained a document written in Hungarian, which I couldn't read, but appeared to be some sort of receipt or bill of sale. It was followed by photocopied pages of what looked like a personal journal or ledger, row upon row of precise handwriting. Fascists, it seems, have always been diligent record keepers.

"I can't read Hungarian," I said.

"There's a translation attached to the back of the file."

I slid the contents aside and began to read the documents as Ms. Mockley explained to me that the first was, indeed, a bill of sale, a receipt for the painting in the file. It was signed by my grandfather and dated April 12, 1944, and recorded a tiny sum—350 pengő, about twelve dollars. There was a lot of this sort of thing going on during the war, Ms. Mockley explained, as though I didn't already know, Jews forced to sell their art at a fraction of its real value, and the ludicrous mania for documentation accompanying these sales to somehow legitimize them as something other than the thefts that they were. I nodded dumbly as I studied my grandfather's signature, his expansive, elegant cursive.

But it was the journal entries, Ms. Mockley explained, warming to her tale, that told the real story. In fact, my grandfather had traded this painting to Halasz in exchange for transit documents to get his family out of Budapest to London. Here, Ms. Mockley grew somber.

"Halasz writes in his journal that the documents did not arrive in time to save your grandmother's life."

I would like to say I performed well, that I held her eyes with appropriate solemnity, but in truth, I knew almost none of this. The story of my family's escape had always been a well-kept secret, and here at last the mystery was almost casually revealed. My repertoire of gesture was too limited. I could think of no interesting choices, and so I gazed blankly at Ms. Mockley.

My shock must have been apparent. "I'm very sorry," she said in that remorse-free fashion unique to bureaucrats.

"Is there anything else?" I asked.

"Oh, yes, quite a bit more."

Budapest Street Scene, it appeared, had recently been added to a database of unclaimed war paintings, following the death of one Cassian Yuhaus, its last owner, who acquired it under murky circumstances, presumably from Halasz, although no further documentation could be found. He subsequently lost it to the IRS as part of a tax settlement. The painting was in storage at the National Gallery in Washington, D.C., due to wartime gaps in its provenance, but, Ms. Mockley explained, the Americans were responsive to legitimate claims put forward, and the documentation found in Halasz's apartment appeared sufficient to award the custody of the painting to me, assuming there were no competing claims to sort out. She paused for effect, an amateur in these matters, but her material was strong enough to survive her earnest, drama club delivery.

"The present estimates suggest it is worth anywhere between two and three million dollars."

She sat back, satisfied with her performance, and my hand trembled as I picked up the photo and regarded the painting, quite certain now where I had seen it before. After a moment, I set the picture aside and met Ms. Mockley's eyes.

"Look, my father is the one you should be talking to, not me. Béla was his father. Why aren't you giving this to him?"

Ms. Mockley delivered her last surprise, her iron eye contact with me never wavering.

"We tried. He didn't want it. He wouldn't even come and discuss it with our New York office. Do you have any idea why that might be?"

Well, my first answer would be that if my father were to say no, it was because he had determined that there was nothing in it for him. But that was clearly not the case here. In fact, the opportunity seemed tailor-made for him, a man who reveled in getting something for nothing. Whether he was submitting family vacations as tax deductions to the IRS or screwing over the union painters who worked for him, nothing gratified him more than the idea that he had gotten away with something. He was a man who viewed getting too much change from a purchase as free money. No, Ms. Mockley, when it comes to my father, I can offer you nothing useful, not a glimmer of understanding or insight. I did not realize that sitting there in your office, but that's been the truth all along.

MY FATHER TAUGHT ME NOTHING.

There is no judgment implied in this, merely observation, though I know how it sounds. On a practical level, he never taught me to fish (though we went fishing), to throw a ball (though we attended ball games), to change a tire, to tie a knot, or whatever it is that fathers seem to pass on to their sons at one time or another. He also never taught me the more essential things—right and wrong, how to read a stranger, how to love. That this omission went unnoticed by me for so long is, in itself, telling.

I suppose there is one thing he taught me, though I am certain he did so without meaning to. When I was a child, I built plastic models of World War II airplanes. I had no real interest in aviation—I couldn't tell a Spitfire from a Messerschmitt, and I still can't—but there was something irresistible about the promise of the photos on those little boxes. If you were patient enough you could, with the right paint and decals (sold separately), create a marvel of simulated flight from dull gray pieces of plastic. But I was neither steady nor patient and my planes all resembled the air force of a banana republic. One afternoon, I was putting the finishing touches on a Messerschmitt Bf 110 Zerstörer. I was oblivious to the fact that it was a German plane; I was captivated by the distinctive shark's teeth decal, which, because I'd placed it askew, now appeared to smile unthreateningly. My leg began to cramp and I leapt to my feet, upending a small bottle of hunter-green model paint that spread over the edge of the newsprint I had laid down and soaked into the carpet like an alien bloodstain. At almost the same moment, my father knocked at the door. I never understood why he knocked, because he never waited for permission. He just entered, as though every room in the house were his birthright, and he summoned me to assist him in some task about the house. At the sound of his knock, I had reflexively kneeled into the stain, hoping to cover it from view with my pant leg. I nodded and said I would be along in a moment, a time frame that never suited my father. He studied my unnatural position—I was contorted like some crippled beggar—and must have seen the paint bleeding out from beneath my knee, because he grabbed me by my collar and hoisted me upright, exposing my folly. *What did you do*, he roared, with a rage out of proportion to the offense. He didn't wait for my answer, which was, after all, unnecessary. Snarling, he brought his own paint-stained work boot down hard upon the Zerstörer and crushed it. My mother pleaded from the doorway for him to calm down but, his fury unspent, he raised his hand high—I still remember the paint flecks beneath his nails—and brought it down hard repeatedly on my backside until I wet myself and he released me in disgust and disappointment.

In my teenage years, I learned to lock my bedroom door, as I did one Saturday morning when my college grades arrived in the mail. I'd flamed out that semester, distracted by the toxic haze of a romance gone awry and a newfound devotion to weed. The sheet in my hand was a welter of red, and I panicked as my father pounded at the door, insisting he be let in. I stuffed the indictment into my back pocket, and as I opened the door, he nearly fell into me, flushed and disheveled and demanding my grades.

"I . . . I don't have them," I stammered.

"What are you talking about?" he bellowed.

I repeated myself, stalling. "I don't have them."

"Did you flush them down the toilet?" he asked, bristling with suspicion, supplying the very course of action that he himself would have taken, one that had not occurred to me. But I knew a lifeline when I saw one. Only in the ways of deception could I claim him for a role model.

"Yes. I did." I hung my head in an excellent facsimile of shame, already the promising performer. There was a beating, of course, but the older we both got, the less the lashings stung. More important, I'd bought the necessary time to forge a replacement set of grades, one that told a less dire story than the grades I'd supposedly flushed.

This, I suppose, is my father's legacy, the ease of the lie, the comfort of the half-truth. The actor born in fear, borne by fear.

DAZED, I LEFT MS. MOCKLEY, clutching the buff folder like a life preserver. I felt light-headed, disoriented, as I tried to banish thoughts of the Arrow Cross, to force aside images of my grandmother dead in the waters of the Danube, another distended human cork bobbing in the river. And this yarn of exit papers and stolen paintings? It felt like something out of *Casablanca*, although in the space of ten minutes, an Australian bureaucrat had told me more about my family than I had ever learned from my father. I dialed Tracy, but the call went to her voice mail, something that had begun happening more often. I hung up without leaving a message. It was all more than I could absorb, so apparently—I say "apparently" because I have no memory of any agency—I wandered down to the library and headed into the art department. I found a large, musty old catalogue raisonné of the paintings of Ervin Kálmán and sequestered myself among students, retirees, and the homeless using the computers to look at pornography. One moment I was at the embassy and a moment later, it seemed, I was huddled over the catalog, which smelled of spoiled cheese and crackled as I laid it flat. I flipped through it until I found a striking, full-page reproduction of *Budapest Street Scene*. The brief catalog entry—little more than dimensions and material—ended with the words *Whereabouts unknown*. The book had been published in 1962, before *Budapest Street Scene* reemerged as part of Cassian Yuhaus's tax settlement.

The colors in the library book were far more vivid than those in Mockley's photograph, which I now set beside it. Which was closer to the thing itself? Or was the real painting a third variation that neither picture captured? I wondered how long it would be before I might stand in front of it and see for myself. These questions were displaced by a dozen others: Why hadn't my father snatched up this windfall? Would pursuing this painting bring us into yet another conflict? Did I have the patience, the energy—the curiosity—to see me through to the end, where a considerable pot of gold appeared to wait?

I closed the book and returned it to a nearby cart, and it was only much later that evening that I realized I had left my photo of *Budapest Street Scene* tucked between its pages.

I'VE DESERTED MY POST, and after some restless wandering through the auction house, Virgil ever at my heels like a loyal spaniel, I have come to rest before a display case that contains a toy car. It's a shabby piece of tin, cheaply made. The once-white tires are brown, cracked with age. The thin film that passes for a windscreen is cloudy. Sunburnt flakes of red paint peel from its body. The driver's head is missing. Unlike my painting, this was once a child's toy, purchased for a pittance, designed to bring some passing pleasure to a little boy. Now it sits encased, awaiting a buyer who will shell out a terrific sum—the official estimate for this tattered rarity is twenty-two thousand dollars—only to place it inside another glass case. This fascinates me, the way trivial pieces of our lives assume such importance, while the object itself has only degraded with age.

That brief flare of recognition I'd experienced in Ms.

Mockley's office at the sight of *Budapest Street Scene* continued to glow. Arriving home, I tried again to reach Tracy. Again
no response, though also not unusual when she was working,
and so I went into the garage, where I keep my files, and began
searching through drawers. Although I am not a collector, I am
organized. Collecting was my father's grand passion, the reflex
around which he organized his life. I do not have that kind of
singleness of purpose and I often derided his obsession with
his massive collection of toy cars; an obsession that ruled him,
consumed his time, energy, and money, but also brought him
the only moments of happiness I can remember.

His particular passion was for Corvettes, an affectation,
I suspect, through which he was determined to demonstrate
devotion to his adopted nation. There could not have been a
more potent symbol of America, all open roads and convert-
ible tops and bright, primary colors, though in the garage my
father always kept Volkswagens, oblivious to any historical
resonance. He was a completist by nature, and the basement
of my childhood home was filled with model cars of increasingly rare vintage and escalating value. I hated the things,
the smell of them, the glass cabinets that separated them from
me, the exaggerated care that my father used on the infrequent
occasions when he was required to handle them. As I got older,
I found the whole thing juvenile, embarrassing. I never spoke
of the collection to my friends, who probably would have been
amazed at the sight of it. In truth, I never quite got over my
resentment of my father's willful cruelty—thousands of beautiful toy cars, and I was not permitted to touch, much less play
with, any of them. I was only allowed downstairs with super-
vision, lest the urge to tear a car free from its display and roll
it across the floor overwhelm me. And so, over time, I stopped
going downstairs.

After twenty minutes of searching, I found a file of old family photos that I'd been looking for. Tracy once offered to arrange these pictures into an album, to afford them the presentation that she felt was lacking. But I prefer them disorderly in this file, never sure which picture will come up next, which long-dormant memory will be stoked, flare to life, then sigh back into obscurity.

I withdrew an early photo, in which I'm about four. On the whole, my father seems . . . happy. Happy with me. My mother is busy watering plants in the background, and I'm sitting on his lap, facing the camera. He's holding my arms out, as though I'm his marionette, and there appears to be genuine joy on his face. I realize this sounds less unusual than it probably is, but I can't seem to remember feeling that happiness, *his* happiness. Clearly, it was there, if the photographic evidence is to be believed, but my memories of those early years are featureless, like a vast desertscape.

I pulled out another photo of us standing on a busy Manhattan street. In this picture I'm twenty, taller now than the old man, long hair curling about my shoulders, and although my father is still smiling, he stands awkwardly, at a distance from me, his outstretched arm resting on my shoulder. I appear to stiffen against his touch, but I smile, too. How much are photographic smiles to be trusted? There's a real difference between the two pictures, a happiness in the early one that can't be forged, despite the wan attempts of the latter. What happened to us between these two shutter clicks?

MY BACK BEGAN TO ACHE from hunching over the files, and I was about to go inside to use the bathroom when I found the object of my search. A black-and-white photo about three inches square with a serrated border that might have been cut with pinking shears. A crack runs through the top right corner of the photo, where it had been folded years before. On the back is written *Szantos család, Székely Bertalan utca, Aprilus 1944*. Szantos family, Bertalan Székely Street, April 1944. The photo is of the sitting room in my grandparents' Budapest flat. The room is cramped, the overstuffed furniture leaving little room to walk around. A shaft of light crosses the room from a sole window on the left. There's tea paraphernalia on the lace-covered coffee table in front of a sofa upon which my grandfather reclines, trying to keep his errant son still for the photo. My grandmother leans on her forearms on the back of the sofa, stiff, smiling thinly for the camera. How little she would have had to smile about in April 1944. The photographer is unknown. In the past, I have always been drawn to my father in this photo, first shocked, later dismayed to see how much I resembled him as a boy. Not just in our full-lipped, dark-haired looks but in that same restless apartness. But this time my eye skips past family, past the furniture, the tea, the books on the shelves, and goes straight to the painting on the wall behind them. A third is cut off on the right, out of frame, but there's no mistaking *Budapest Street Scene*, hanging crookedly over the hearth.

I CLUTCHED THE PICTURE, dizzy, my innards seeming to bend as in a carnival mirror. None of it made the slightest sense. My father never said the first word about art—painting, sure, but art? Never—and nothing suggested that his barely middle-class family had enough bourgeois cultivation to gesture in the direction of modernism. Before leaving the garage, I extracted a second file from the cabinet, but this time I did not look inside. With an unsteady hand, I slid the family photo into it and stepped inside the house to find Tracy pacing the living room, talking urgently into her cell phone. She nodded at me as I walked in and kept talking and pacing. She mouthed the word "Brian" to me.

Of course. Brian. The omnipresent third member of our happy household. A lawyer representing a Texas death row inmate with an IQ of 62 named Ricky McCabe, on whose behalf Tracy had been interceding for nearly a year, helping to underwrite his legal team and coordinating an "awareness campaign" for clemency.

She covered her mouthpiece and whispered to me. "Bledsoe is recanting."

I immediately understood the urgency. McCabe was accused of killing a young woman in the parking lot of a bar for refusing his advances. The police built a circumstantial case around him, despite the victim's physically abusive ex-husband and an unsolved string of armed robberies of women in the same area. That her stolen handbag was never recovered and no gun was ever found hardly impeded their certainty. Instead, a perfect storm sent Ricky McCabe to death row: A small blood splatter on his shirt, which he said happened when he found the victim in the parking lot and tried to wake her up. A sole witness, Amelia Bledsoe, sixty-eight, who, driving past the lot at night, claimed she saw him hurrying from the crime scene. A defendant abandoned by a mother who drank heavily during pregnancy, and unable to influence his lackluster defense.

The case had already twice delayed our wedding.

I pursued her hard, my flaxen goddess, proposed early, knowing how rare openings for men like me are with women like her. Yet months after my proposal was accepted, all urgency receded in the face of the life-and-death matters that consumed her time and energy. I confess, I struggled to understand her devotion to the cause. I pressed from time to time, but her answers felt like evasions, platitudes. True, Tracy grew up in a home devoted to causes and mistrustful of the establishment. Or perhaps it was simply the fact that she had been raised with love that disposed her so compassionately to others. But I felt there was something deeper, perhaps darker, driving her along.

I occasionally allowed myself to wonder whether she might be having an affair with the lawyer, Brian, whom I envisioned as tall, fair-haired, a Gentleman of the Old School. I bristled when she spoke to or texted him, which was often. I sat down on the couch and made a mild show of waiting for her to finish.

"Excellent," she said. "Talk tomorrow."

She turned her attention to me at last, dropping down onto the sofa beside me.

"Sorry about that. Big day."

"All around."

"It opens everything back up. Her testimony was such a key part of the original case. Maybe this will make the difference."

"It *is* Texas . . ."

She shook her head at me. "Cynic." She kissed my cheek and regarded me with what seemed to be affection. "How about you? How did it go with that Australian woman?"

"Well, a little weird, actually."

"Weird? How so?"

As my recap of the morning unfurled, I was disquieted by two things. First, although I was telling Tracy the truth, I felt somehow dishonest, like a carnival barker. There was something a bit too staged in my rendition, it felt false even while painting a picture of perfect accuracy. *Ceci n'est pas la vérité*, to paraphrase Magritte.

The second thing I noticed was that, in my otherwise accurate-to-the-last-detail retelling of the day's adventure, I omitted the value of *Budapest Street Scene*. At the time, it struck me as benign. I am forever withholding this or that bit of the truth as suits me, it's just another technique in my repertoire, as every actor learns the fundamental lesson that less is more. But looking back, I wonder if that fact withheld, and not Mockley's phone call, was the real beginning of things.

As I neared the end of my tale, Tracy's phone began bleating, the word about McCabe no doubt having spread. She picked it up and began reading and answering her texts as I spoke. Brian. I was sure it was Brian, and even if it wasn't, it was Brian. I stopped talking and she didn't notice for a moment. Then she looked up at me.

"I'll wait until you're done."

I'd said it evenly, but she registered the rebuke and set down the phone with an apologetic look. She slithered up beside me and, making amends, whispered in my ear.

"Would you like to fuck me now?"

It's her standard invitation, its unromantic bluntness something of an in-joke, the joke, of course, being that the answer is never no. How could I, how could any man, refuse such largesse? And yet.

"Later, I think."

She seemed surprised though not altogether disappointed. She was, perhaps, too focused on the news of the night, and too eager to return to poor, doomed Ricky McCabe to linger on the moment. We said good night and she disappeared up the stairs. I sometimes looked forward to the evening hours after Tracy settled into bed and I could enjoy a little nocturnal privacy. At length, her snoring would echo throughout the house, kettle drums tumbling down a flight of stairs. I find it one of her most charming traits, for some reason. To the world, in magazines and on billboards, she epitomizes refinement, but in the privacy of her dreams, only I know her to be the window rattler she is.

I settled into my study. The house was slipping into darkness but for the spotlight of the desk lamp illuminating the file I had retrieved from the garage. I opened the folder, which contained an old family tree. There was a thick hum in my ears, and it seemed as though the whole of gravity itself had converged upon this printout. Turning the first page required a Herculean effort.

The document had been created a dozen years earlier by an elderly cousin of my father's. I still remember his phone call, his accented politesse, as he inquired whether I could supply a few missing details about my family. I had little to offer beyond my own birthday, but he sent me the completed family tree a few weeks later. Did he chastise me for my ignorance? I'm sure he must have. I hope he did.

It was a confusing document, ten pages of difficult-to-read dot matrix printouts in no apparent order. At the time, I tore the envelope open and flipped through the pages looking for my own name, finding it on the last line, nestled beneath my parents'. Above them, my grandparents', and though I knew the story, I was nevertheless brought up short by the entry for my grandmother, which ended *d. 4-14-1944 in Budapest*.

That was all the attention I gave it, and I filed it away for some unknown future purpose. Now I returned to it, experiencing the same leap in my stomach. But for the first time—how was it possible I was just noticing this?—I became aware of the cluster of names above my father, all siblings of my grandparents, all abruptly terminating with the stark designation *d. 1944 in* followed by a variety of locations: Auschwitz, Mauthausen-Gusen, Budapest. These, I now realized, were my father's aunts and uncles—aunts and uncles he had never mentioned.

I began to flip back and forth between the pages, trying to connect the links and see how far back I could follow. After nearly thirty minutes of fiddling with highlighters and color-coded Post-its, a clear line tracing back to a 1770 patriarch emerged. The lineage sputtered out at that point. But for the first time, sitting alone in my study, I considered the Szabos of nineteenth-century Debrecen, the Lowenheims of Kecskemét, and the Ujvaris of Esztergom. These tributaries of family ran into a wider river than I'd ever imagined, and amid them all, Szantos emerged like a thin green shoot rising out of Europe's rubble. As for Santos, how banal and ugly our variation looked at the end of that long and distinguished line.

I sat back in my chair, awash in my newly uncovered ancestry. An hour earlier, for all I had known, I'd sprung from the brow of my parents, sui generis, and suddenly I was Marley's ghost, dragging behind me an eternal chain forged through the centuries by people who could not have guessed at my existence. Nor I theirs, evidently. Where there had been nothing before, now there was family. My family. My murdered forebears.

It's all right to sneer, Virgil. After all, where did I imagine I came from? I'd given the document and its stark contents so little consideration when I received it. Why was I so incurious, so content to be ignorant for so long? I looked back at the photo I had retrieved from the garage and thought of the cataclysm gathering beyond my grandparents' increasingly frail walls.

So many names. I bowed my head toward the file and fixed

my energy on them, as though my belated guilt could erase decades of neglect, my efforts punctuated by the occasional snore issuing from the bedroom. Szabo. Lowenheim. Who were these lost people? What had unfolded between the *b* and *d* that bookended each slight entry? Eventually, I returned the tree to its folder and stowed it in my drawer, uncertain what to do with it next. It had told much more than I'd imagined, but much less than I'd needed.

THERE'S A PHOTOGRAPH OF HITLER in which he stands before some so-called degenerate art, looted from its Jewish owners. The painting that has drawn his attention is a self-portrait of Kálmán as a soldier on crutches, one leg torn away, his ham-hock stump tattered and exposed. It conveys Kálmán's penetrating terror of the first great European war, into which he was swept. The painting is arresting in its raw vulnerability, his pallor the color of urine, his face pierced again by those flat, vacant eyes that mark most of his interwar paintings. Of course, it's easy to see who the true degenerate in the photo is. There's a Neanderthal vacancy in the idiot grins of *der Führer* and his drooling cohort as they stand, braying like asses, in front of paintings they are ill-suited to grasp, a mocking that must surely conceal the rage they feel at their bewilderment. Wherever he was at the moment—the timeline suggests a Davos sanatorium—Kálmán must have shuddered under the scrutiny, felt the footfall upon his grave.

This is all conjecture, true, but conjecture is all I have left. Please, sir. Just the facts. Rachel, too, was concerned with the facts. At first. And in the end, facts provided little comfort for Tracy. All right, Virgil, you plodder. The agreed-upon facts about *Budapest Street Scene* are these:

It was painted by Kálmán in 1925, the period during which scholars agree he was at the height of his creative powers, a leading figure in the European avant-garde, despite his refusal to relocate to Paris permanently. This refusal most likely bought him the mixed blessing of four more years of unhappy life, keeping him out of the Nazis' grasp until 1944. The painting was sold in 1927 to a thriving coffee merchant named Imre Weisz, following its appearance in a group show at Budapest's renowned Geszti Gallery. The Weisz family owned *Budapest Street Scene* until 1944, the year in which Kálmán took his life, the Germans took Budapest, and the painting disappeared along with all the other Weisz assets and, finally, the Weisz family itself. It did not reappear until 1967, when it surfaced in the collection of Cassian Yuhaus.

Into this narrative I was now obliged to insert the story of my grandfather, who somehow came into possession of the painting after Weisz, and tried to use it to buy his family's way to freedom, too late, too terribly late. After that, via routes yet unknown, the painting traveled from Halasz to Yuhaus, but the real mystery, though scarcely the only one, was how my grandfather got his paint-stained hands on it to begin with. The easiest solution surely would be to call my father and inquire.

Ah. *Easy.* According to what facile definition of the word? There was nothing easy that passed between us. I was afraid of him as a boy, terror unmixed with the admiration my friends felt for their fathers, and—snicker though you might, Virgil—in truth, I feared him still. Not in the same way, not in so primal a manner—when I was a boy, the sound of his approach down the hallway could make the hair rise on my neck—but fear, nonetheless. Perhaps that's why Kálmán's terrified, crippled soldier moved me so. No, calling him and asking would not, in fact, be easy at all. My mother, however, was a different story.

But her answer to my questions about *Budapest Street Scene*, about the Lowenheims and the Ujvaris, was the same opaque reply she'd given me throughout the years whenever I ventured the occasional query about our inscrutable patriarch:

"Ask your father."

There was something touching about my mother's refusal to discuss anything more to do with my father or his family, a naive belief in the restorative value of clean breaks. Her break could not have been cleaner. When she divorced my father five years earlier, the timing, like most things to do with my mother's second act, was dramatic, unexpected, bordering on the melodramatic. Within a month, she was ensconced in a Paris apartment, having a go of it as, yes, a painter, sustained by alimony and an unflappable self-regard. I'd given her experiment a year, but she was still plugging away out of a small studio in the nineteenth arrondissement, and even enjoying a modest success, at least by the Churchillian measure of leaping from failure to failure without a loss of enthusiasm. By dint of sheer perseverance, a tiny circle within a circle within a circle of Parisian art types had begun to take notice of her, which only reinforced her willfulness. And so, she was disinclined to make things easy on me.

"Ask your father." *Ask your alleged father*, when she was feeling mischievous.

"I'm asking you. At transatlantic rates, I might add."

"You can afford them, son."

Her interest in the topic of *Budapest Street Scene* exhausted, my mother commenced one of her conversational free-for-alls, something I have never had patience for even when the calls were local. She tends to burble on, free-associating all manner of topics long past my fragile point of interest. This monologue included complaints about yet another Paris metro strike; a detailed recapitulation of a standoff between my mother and her landlord, an avowed anti-Semite, she was convinced; a tiresome extended review of a gallery show by one of her artist friends; and something to do with her acceptance to a prestigious artists' retreat somewhere in the Pyrénées.

"Bliss," she sighed. "No phones, no TV, no radio, no Internet. Nothing but total isolation, light, and painting for a month."

"Hmm."

"Matt, are you even listening?"

"Hmm? Yeah. What—"

"Honestly, I don't know why you call. How's Tracy? Still charmed by your attentiveness?"

"For the moment," I answered, ignoring her sarcasm. "Mom, please, about this painting—"

"Ask. Your. Father."

My mother confuses me, although this was not always the case. During my childhood, there was something comforting if unexciting about her. Although as I cast my mind back across those years, I am once again hard-pressed to fill in too many details. She was a terrible cook with, even worse, a limited culinary range, so it wasn't just bad food, it was the same bad food over and over again. I would like to say she tried, but I'm not sure that's true, and I'm also not sure she ever cared about just how dreadful it all was. To her, another dry pork cutlet was good enough.

She was indifferent to the news of the world. American-born, she didn't share my father's sense of urgency about the Communist threat. I remember taking him to see the Big Sur coastline during one of our few, doomed attempts at bonding. Looking out across the endless expanse of sheer cliffs and boiling surf, he muttered, "The Ruskis would love to get their hands on this." *And do what with it*, I thought but did not say.

My mother, at least, would have enjoyed the view. She drank moderately, which was when I found her most entertaining, as she was especially gifted at impersonating my father's Hungarian circle, not just their accents but their blowhard bonhomie. Not a sentimental woman, my mother. In the baby book she threw together to commemorate my birth, she entered the following physical description: *Ugly. big nose*. My mother, to be fair, insists she wrote *Ugly, big nose*, the "ugly" intended to modify "nose" and not to serve as a blanket appraisal of my appearance. Like constitutional lawyers parsing the second amendment, we have debated the existence and significance of that comma for years. I see it as a period, but perhaps that is how I want to see it.

And then, without warning, she changed. No, changed is too mild, she transformed. In the year leading up to her divorce she emerged a full-blown, middle-aged bohemian. She was nowhere to be found for all the museum openings and opera outings, and the ancient Singer sewing machine that had rattled throughout my childhood, the sort that disappeared as though through a trapdoor beneath the table, was replaced with canvases, paints, charcoals, watercolors. I wondered what my father made of all this. I imagine it would have felt like a provocation. I'm not sure my mother didn't intend it that way. She was usurping the family business, and now the house was filled with the smells of oil paints and linseed oil, not from my father's work-stained clothes but from her increasingly inspired canvases.

By then I was living in Los Angeles, my career well established, but I would visit them from time to time and found myself unable to recognize my mother. I was secretly amused by my father's irritation at her hitherto-unseen displays of will, of opinion, of independence. But if I am honest, the change discomfited me as well, and when my mother first announced she was leaving my father, I was caught off guard by what now seems an entirely logical denouement of the little melodrama she had cast herself in. I tried to get details, to have her explain to me this rupture, but then as now her rejoinder was ineluctable:

"Ask your father."

Will it surprise you, Virgil, to learn that I did no such thing?

My mother had finished her exegesis on the Parisian art scene and executed another one of her high-wire conversational shifts. "You know, I'm looking at my phone book," she murmured, "and there are ten dead people in it already. Ten. That's depressing. There are too many dead people in my phone book."

"Mom, please. Can we have just like a second on point here?"

She paused for a moment, and I could imagine her posing with her cigarette—another habit adopted late in life—looking out her tiny window with its fractional view of Sacré-Coeur, deciding how much to reveal. I considered my own contrasting view: Through the window of my study, I could see Tracy in the garden, cell phone propped against her ear, making her weekly effort at resuscitating our rosebush that had, to date, resisted all her ministrations. I heard a flutter of a sigh, like moth wings flapping, and my mother began talking.

"You know, this flat reminds me a little of the awful apartment I had in the Haight back in the late sixties—"

"You lived in San Francisco? I didn't know that."

"Of course you did. I've told you that before. Many times. Anyway, I was in San Francisco and I was in an apartment that was always either too cold or too warm and never at the right times. And I distinctly recall . . ."

My mother spoke on, another monologue, her performance specialty, and my attention drifted. I tried to imagine her living in Haight-Ashbury in the 1960s in paisley blouses and heart-shaped glasses, dispensing free love and smoking pot in her rickety walk-up, but I couldn't make the image cohere. She was saying something about a man and an offer of marriage, but now my attention had settled back on Tracy down in the yard, struggling with her rosebush. In the past, there was something touching about her refusal to give up, although I was certain that no rose would ever bloom on her benighted branch. Now, however, there was something about her dedication that irritated me. Sweating in the sunlight, cell phone tucked between her ear and shoulder, her taut biceps twitched with effort, her stomach flat even as she leaned over. If this had been one of those awful movies I make my living appearing in, she would have felt my eyes upon her and looked up at me. But she remained bowed over her project, talking urgently to Brian, surely.

I could tell from my mother's cadence that her story was coming to an end.

". . . but, of course, by then it was too late, and I never got the chance again. And that, my son"—she closed with a flourish—"is your father in a nutshell. Do you see?"

I realized she was waiting for a reply. Hot, angry sweat pricked my forehead. She'd told me something, something key in her estimation, and I'd missed it. Now, knowing my mother and her fallible sense of the critical, it's possible that, in fact, whatever it was she'd told me was tangential, or not even relevant. It wouldn't have been the first time. Which accounts for my habit of tuning her out. I imagine an accounting of the moments I have glossed over in a similar fashion would keep the recording angel busy indeed, a damning encyclopedia of

regret. Whether her story contained a warning, advice, a bene-
diction, I would never know, it was lost to me now, and my
vanity, or something more sinister, ensured it would stay lost.
How easy it would have been, I now understand, to have donned
my most confiding voice and say, "Mom, forgive me, I was looking out the window at my fiancée and was so captivated that I
missed all that. Can you tell me again?" She would have liked
that. It would have sat well with her romantic disposition.

"Okay. Something to think about," I ventured. "Thanks."

I hung up the phone with vague promises about a future
visit. I glanced back out the window into the garden. Tracy,
deep in conversation, had abandoned her roses but not her
phone. I tried to get her attention, wanted to wave, blow a kiss
perhaps, but she remained absorbed in her call and didn't turn
around.

TWO WEEKS AFTER the Mockley interview, I still hadn't spoken to my father. Instead, I invested my time and energy in becoming an authority on Ervin Laszlo Kálmán, who, though dead, seemed far more approachable. I filled pages upon pages with dates, places, names of intimates, all manner of historical data. The pages were cross-referenced and color-coded—one has a good deal of time on one's hands between takes on a film set. On a separate sheet beside these, as a comparison, I thought it would be interesting to write down every related fact I could recall about my father. I have kept that single, limp sheet, have it with me still, crumpled in my pants pocket, although there is no need for me to look at it. Its silent reproach has accompanied me on this journey, traveling to Budapest, to New York, to my father's hospital room, to Rabbi Wolfe's congregation in Chicago, to Rachel's bed. I could, at any number of moments, have begun to fill up that lonely page, but it remains blank to this day. Rachel asked about it, finding it among my belongings in my little Hungarian hotel room. I saw pity in her eyes as I explained.

My Kálmán archive—which now contained a certified letter from the World Jewish Congress bearing a referral to a law firm well versed in matters of restitution and prepared to offer any required legal assistance in recovering *Budapest Street Scene*—was installed in my trailer, where similar archives in similar trailers had been situated over the years. My entire education has unfolded in tiny mobile units like this one, filling the endless numbing hours of downtime reading all the books I could get my hands on. There was the summer of Hemingway and Fitzgerald while I worked on a tent-pole science fiction movie for Warner Bros. I remember reading all of Faulkner, Joyce, and Woolf during my one year as a series regular. I became obsessed with quantum mechanics and read dozens of books I didn't really understand while I had a recurring role on a popular sitcom. Along that continuum, my Kálmán obsession was merely my latest in a series of distractions. That's always been my method, if I can be said to have one, using each new job to hole up and continue my irregular learning, plugging up the potholes of my scattershot education.

I was in the middle of a recurring guest role on a hot new cable drama set in an American embassy in China. Two episodes into a five-episode commitment, with a character with a name, and an actual "arc" (I was set to transform from amoral to honest). It was the kind of role that might bring awards, reviews, that elusive next level of recognition. Mostly, though, I had time on my hands. I have been successful in my profession long enough that my on-set accommodations, though modest, are comfortable. There is a hierarchy of these things on a film set, as with all creature comforts, doled out in quality and quantity according to one's station, and the muscle of one's representation. Do I stare covetously at the deluxe, plush, lined trailers of my A-list costars, their refrigerators an endless bounty of ambrosia and elixirs? Of course I do. Or, rather, I used to. I've learned to modulate envy, reconciling myself to my permanent C-list status. It's an essential survival skill in Hollywood, where someone is always doing better than you are, and more often than not it's someone you loathe. That kind of eternal tote board can consign you to madness, so I have concluded over time that being on the list in any capacity is preferable to the alternative. As long as my tiny refrigerator is stocked with the bottled water of my choice (Volvic) and I have a quiet place to read, I count my blessings and remind myself that my paint-stained father actually had to work for a living.

It was Kálmán's father's work—he was a tailor of some distinction—that brought the family the two hundred kilometers west to Budapest from Debrecen, Hungary's second-largest city. It was 1891 and Ervin was eight years old. Three years later he entered the gymnasium, the prestigious Hungarian secondary school, where his teachers encouraged his artistic inclinations, to the consternation of his parents, who envisioned a more traditional vocational path for their sensitive son. It was in reluctant accordance with their wishes, a schism that Ervin never fully resolved or forgave, that he entered technical college in 1904, but the brief exposure to art had done its work.

I was sitting in my trailer, waiting to be called to reshoot a scene—a rarity but something that had been happening with increasing frequency on this project, the director somehow unable to get what he was looking for from me—when I realized that I had only a vague memory that my father hadn't finished university, but I could not remember where he had matriculated. Had it been a trade college, too? Had he told me and I'd forgotten? More likely, I had never known the answer. I certainly had no idea where he'd gone for his primary education, or when. For that matter, I was also unsure whether his family was born in Budapest or arrived from elsewhere, like the Kálmáns. I pulled out a fresh sheet of paper and labeled it, simply, *Dad*. A production assistant knocked and advised me that I would be needed on set in ten minutes. I pulled one of the timelines I had assembled about Kálmán's life, set it beside *Dad*, and looked at it more closely.

It was at college that Kálmán befriended Gyorgy Heti, whose name today is remembered for having urged Kálmán to contemplate the life of the artist. It was also Heti, an opium addict, who introduced Kálmán to the pleasures of narcotics. Some of Heti's sketches survive to this day and they remind me of nothing so much as my mother's earliest efforts. There's something plaintive and earnest about these Budapest cityscapes, clichéd renderings of iconic sights such as the Chain Bridge and the Fisherman's Bastion. Of greater interest are the letters he wrote to Kálmán, impassioned missives about the role of the artist, the sanctity of painting, and a dozen other points that Kálmán would steal in later years, rolling them into his Duna Manifesto, often transcribing pages of Heti's letters verbatim without crediting his friend, who had by then disappeared into the mud and snow of the eastern front.

Tapping the pen to my temple, I sought to note something comparable about my father, nothing more perhaps than the name of his closest or oldest friend, when I realized that I could not recall meeting any of my father's friends. There were acquaintances, certainly, but my father avoided intimate companionship. I would watch as he hung up the telephone with someone he had known for years, only to mutter *idiot* as he retreated to his cellar full of toy cars.

The more I learned about Kálmán, the barer my father's page felt. For example, whereas I knew that Kálmán finally broke with his parents and left college in 1907 to pursue his art full-time, I could not remember whether my father had left college or been ejected. And when I read about Kálmán's success in arranging a small allowance from his parents to enable him to move to Paris, it merely underscored that I had no idea whether my father ever lived outside the family home, ever sought his independence as a young man before his great leap westward.

I remembered packing my bags for my own great move to Los Angeles. I filled two medium suitcases and had five thousand dollars in my pocket, all of my savings. My father watched me pack and inquired how long I intended to give it. It was, I suppose, a reasonable question but to me it underscored how little he understood me. I paused in my hurried folding, looked up, and said—quite self-importantly, as I recall with some shame—as long as it takes. Now, as it happened, as long as it took was not very long at all, but neither of us had any way of knowing that at the time. He looked at me with an indecipherable sadness, nodded, and left. What was he feeling? Perhaps he was saddened by my certainty, a melancholy echo of his own youthful vitality. Or perhaps he felt nostalgic for his own great youthful escape, crossing the border hours ahead of Soviet tanks in October of 1956, and arriving in America without a friend or a word of English? Is it possible that he was simply sad at the prospect of not seeing me for many years? That's a possibility I cannot bear to consider, not now.

My cell phone rang. I glanced at the display—Mockley. She had been hounding me for days, eager to know what steps I was taking toward "resolving the matter," as she put it. I ignored her call, as I had the others, though I knew I couldn't continue to do so indefinitely. I pulled the World Jewish Congress letter from the file. It said I would be hearing from a Rachel Steinberg, Esq., who would guide me through the restitution thicket. At that moment, the production assistant returned and I was shuttled onto the set, maneuvered into position, my feet on bits of tape as lights were adjusted around me. But my mind was still thrumming with shame, with questions, with . . . with what else, Virgil? I must have sensed something gathering, my mind was full of my father's absence, his blank page. I was abstracted, my performance off, to the growing irritation of the director and the crew. It's a desperately expensive business, after all, and my unreliability was costing the production no small sum. But my mind kept trailing back to my papers, my research and, above all, my father's single empty page, and now I became angry at how much I knew about Kálmán's life, how thoroughly it has been documented, examined. What makes one life more worth examining than another? My father left the world no art, it's true. But can that fact alone account for the disproportion in interest, in information? Can it justify the many full pages against the single empty page?

These questions exhaust me, Virgil. All these months with so little answered. Even now, I can feel the weight of his blank page in my pocket.

I remember playing Hamlet in an amateur theatrical production shortly after I arrived in Los Angeles, when I was still under the illusion that such vanity productions had any career value. But for all the aching earnestness of the affair, I comported myself with some distinction, made some interesting choices, as actors like to say. I was a natural Hamlet, I had the melancholy part well in hand—again that sadness, that useful sadness—even if no one would mistake my brooding Semitic countenance for Danish. But something deeper in the role spoke to me, something off the page. Was it the fear at the first sight of the Ghost Father? Such a familiar fear. I knew that tightening in the chest all too well. Or perhaps it was the sense of thwarted promise, of things that were simply never to be. No throne for our hapless lad, no love, not even, in the end, life. Or was it the obvious take, the young prince's chronic indecision, his inability to do the one necessary thing, that so resonated with me? After all, the drama of *Budapest Street Scene* was going nowhere and still I balked at the one step remaining.

I flubbed a line I had been trying to get right, and the director, his frustration evident, called an end to the day's shoot. He pulled me aside to register his concerns and I made a great show of listening with deference and interest, and promised him things would be different in the morning. There was something in his manner, Virgil, and it occurred to me that I could lose this gig, something that had never happened to me. I wasn't about to let it happen now. Things would be better after the holiday break, I assured him. Whether he was mollified or not, I can't say, but I was excused and I returned to my trailer, where I was greeted by a photograph from my archive that brought most of my visitors up short. It's a photo of Kálmán, dead, his head surrounded by a halo of flowers arranged to hide the hole in the back of his skull. Why did I choose to display this photo so prominently, taped up at eye level on the door of my wardrobe? There was something about his mouth cracked open as if he had expired midsyllable, about the emerging razor stubble (I wondered about the diligence of Hungarian undertakers), about the fact that it was a photograph of a dead man, that I could not look away from. I'd not yet been in the presence of a dead body, and something about the finality of the image made me slightly dizzy. I would look back and forth from his head to his paintings, trying to connect creator and created.

I picked up the letter from the World Jewish Congress and looked it over one last time before sliding it back into its file. I couldn't continue to cower in my trailer from the long arm of Ms. Mockley. There was one thing left to do.

To call or not to call. That is the question. Angels and ministers of grace defend us. Mark me.

VIRGIL APPEARS SUFFICIENTLY CONVINCED of my harmlessness to have begun a game of solitaire, which he attends with a dogged consistency that's almost touching, though the cards do not favor him. Once or twice, a groan floats my way as yet another unwanted red king is turned over. I loathe the tense tedium of card games. My father played cards every Friday night at a Hungarian social club in Manhattan. Social club. The words evoke images of a world so foreign, a world in which people might socialize for no other reason than shared nationality. My father's mood was unfailingly bad the day after he'd lost, which was often, and he railed against the stupidity and—the greater sin in his view—the timidity of his partners who had no killer instinct. Those were his words: *killer instinct*. Something he imagined he possessed in abundance.

When I was ten, he had occasion to visit the Club, as he called it, in the middle of the day, and he took me along on an errand, the purpose of which is long forgotten. I'd only heard talk of it and had constructed such an elaborate fantasia of glamorous men and women, music and danger, that I leapt at the opportunity to see firsthand where my father spent his Friday nights.

I suspect my disappointment was palpable as we mounted the steps of a sagging brownstone in Yorkville, the Hungarian neighborhood of Manhattan, off Second Avenue in the mid-eighties. A battered green steel door embedded with a small square of safety glass gave way to a narrow corridor littered with refuse. Broken mailbox doors dangled at odd angles like decaying teeth. As the elevator approached, the silence was punctuated by the *thunk* of each floor brushing past. My bladder tingled as it often did in exciting situations. The door slid open in quarters that disappeared into each other, and we stepped into the tiny cab. My father let me press one of the six raised black buttons, and the floor number glowed amber. The elevator reeked of ammonia.

We stepped out and walked down the linoleum-tiled corridor. My ghost father's footsteps rattled along cream-painted cinder blocks. We arrived at a dented and scratched olive door with a security eyepiece and a doorbell bearing the legend THE TOWER CLUB. As I looked around for evidence of a tower, my father pressed the black lozenge firmly and a full, round chime answered. The door was opened by a middle-aged woman with orange shellacked curls, rhinestone-studded glasses, an architectural bosom, and eyebrows drawn at a rakish angle. This was Ildiko, and she smiled at the sight of my father, beckoned him to enter, and cooed over me, applying special accented ministrations upon the much discussed but never seen prodigal son. My father transformed, became Gabi the boisterous, jovial charmer, a creature I'd glimpsed at dinner parties. It was a bravura turn, and I do know about such things. The scope of the part was small—a critic might even call it one-note—but he owned it and delivered a convincing if broad performance.

Ildiko's interest in me spent itself quickly, and she assumed her place behind a bar stocked with dusty bottles of Crown Royal and Cinzano, speaking rapid Hungarian into a black telephone, and I was able to take in the room. What struck me first was the smell: stale, like the cosmetics section of a cheap department store. The combination of scents laced with cigarette smoke and Ildiko's hair spray should have been revolting but I swooned.

There were eight round tables covered with white tablecloths, nearly all of which were cratered with cigarette burns. Abandoned half-full glasses with cigarette butts floating in them. Two of the tables were occupied. At the first, three men my father's age were playing cards. It was to this table that my father attached himself, with an admonition for me to stay put and not bother anyone. But it was the players at the second table who riveted me.

Two elderly men sat in old military uniforms. One of the two was emaciated, his stubbled turkey jowls disappearing into his collar, which sat loosely around his blue-veined neck. All gray wisps, he seemed to vanish within his uniform. His friend suffered from the opposite problem, straining at the buttons of his jacket, constantly tugging at his waistband for elusive comfort. Moth-eaten ribbons rested upon their chests. Tarnished medals failed to catch the light. There was an absurd formality in their posture. Despite their dotage and infirmities, they sat rigidly upright with a wan, martial dignity. I strained to listen as the thin one drew a card and threw what I took to be some chips into the pot.

"I see your twenty thousand Romany souls, and raise you five thousand souls."

The fat general perused his cards once more and nodded decisively.

"I raise you a hundred thousand Bulgarian souls."

A terrible expression crossed the thin general's face, as though a herald had just delivered the worst possible news.

Bottom lip trembling slightly, he set his cards facedown and spat an obscenity. The fat general nodded, as if in agreement, and collected his winnings—not chips but a pile of multicolored bottle caps intended to represent the souls in question. Fanta oranges, Pepsi blues, Sprite greens, Coke reds. Ildiko noticed my interest and leaned over the bar to whisper to me.

"The fat one, he commanded five thousand men in Hungary. Terrible battles in the war, almost died during the siege of Budapest. Now he is a janitor. The skinny one, he led three battalions, was tortured by the Germans. Told them nothing. Here, he delivers newspapers." She leaned in close. "They say the fat one pushed Jews into the Duna. Who knows?" She shrugged, a gesture meant to explain all tragicomic inequities to me, and I wished I was old enough to decipher it. I glanced over to where my father was kibitzing with his buddies, and saw that he had noticed my interest. He looked at the two generals with distaste and, after thumping his friends theatrically on the back, rose and collected me. Effusive goodbyes were exchanged and we found ourselves in the hallway waiting for the elevator.

"What is the Duna?"

"The Danube. A river in Budapest."

"The woman told me she thinks the fat man pushed Jews in the river. Why did he do that?"

My father did not answer. Though I didn't realize it at the time, he was continuing a lifelong pattern of not discussing the war. I persisted.

"Who were those men, in the uniforms?" I asked.

His reply was clipped, tense. "Nobody." The elevator arrived and we stepped inside. My father pressed the ground-floor button, depriving me of my little pleasure, but he rested his hand on my shoulder, a rare bit of physical contact that gave me even greater joy. Then he spoke again, hoarsely. "Ghosts, Mátyás. They are ghosts."

He jabbed at the ground-floor button, eager to get me the hell out of there. I was never invited back to the Tower Club, which was demolished last year to make way for a luxury condominium. My two generals are surely dead by now, though I imagine them taking their game of souls elsewhere and continuing it until the moment when their own souls would be collected on another, larger table.

YEARS AGO, I WROTE DOWN THE FEW THINGS my father and I had in common. I kept the list in my nightstand drawer, handy whenever I had an uncomfortable interaction with him, a touchstone of sorts. It wasn't a very long list, nor a particularly deep one: We both liked to drive fast, recklessly even. We loved dogs. We both hated to shave. There was something I loved about his prickly stubble, his five o'clock shadow typically settling in around three o'clock, a characteristic I've inherited. I continued to hug him well past the age he thought such displays appropriate and he finally called a stop to it after my tenth birthday, when I was instructed to address him henceforth as "Dad," my preferred "Daddy" having been deemed unmanly. With the banishment of Daddy, the hugs also came to an end, though to this day I can still summon the sharp pricks of his incipient beard against my always tender skin, something comforting, reassuring in the pain.

I lay in bed, watching Tracy prepare for her shoot. It was the last day of the year. The curtains were parted, the room suffused with the warm blue of a clear Los Angeles winter morning. Despite the early hour, Tracy was already dressed and was assembling the day's necessities: iPad, water bottle, and a

small army of moisturizing lotions disappeared into her Brob-
dingnagian bag.

"You're going to be late, aren't you?"

She shrugged. "Only a little. They're always behind anyway. Eager to get rid of me?"

I smiled and twisted the sheet anxiously around my ankle.
"Of course not. Come here."

She leaned in to kiss me goodbye, and I held her wrist and
fingered the scar on her radial. It's a tight little bug of a wound,
the remnant of a burn her kid brother gave her as a child. He
was, he said, unnerved by her perfection. She'd long forgiven
him—it was the tiniest of marks—but I always marveled at
how he'd left his permanent imprint on her. I kissed her wrist
gently. Her engagement ring was absent.

"No ring?"

She shook her head. "No, it's too easy to lose at these
ocean shoots. I misplaced it last week and it freaked me out.
It's safer here. That's okay, right?"

I smiled and released her hand. "Of course, it's fine."

She sat on the edge of the bed. "So. Big day?" she asked.

I shrugged. "Well, you know."

She sighed, opened the drawer, pulled out my list, and placed
it on my stomach. "Call him. And give him my love."

She kissed my forehead and began to head out. "Cell phone,"
I called after her. She stopped, returned to her bedside, un-
plugged her phone from her charger, and hurried out with a
goodbye smile in my direction.

After she left, I remained motionless for several minutes,
dreading the task that lay ahead. Finally, I propped myself
upright against two pillows and studied the list as I auto-
dialed his phone number, as though intense focus on it might
raise some kind of protective shield around me. Pointless. I

was sure my heartbeat could be felt through the phone. After seven rings—my father rushed for no one—he answered the phone.

"Hi, it's Matt."

"Oh. Hi."

"How are things?"

"Not bad. Same as alvays. You?" The *w* in "always" softened into a sludgy *v*.

"Okay, thanks."

"Good."

"Tracy sends love."

"Same to her." The only warmth in his voice.

"Will do."

"Are you vorking?"

"Yeah. A recurring guest star on cable. Five episodes."

"Congratulations. Good money?"

"My quote."

"Vhat's that these days?"

I told him the figure. Once it gave me pleasure to flaunt this information. Now it felt petty. There was a long silence. Then:

"That's a lot of money."

"Yeah, you know, after taxes, commissions, it's not as much as it sounds."

"It's a lot of money, Mátyás."

Dogs. Shaving.

"Yeah. I guess it is."

"Well, thanks for calling."

"Hang on, I need to ask you something."

He hesitated. "Sure."

Why must you always be such an inscrutable, remote, self-righteous bastard?

63

"The Australians called me. What's the deal with this painting, Dad? They said you didn't want it."

The ensuing silence was so long I thought we'd been cut off. "Dad?"

"I don't."

"You don't what?"

"I don't vant it." *Vhy not?*

"I don't understand, Dad. This thing is potentially worth a few million dollars. Did they tell you that?"

"Yes."

"And?"

"And what? It has nothing to do with me. Or with you."

"What the hell are you talking about?"

"Don't talk to me like that."

Fast cars. Dogs. Dogs.

"I'm sorry. But Dad, please. You never told me . . . I never knew your family owned art."

"There are many things you don't know, Mátyás." Rebuke, not invitation.

"Well, why don't you change that? Tell me about this painting. Tell me why you don't want this money."

"There's nothing to tell. No story, no painting, no money."

"Well, that's helpful." He hated sarcasm, it drove him batshit, so it was always my fallback tactic. But this time, he surprised me. After another long silence, he struggled as he spoke with what appeared to be—and how I resist the word even now that all is known—sincerity.

"Mátyás. You must listen." He sighed. "There is nothing there but loss. Heartbreak. Everything connected with that painting is . . ." His voice fell to a whisper. "This one time you must trust me to . . . to keep you safe."

My father had never spoken to me like this before. Not

once in all the years of my life. It was the father I'd dreamed of. So simple, so direct, so genuine. It could only be a scam.

"Yeah. All right, Dad. Whatever you say."

Another protracted silence. Then: "Kiss Tracy for me." And his inevitable send-off: "Pushpushpush."

And just like the Ghost Father, he was gone, dissolved into the morning mists. I held the phone in my hand. The bed-sheets were soaked with sweat, as though I had just completed a marathon. It seemed unimaginable to me that he'd hung up, that my father, the schemer, the pursuer of angles, could be so unmoved by this pot of gold. For a moment, I considered the impossible notion that he'd told me the truth, that there was a bucket of horror at the end of this rainbow, but I discarded it as quickly as I'd considered it. It was far too early in the tale for such momentous shifts. Fortunately, thanks to the World Jewish Congress, I had a contingency plan.

THESE ARE THE THINGS I associate with Rachel, with the first time I awoke beside her: dusk in the city as the streets downshift with evening traffic, taxicab headlights plangently illuminating the avenues; the tiny crooked streets of Paris's Jewish quarter; bundles of fresh vegetables overflowing the stands of a weekend farmers market, earth-covered mushrooms especially; bales of hay, warm and pungent under the midday sun. It's such a dreadful cliché, but I watched her as she slept, my arm trapped beneath her head, the thick, ropy strands of her wheat-colored hair cushioning my bicep. In my small Budapest hotel room, I found myself uneasy at the transgression I'd committed, yet tranquil within Rachel's perimeter. She twitched, a nocturnal rabbit staying one step ahead of dream foxes. I watched her face for some hint of subconscious distress but instead she seemed to smile, knowingly. I marveled at contrasts. Where Tracy's hair was flaxen and silky, Rachel's was rough-hewn and unruly; Tracy's skin was so flawless as to appear untouched, whereas Rachel's bore the traces of a dozen slights and imperfections over the years. And yet I beheld in her a serenity I could not understand, an ability to attend life's daily outrages with such repose. It was the same serenity I would come to see in Rabbi Wolfe, although I thought her a fool for not raging against the dying of her light. In Rachel's case I envied it, coveted it.

But at first, long before all that came to pass, she was my lawyer and I her client. When she returned my call a few days after the new year, she explained that her assistance was being provided at a reduced rate in light of the historical importance of the case, but with the full resources of a heavyweight Century City law firm behind it. That she felt a strong personal conviction about matters of restitution. That she would be honored to play a role in reuniting me with my property.

Before I called, I visited the law firm's website, where I found Rachel's profile and photo. She was, it appeared, a newly minted partner, the youngest at the firm at thirty-three, I would learn later. It was fortunate that Tracy's jealousy had receded, I would not have been able to reassure her about this one. On the one hand, it seems hard to imagine any additional impetus to pursue this claim was required; Ms. Mockley had given me millions of reasons to proceed. And yet, was there something about Rachel's photo, about the way she looked, that drew me in? It wasn't merely that she was beautiful—she was, is, but we mustn't forget with whom I was sharing my bed. Did I already perceive that serenity? Can it be that there was something familiar about Rachel? Something in her eyes, in the curl of her hair, that whispered "home"? Or am I just rewriting the story now that the facts are all known? I wouldn't put it past myself; I've always been one for jumping to the last page of the script, unwilling to dwell in uncertainty for too long. It's something that has frustrated the better directors who have worked with me, who wish I was a bit more "organic" or "genuine" or "free," to use the many words they employ to try to get what they want out of me. But I think the word they are all avoiding is "honest."

I don't know what I expected to find in Rachel's office, what manner of exotica I imagined would greet me. Undulating palms? Jasmine incense? Dead Sea salts? Why was I so intently on the lookout for exotic signifiers? I was thus unprepared for the quotidian reality of a successful young partner's office: chic, modern, all streamlined elegance with smog-streaked views, and almost no personal touches of any kind. I was more than an hour late for our meeting. I had forgotten just how bad Friday afternoon traffic on the Westside of Los Angeles could be, the avenues clogged with multicolored metallic beetles, especially in the weeks after the holidays when all the vacationing commuters were back on the road. It's a privilege of my lifestyle that I am largely able to avoid the circadian tos-and-fros of Los Angeles's workaday traffic patterns. As a result, I hurried into her office, breathless, ashamed, at nearly four-thirty. Rachel's manner was impenetrably apologetic.

"I'm really sorry, Mr. Santos. My assistant tried to reach you. I'm afraid it's gotten too late for our meeting."

"Matt. Please. I'm sorry, traffic was positively biblical. A plague of Priuses."

Did she smile? I don't remember. I have pored over every gesture, every inflection, every moment of that first meeting and now the impressions are rubbed smooth like sandstone beneath centuries of waves. I think she smiled. Does it matter? Surely not. And yet, it mattered to me at the time. With the likes of Tracy at home, what did I imagine I was up to with this . . . with this what?

This Jewish girl? Can I possibly have been thinking that?

Why do the words desert me so suddenly, Virgil? We both know a shortage of words is not my affliction. "You're the one for the pretty speeches, the poetry, the eloquent statements," Tracy would complain later, after all began to fester, exposed to the light. But now? Here? In this first moment? Did I know something?

Gah. Let me begin again. I walked into Rachel's office, apologizing in my most charming manner for my tardiness. She was equally apologetic, and expressed consoling sympathy about the vagaries of Los Angeles traffic. But she was firm in her insistence that we would need to reschedule, there was no longer enough time left in the day for what needed to be done. I glanced at my watch, four-thirty. Did I register the surprise I felt? What ambitious Los Angeles lawyer calls it a day before six? She noted the look, she told me later. She didn't much care for it, recoiled from its implication. But she said nothing. Instead, as she gathered her papers, she gave me an outline of what the restitution process was likely to entail and how little would be required of me. A few signatures, an interview, but the effort of preparing the documentation to be submitted on my behalf was to be almost entirely Rachel's. She would pull all the pieces together, submit my application, and then we would see. The only complication she could envision was the possibility of a competing claim, but her preliminary research showed none had been filed.

She paused over a photocopy of the picture of my father's Budapest living room.

"It might help to get this authenticated. It's such a compelling piece of evidence. Do you think your father might sign an affidavit? It could be useful later."

I sighed and shook my head. "I wouldn't count too much on his cooperation."

"So I've heard. That's weird, don't you think?"

"Everything to do with my father is weird."

She smiled and set the photo into a file, which she slid into her briefcase. "Well, weird or not, I'm hoping it will be fairly easy as these things go." Her tone suggested the meeting had come to an end, but I was not ready to quit her so quickly.

"It can't be as easy as all that. I mean, that's it? We're done?"

"Well, no, it's not *quite* that easy, it's true—which is why I'd like you to come back next week. We can do this on Monday. I have an opening at three. You'll have the weekend to plan your route and be on time," she said, and rose with a smile. "My assistant will book the appointment."

I rose with her. "Won't he wait just a little?" Nervy boy.

"He will," she said, looking at her watch again. "But sunset won't."

How did I overcome the deficit of that initial impression, my tone deafness, all the cues missed, the signals read incorrectly? It was a disastrous performance on nearly every level. And yet, just a few weeks later, we would be standing in a museum together, looking at paintings. I'm sure there was a path from the one moment to the next but I can't seem to remember it. Does it seem portentous to say we were guided there? Of course it does. But based on what happened next, I am left with no other suitable explanation. We went through our obligatory goodbyes and confirmed our contact information. Rachel picked up her briefcase, to underscore the finality of the interview. I followed her to the door of her office. Then it happened.

Throughout this tale, I have encountered moments that have seemed, in turn, like the ones that changed all that followed. Perhaps they all have been, in their way, the story beginning anew over and over again. Mr. Calvino, allow me to present Mr. Escher. You two will have much to discuss. But this, this truly was the beginning of the things that turned out to matter most. As I followed her through the door of her office, I watched as she reached in passing with her left index finger and allowed it to graze a mezuzah she had affixed to the doorframe. How can I explain that touch, its effect on me? I vibrate with it still, that gentle stroke. I replay the moment again and again, trying to understand how so simple a movement could have unleashed so much in me. I was startled by the intimacy of the thing, how joined to the mezuzah she became in so fleeting an instant. It electrified me. It wasn't that I wanted to be the mezuzah, to feel the shock of her finger trailing gently across me. Rather, I wanted to feel for myself whatever it was that had animated the gesture. I wanted to understand this profound, silent serenity, this reverie; to know how she had accomplished this astonishing feat of seeming substantial and ethereal at once, of being transported by a devotion that was not reflexive but ran deeper than consciousness.

More questions. As though there weren't enough already. But these burned with a different intensity, an urgency that my father's painting, for all its millions, could not match. Much later, I asked Rabbi Wolfe about mezuzahs in one of the few pleasant conversations we had. I wondered if their placement in workplaces was normal or sanctioned. She advised me that, according to *halakhah*, that arcane and complicated body of Jewish religious law, every doorway in a Jewish person's home or business that leads into an area fit for human habitation or in which a person spends significant amounts of time requires a mezuzah. I remembered, with shame, the mezuzah on the front door of my family home, mummified under dozens of coats of old paint. As a boy, I asked my father about it, and he shrugged and informed me it had come with the house.

I know it is time to talk about Rabbi Wolfe. She's hovered at the perimeter of events long enough, a spectral presence, and she deserves to be admitted. To be faced. Her role in this affair is, after all, decisive. But I'm not ready yet. Of all the aspects

MARK SARVAS

of this saga, I find her the most vexing. I cannot even describe, with any certainty, my feelings about her. Anger? Sorrow? Pity? A strange kind of love? A hard woman to know, our rabbi, and an even harder one to like. Wisdom without warmth. Yes, she looms large. But her hour upon the stage will emerge soon enough. Patience, Virgil. Trust the tale, not the teller.

I T'S GOTTEN STUFFY and warm in here, which surprises me. I would have imagined the climate-control apparatus ran all night to protect the auction house's ill-gotten gains. Apparently that is not the case, although I suspect some intricate network of devices and quivering needles in the back is poised to bring a vast lumbering array to life to adjust things should a certain critical point be reached. The thought is comforting—to be looked after, provided for, responded to—and I find myself longing for so convenient an arrangement to regulate my own disorderly affairs.

I can feel the coarse bristling fabric of my chair's backrest dampening my shirt. I have thought to ask Virgil to run a little air through the place, but the reproachful look he gave me when I pulled the chair over leads me to believe my request would not be warmly met. It was a defeat of some kind to sit down, puncturing the effect I'd worked so hard to establish: the intense, solitary brooder of unknowable depth.

The painting has changed yet again, transformed beneath my scrutiny as the hours pass. To what can I attribute this latest evolution? I have spent so many hours with my attention fixed on this canvas that it's difficult to imagine there is anything left for me to discover. Perhaps there isn't. It isn't that new details emerge. Yet the character of the whole keeps shifting. Certainly, the painting seems softer to me now, its edges smoother and less forbidding than they seemed just hours ago. The blues, in particular, once electric, now seem to pulsate thickly, slowly, like an aristocratic heartbeat. Whatever the truth of it, it is surely a different painting now than it was months ago when I first stood before it with Rachel at my—

But I get ahead of myself. *Patience, Matt*, as the old man would say. For now, the painting. The thing itself, here on the wall before me. My thoughts return to the human hand that painted it, long lost, reduced to dust in blood-soaked European soil. Could Ervin Laszlo Kálmán have imagined, in his wildest dreams, that his work would last? He had his ambitions, amply documented. But his world was so riven by tragedy, did he merely cast his forlorn children into the world and hope for the best?

Lest I judge this wayward father too harshly, I remind myself that, like the rest of Europe's youth, he was summoned up and flung into the charnel house. He entered basic training late in 1915, and records indicate that the emperor found him an inferior specimen, sensitive and unsteady. When he should have been learning how to operate his artillery, he was discussing the finer points of synthetic cubism with other artistically inclined soldiers.

He did not last long on the front, having a complete nervous collapse in the spring of 1916, undone by the carnage at the Battle of Lutsk. He squatted in a trench soaked with the blood of a childhood friend who bled to death from a severed leg, the leg Kálmán would later commemorate in his self-portrait. He was discharged and sent to a sanatorium, where he was treated for what they used to call "shell shock" with morphine and veronal, beginning a lifelong addiction. He lost thirty pounds and was plagued by nightmares. He frequently shat blood. Under the patient ministrations of his doctors he began to make some progress until he learned of his friend Heti's death in July of 1916. He collapsed again and did not lift a pen—or a brush—for another year, during which he was in and out of a variety of mental hospitals.

Things began to turn for him late in 1917, a year in which he resumed his correspondence with other artists, most notably his lengthy discussions of color with Matisse, whose influence can be seen in his famous bather paintings of that year. These were the first big canvases Kálmán had undertaken since his conscription, and they showed the mark the war had left on him, as I would see for myself in a few weeks at Rachel's urging. They are the first of his works now accorded masterpiece status. He briefly managed to overcome his addictions and, with the war's end in 1918, he returned to Budapest to mourn the deaths of his many friends. But before returning to Budapest, he spent three weeks relaxing at Lake Balaton.

This particular fact has always stood out to me for the simple reason that as a child I spent two summers there, at what we used to call sleepaway camp, on the banks of Eastern Europe's answer to Lake Tahoe. It admitted one foreigner of Hungarian extraction for every twelve native Hungarians, and was my mother's idea, this insistence that I should have some connection to my heritage. My father could not have cared less. I was a miserable and lonely nine-year-old and wrote my parents plaintive, prestamped postcards begging to be brought home, postcards that went unanswered. We were taught Hungarian every day, not a word of which I have retained. We were fed Hungarian meals. We were taught to sing the Internationale, which would have incensed my father had he known. It did not occur to me at the time to use this information to expedite my passage home. The legendary Santos opportunism was, in my youth, a recessive trait.

And—for some reason, this is the thing I remember most, though I can't say why—it was there that I first saw an uncircumcised penis. Get your mind out of the gutter, Virgil. It isn't like that.

I remember the dead, still air of my dormitory room, much like the dead air here in the auction house. The room was long and narrow, marked by two rows of single beds, each equipped with a small particleboard closet and chest of drawers. A row of clerestory windows admitted light but no views. My closet was cleaned out early on by light-fingered Hungarians enamored of my American T-shirts and candies. This remains my only experience bunking down with large numbers of males—there were probably thirty of us in the room—and I imagine it's similar to being in the army or in prison. The almost continuous feeling of vulnerability, of exposure. Friendships born of necessity, protectors and patrons. We foreigners hung together, whispering our impenetrable English codes late at night, enjoying our apartness and privilege over our backward, Eastern European brethren.

After our daily swim in the lake, we would all return to the dormitory to change out of our wet trunks. Ridiculously modest, I would position myself beneath a towel held into place by my chin pressed to my chest, and try to change with a minimum of exposure. My maneuver was a source of much mirth in the room, especially among the more exuberantly naked of my peers, who discarded their trunks and ran around flicking wet towels at each other. I remember being startled and repulsed by their hooded members. I had, after all, limited experience with the male organ, exclusively my own, which hadn't yet begun to interest me, and so I assumed there was something defective about them, some peculiar foreign variant. But there was something more about these boys. I couldn't help but contrast their tall, supple power with my own scrawny limbs, and although there was obviously something wrong with them, I envied the effortless grace of their movements while I hid beneath my terry-cloth tent. Later, I approached Geza, one of my counselors, a mere teenager himself with whom I'd formed a vague, brotherly bond as the weeks had dragged by. I drew a picture of what I had seen and tried, in broken Hungarian, to elicit an explanation. He looked curiously at me, gestured toward my own package, and asked, "*Zsidó?*" I did not understand, and after a few minutes of fruitless gesturing, he drew a Star of David on a sheet of paper and pointed inquiringly at me. I hesitated, and executed a movement that rested uneasily between a nod and a shrug, and that was how I came to realize that *zsidó* meant Jew.

Did Geza's attitude toward me change at that moment? Yes, I believe it did. Weeks later, I was being punished with one of my friends for talking after lights-out. There was something sinister about the way Geza extracted us both from the dorm and took us out into the warm, honeyed night, where he had us squat barefoot in the gravel. I didn't understand, at first, but as the minutes passed, I came to see that the discomfort of the position was the point, and I was forced to maintain it even after the pain had become excruciating. To be fair, the same penance was required of my bunkmate, about whose religion I have no specific recollection. But it seemed to me that Geza—lithe and lean and blond like my bedfellows, or so I remember him now—was deriving considerable pleasure from my suffering.

Or is that merely the way I remember it, the inevitable Woody Allen trajectory of all this? Once you embrace your inner Abraham, all you can see are anti-Semites lying in wait? Yet I felt myself an outsider among those boys even then. A strange fear gripped me as I lay in my row beneath my thin blanket, long before I had learned enough history to compare it to images of other rows of people sleeping in camps. Yet when my father announced, the following year, his decision to return me to camp—my opinion was not solicited—I did not protest. Why was I so compliant? The obvious answer is that fear of my father's displeasure was greater than my fear of whatever I imagined awaited me at camp. But was that reasonable? Would he have thrown me back if I had told him what I was facing? Is it possible that I have read him wrong my whole life, failed to give him the credit he deserved?

Hah, look at you, Virgil, all knowing smiles. You've caught me out. Of course not. Performance still, to the end. The old man wouldn't have given me a second's thought once the flight attendant took me, the unaccompanied minor, to the plane bound for Budapest. *O Father why hast thou forsaken me?* Oy. Great-grandpa Szabo is no doubt rolling in his . . . in his what? There was nothing left of him but ash and smoke.

IN THE SIX WEEKS that followed my first interview with Rachel, events proceeded with a frustrating dullness. Given the remarkable intensity of that first meeting, I imagined that our follow-up would attain similar heights. But the second visit consisted of signing an impossible number of legal documents, insistent red adhesive arrows directing me again and again to scrawl *Mathias Santos* across a variety of dotted lines. I think I bought a baseball team. To this day, I can't really say what I signed. I'd like to say I trusted Rachel so implicitly that I gave myself over to her, but the truth is I have always been careless about such things, to my agent's irritation.

Once the paperwork was signed, there was dismayingly little needed from me. The documentation required by the government, arcane and overcomplicated though it was, could be generated with minimal involvement at my end. The question of authenticating my father's photograph was raised again, and then deemed unnecessary in light of Halasz's meticulous journals. There were a few one-question phone calls, and a single interrogatory as well as a few documents requiring notarization. All of this was followed by weeks of silence.

I was suffused with a feeling of anticlimax. The echoes of that first meeting continued to reverberate, and I was desperate to feel *that* again, that purpose, that, dare I say it knowing how it will sound, love? And so it came to pass that after several weeks of quiet, I made my way to a small shop that carried Jewish specialty items. I had decided to buy a mezuzah of my own, as though this might restore in me the quiet ecstasy I'd beheld. I am aware of how foolish, how pathetic that sounds now, but if it is any consolation, it felt foolish and pathetic even then. I headed down to one of the Jewish neighborhoods that dot Pico Boulevard, and I stumbled more or less at random into a store called Solomon's. Yes, I know . . . Would I make that up?

The shop was sunlit, although a faint odor of dust permeated the space. Moving through the store, one traveled from the general-interest books in the front, through the religious accessories in the middle of the store, to the storehouse of religious texts in the rear. The character of the handful of customers seemed to progress along similar lines: two women in jeans and T-shirts perused the menorah selection, while an elderly bearded Hasid fingered a Babylonian Talmud. I asked the Orthodox twenty-something behind the counter where the mezuzahs were, and he directed me to the middle of the store, barely looking up from his text. Did he know a poseur when he saw one?

I wandered past the kippot, the tefillin, the yahrzeit candles—how easily these trip off my tongue now, and yet how alien they were to me just months ago, neglected for a lifetime—and stood, bewildered, before a display of mezuzahs. There were mezuzahs of pewter, of wood, of frosted glass, of bronze. There was one covered with handmade sequins, and another in the shape of Batman. There were sports icons, maps of Israel, olive branches, and a true monstrosity, Noah's Ark in pewter and colored enamels. There was even one made of stone recovered from an archaeological site on the Temple Mount, holding out the possibility that it might contain a piece of the ancient temple. The prices ranged from the cost of a movie ticket to hundreds of dollars. Which would I buy? I certainly couldn't be seen buying the cheapest—my browsing had caught the attention of the young ladies.

I focused on a simple bronze mezuzah, sleek and unob-trusive. I reached out my finger and stroked it. Nothing. That astonishing feeling that had gripped me in Rachel's office was nowhere to be found. My gesture felt false, mannered. How could I imagine devotion would inhabit me so easily, un-earned? I felt my cheeks redden with disappointment and self-reproach, and I looked up around the room, certain everyone had been watching. The two women were busy among the books and the cashier was still deep in his studies, but I became convinced that they knew exactly what was unfolding, and had averted their eyes to spare me disgrace. Only the old man with the Talmud held my eyes, briefly, inscrutably, and returned to his text.

The bell over the front door chimed, and I looked up as

a father and his young son, maybe nine or ten, walked into the store together draped in prayer shawls. The boy took in the store's wares with delight, and together they walked up to the counter, where they fell into easy conversation with the cashier, whose countenance thawed at the sight of them. As they spoke, the father laid his hand on his little boy's head, and the boy raised his head to meet his touch. I felt something pierce me and I hurried from the store, buying nothing.

I returned home to find a short e-mail from Rachel. Our petition has cleared the first level of review, she informed me, with a startling matter-of-factness. *Budapest Street Scene* was one step closer to being back in the family where it belonged. Her words. Not mine.

I T WAS IN 1919 that Kálmán, in characteristically short
order—the man was unreflective about anything not in-
volving canvas and paints—met, fell in love with, and
married Ágnes Orban, a nurse who had tended to him
during one of his brief stays in a Hungarian sanatorium. It
was obvious to Kálmán that he could only survive with a help-
meet, someone committed to regulating his daily life in such a
manner that he could free himself to paint. It is agreed that
the *Budapest Street Scenes*, the monumental works that follow
their union, belong as much to Ágnes as to Kálmán. It was
under her steadying influence that Kálmán was able, in 1920,
to be considered for and awarded a professorship at the Hungarian University of Fine Arts, a position he would hold for
four years until he relapsed, his veronal-soaked lectures a disgrace the university would no longer tolerate.

Thus began 1924, Kálmán's lost year, the year in which he
might just as easily have died, rendering him little more than a
footnote to modernism. But this time he had Ágnes, who saw
him through the crucible of withdrawal. She helped him tame the
hard white flame of addiction, and the Kálmán who emerged was
a different man, tempered in a way that allowed him, a year later,
to begin painting his famous street scenes. That these paintings
were done from memory strained through the haze of narcotic
withdrawal made them no less vivid, as disturbing in their day as

they continue to be in ours. He painted them in a frenzy, a com-
pressed period of weeks that saw him create six distinct views
of the street. The angles change, the palette adjusts, the compositions alter slightly. But a darkness, a sharp-edged foreboding,
informs each variation. Two were lost in the war, presumed destroyed by the Germans. One is in a private collection of a
Japanese banker. One is on permanent display at the Museum
of Modern Art in New York, and another hangs in the Kunst-
halle in Hamburg. The last of the six is before me now. Could
I imagine similar greatness coming out of a marriage to Tracy?
Would she inspire me, protect me, if only I let her? And if she did,
would I be capable of anything beyond the usual half-measures?

I awoke to find Tracy sitting up in bed, sending texts, her
morning ritual. It's something that has always bothered me,
this electronic attachment that leaves me feeling supplanted.
But Tracy has always been much more in the world, and of it,
than I, so I suppose it's natural that my own neglected phone
should continue to slumber while hers lights up like a slot machine delivering a jackpot. There are, for her, always friends to
be greeted, arrangements to be made and, of course, a cause
to fight, although the last few months had been bleak. The
recanted testimony had not moved Texas authorities as she'd
hoped, and the execution date remained fixed on the calendar,
looming in mere months, which meant even more Brian time
in our lives. Just the night before, she'd hosted a fund-raiser
with him. I was asleep when she came home, so she didn't know
about Rachel's latest. I watched her for several minutes in a pose
of mute indignation, waiting for her to notice I was awake, but
she was engrossed. I finally spoke up. A performance is only a
performance if someone is watching.

"You two should just get a room already," I said, with
forceful levity. Tracy looked up from her phone.

"Good morning. Have you been up long?"

"Hours."

"Dick. Hang on, I'm just finishing up some stuff from last night. We did well, I think. We might have cleared thirty thousand." She finished up her typing and set the phone aside on the bed.

"That's excellent. Congratulations. I'm sure Brian must be pleased."

"Was that a dig?"

I shrugged. "Little. It was a little dig." She looked at me with what I hoped was fondness but could just as easily have been mild disdain. I pivoted and told her about Rachel's e-mail.

"That's fantastic. Congratulations—that's exciting."

"It's a good start. We're not there yet but . . ."

"Should we celebrate?"

"What did you have in mind?"

She climbed atop me. "Do you want to fuck me now?"

I kissed her. "I like the way you think."

I have always enjoyed morning sex the most. Perhaps it's the promise inherent in the new day. Perhaps I just like to see what I'm doing. I admit a weakness for the sight of the golden cross Tracy wears around her neck, dangling over me, between her breasts—there's something irresistibly transgressive about watching it swing as she sways atop me. We were well on our way when her phone began to buzz, and she glanced in its direction.

"Don't. You. Dare," I warned her.

She complied but I could see the distraction had begun to set in. Fucking Brian. I grabbed the buzzing phone and threw it across the room, into an armchair, out of reach, out of sight.

LATER OVER COFFEE at our breakfast bar, Tracy filled me in on the case. An appeal had been filed with the Texas Supreme Court, though they held out very little hope on that front. They already had their eyes on a U.S. Supreme Court appeal, and the fund-raiser had been held to help defray those costs. As Tracy spoke, I worried for her, wondered how she would withstand the blow if things did not go her way. But I also admired, even envied her commitment. Years earlier, I had tried to teach her chess. There was something I found erotic about sparring over a chessboard, and she gave herself to the study of the game. She mastered the basic moves quickly and even showed a knack for strategy. But I beat her each time because she was reluctant to attack, to capture. It felt aggressive and wounding to her, I think, and so she played defensively. At the time, I thought of my father—no killer instinct would have been his diagnosis, and it was mine. I thought she was too kind to fight. But I have come to see, as this case unfolded, that I was wrong. Chess was my thing, she did it to humor me. But to this cause she was committed, she had conviction, something that eludes me even now, as I continue this absurd pose in this darkened room alone with this painting. Aware of my own shortcomings, I would periodically test her convictions.

"Tracy, that all sounds great and you know I'm behind you in this, right? But . . . well, what if you're wrong? Have you thought about that? What if he *did* do it?"

"He didn't. There's no way. He's a mental child. It's impossible."

"You think children aren't violent? Have you been to a playground lately?"

She shook her head with a kind of tender scorn, the memory of which now aches.

I remember late one evening coming upon Tracy as she watched a video on her laptop. Ricky McCabe spoke to an unseen interviewer from behind prison glass, his hands cuffed, his expression desperate. His skin was mottled with acne, pale against the orange of his jumpsuit, his dirty hair in a sort of pageboy cut that didn't suit him. I didn't really listen to what he was saying, I was paying more attention to Tracy and her reactions. As she watched, she would occasionally sigh, no, more a shudder, almost a sob. At other times she would cover her mouth or wipe a tear. At the end of the short video, McCabe seemed to be addressing her directly and implored, almost in a whisper, *"Please don't let me die."* She seemed to nod almost imperceptibly as she closed her laptop, some ineffable contract executed. It was hard not to be moved.

I tried again, softly. "You weren't there. You can't be sure."

She set her coffee mug down on the countertop and looked at me with what I was now certain was mild disdain. Was I exposing my essential faithlessness at last? I don't know, Virgil. Either way, I extracted the concession I was looking for.

"No. You're right. I can't."

"So what if you get the story wrong? Then what?" Why did I press? I thought at the time I was being competitive; being, as she had averred, a dick. But now I think I was, without realizing it, looking for guidance.

She thought for a long moment, then took my mug and hers to the coffeepot for a refill. "Then you hope for another chance to set it right." As her words sank in, she piped up with forced casualness from the coffee machine. "Oh, hey, there's something else I have to tell you."

Nothing good has ever followed this preamble. I steeled

myself and turned to face her, curious, and I could tell she was uncomfortable under the scrutiny.

"So. I didn't want to ruin the mood. I spoke to your dad yesterday. He's coming to visit."

"He— You what?" Of all the possible things she might have told me, this never made my radar.

"Yeah. Some toy show in Glendale in a couple of weeks."

She placed the refilled coffee mug in my hand. I set it aside.

"Why is he calling *you*?"

"Gee, I don't know, Matt, maybe I'm nice to him?"

"You laugh at his shitty jokes."

"They're no shittier than your shitty jokes."

I pushed the coffee mug away and slid deeper into the chair, as though it might somehow protect me. "He hasn't been out here in . . . I dunno, ten years? More?"

"I guess it's a big show."

"It's the same show they hold every year."

"Well, he seemed excited."

I laughed. Oh, Virgil, how I laughed. The idea of my father being excited to see me was so absurd, so obviously a construct of Tracy's wishful thinking that I could not restrain myself. I laughed but I should have loved her for it. Her cheeks flushed.

"What's so damn funny?"

"The idea of my father being excited to see me is funny. He hasn't been excited since the night he conceived me. It's this painting. It's got to be."

"Well, whatever you think, he's coming. Maybe you should be nicer to him," she said, poking my chest.

Tracy left me to prepare for her favorite gig—a bikini shoot at the beach for Harvest Moon, a catalog she'd been modeling for for five years—and I turned over this latest, distressing development. I wasn't sure what troubled me more: that the old man would shortly be descending on me, bringing his own brand of *Walpurgisnacht* to town; or that he and Tracy were on cozier terms than I'd realized. What con, what scam, what new malefic angle was he working now? I felt the hair on my neck stir as it hadn't in years. As soon as Tracy walked out the door for her shoot, I went up to the bedroom, pulled my talismanic list from the bedside drawer, and called him, though I had no idea what to say. It didn't matter because he didn't answer the call. I left no message, tossed my phone aside, defeated. First Brian. Now my old man. Everyone, it seemed, had a stronger claim on Tracy than I did.

I hoped a long, hot shower might steam away my worries. But even after nearly a half hour beneath sizzling needles, I could still see that stubborn, familiar sadness in my eyes as I shaved away the night's growth. As I was drying my face, I heard an urgent buzz from the armchair. Tracy's phone was rattling away, forgotten where I had chucked it earlier. I was pleased at the thought of her forced disconnection from Brian, when my own phone jumped with an incoming text: Tracy, on a borrowed phone, asking me to run her BlackBerry over to the shoot, seeing as I was the one who had tossed it onto the chair. Okay, I tapped out, and picked up her phone. I looked at the screen. Missed call. Brian Bettersea. Really? Bettersea? Who makes these names up? It dawned on me that I hadn't known his last name before this moment. I was tempted to look through her texts and messages, but I set the phone down, maintaining my reasonable facsimile of integrity. It would do for now.

NO MATTER HOW LONG I live here, I never lose the quiet thrill I feel exiting the McClure Tunnel at the end of the Santa Monica

Freeway to find the Pacific Coast Highway unfurling before me. There's something bracing about emerging from this brief stretch of darkness onto the dizzying ribbon of asphalt beneath cloud-streaked skies, alongside an opal seascape flecked with whitecaps. I open all my windows and my sunroof and let the salty tang of the Pacific envelop me as I luxuriate in the genius of my decision to leave New York.

The road was wide-open as I sped toward Malibu, my thoughts drifting to Tracy, her BlackBerry on the seat beside me, tempting me with its secrets. She'd been typing into it the moment I first laid eyes on her, in an elevator in Beverly Hills. My film agents were located in the same building as her modeling agents, two floors apart. I held the door for her in the lobby as she stepped in, head down, typing. The door closed and she continued typing.

"Floor?" I finally asked.

"Twelve," she answered without looking up. "Thanks."

I pressed twelve and ten, and regarded her with interest, waiting for the inevitable moment when her signal would be lost. It arrived, heralded by an irritated sigh. She looked up and I nodded in sympathy. I, who am so rarely at a loss for words, was dumbstruck by her beauty.

"They need cell signal boosters in these things," I finally managed.

"That," she said, "is a brilliant idea." Then she paused, recognizing me. "I know you."

That was the year I was a regular on my ill-fated cable sensation, the only time in my life I've been recognized with any kind of regularity.

"I love that show. You're so good," she said.

I blushed. Yes, Virgil, I blushed. Even the tips of my ears lit up, a pink wash that quickly turned bright red. Thanks to the highly polished steel walls of the elevator, I was confronted with an infinite series of my crimson mug. Well, thank you very much, was the best I could muster. She smiled and touched my arm.

"Don't be embarrassed. It's true."

The door opened at ten. My floor.

I held my hand out. "Matt."

She took it. "I know. Tracy. Nice to meet you."

We stood together for a moment. "Your floor," she said.

I hesitated. Then: "It can wait."

I let the elevator door close.

I ASKED HER TO COFFEE on the spot, which was against type, for me. I am no fool, Virgil, I know when I am punching above my weight. But I was buoyed by my momentary fame, drawn to her friendliness and approachability, and I asked her with, I fear, little finesse. She demurred—she was meeting with a new client—and I was reconciling myself to rejection's stinging embrace, when she proposed dinner that night instead. I felt like the man at the car rental counter who has just been told his reserved Honda is sold out but there's a Jaguar waiting for him instead. I recommended a favorite sushi spot nearby.

She thrilled me as she entered the restaurant. Heads did turn, then and now. My Tracy commands a room, it's not so much a gift as a birthright, that same ease I saw in my Hungarian campmates.

My Tracy. Old habits.

She was late, always late, I would learn, her internal clock set at a permanent forty-five-minute delay. Even when I used the time-honored technique of padding departure times, Tracy maintained the forty-five minute window without fail, some inner gyroscopic mechanism inexorably attuned behind time's flow. But I would forgive her lateness the moment I laid eyes on her. Her casual attire was unvarying and simple—white blouse and slim jeans. The only deviation would be in her black boots: ankle-high to knee-high. She would have been at home in Silver Lake or Milan, but somehow she had landed here in this cramped, noisy sushi joint in Beverly Hills.

Amid the black lacquered dishes, moist towelettes, and vintage sake, she was expansive, open, and I admired that, even as it terrified me. She told me stories that night; the sociology professor who made a pass at her; the married law partner who'd courted her; her hippie parents, who still lived in the same house where she'd been born in Sedona, her mother's placenta buried beneath a tree in the yard. She received the salmon sashimi on her tongue as though taking a communion wafer. No rice, and only a dab of low-sodium soy. We learned that we both enjoyed billiards, though I would discover, at considerable personal expense, that she was deadly, far more accomplished than I. She found the stories I told about my father entertaining.

We kissed that first night, drunk on sake, on the grassy median dividing Santa Monica Boulevard as the evening traffic whizzed by. It's an odd place, I have come to see, for a kiss, and although it seemed spontaneous at the time—I simply reached out for her as we were crossing back to our cars, my finger latching onto her belt loop—I think there was something of an announcement to it. Look at me here, kissing this goddess in the middle of the boulevard! How far this Santos has come. Saying it to the world. To my father. My implacable audience of one.

Tracy's ringing phone interrupted my coastal reverie. I glanced at it, irritated, expecting to see Brian's name in the caller ID again. I was wrong. It wasn't Bettersea.

Look, my Lord, it comes. It will not speak; then I will follow it.

I SAT IN THE PARKING LOT commandeered by the photo shoot, my heart racing, a steel taste filling my mouth as I scrolled through Tracy's calls. The expected calls and texts from Brian were there, some ending with "xo," which caused flickers of jealousy. But I blurred past those as I tallied the number of calls between Tracy and my father. Almost half a dozen. Most calls were brief, just ten minutes or so. But one was nearly an hour. I was certain he and I had not talked that much since I'd moved here.

The shimmering ocean and the wide green umbrellas marking the location of the shoot had fallen away before me and I could see nothing but gray. I was livid but also terrified, mistrustful. What were these two up to? Why had neither of them told me they were talking? My father's unscrupulousness was a given but Tracy had always been honest with me. All at once, I felt on the outside of something. I scooped up her Black-Berry and made my way toward the makeup station and craft services.

The setup was modest, the Harvest Moon catalog falling several notches below Victoria's Secret, and a few above JCPenney. But they had always been reliable employers, and over the years Tracy had become their cover model. A temporary makeup station had been set up on the edge of the parking lot, not much more than a director's chair, a large mirror, and a card table scattered with a bewildering assortment of brushes and pencils and powdered colors. A bored stylist with magenta hair and a dozen facial piercings lounged in the chair, absorbed by her phone. Another table offered a spread of bagels, fruit, and cottage cheese. Coffee and bottled water were also provided. I opened a bottle, picked up a copy of the latest catalog from the table, and glanced over at a straw-haired woman in a pantsuit who was watching the shoot. Abby, the client rep. She noticed me and gave me a rabbity smile and a small wave. I nodded back as I flipped without interest through the catalog.

Tracy was about a hundred yards down the beach, with Antoine, her usual photographer, and his two assistants, who held up light reflectors. I watched her as I had many times before, admiring her focus, her unshakable professionalism. She seemed blissful, serene, unselfconscious, at once present and miles away, within her own little bubble. I once asked her what she thought about when the camera was clicking away. Her answer was disappointingly prosaic—that she was considering the angles, the light, thinking about how to make the shoot look good. But she also admitted that, with intense photographers, the world would sometimes fall away and she'd find herself locked in this electric, private communication. Tracy and Antoine had a long, storied history. They'd been lovers early in her career, and so that intensity would sometimes show itself and, of course, it bothered me. But not today. Not even the unexpected appearance of my rival could sway me from my purpose.

My rival. Would you listen to me?

But it was then that I noticed *him*, standing midway between our little encampment and the photo shoot. He belonged back here with the rest of us but he had approached the zone of intimacy, the edge of the bubble. He looked out of place on the beach, wearing a tailored dark suit. In my fevered imaginings, I'd always pictured him six-foot-something, blond hair and blue eyes. To my chagrin, the bastard looked just as

I'd envisioned. Immaculately coiffed, broad-shouldered, all he needed was a brown shirt and he could have been a recruiting poster for the Wehrmacht. Antoine lowered his camera—even his tattooed muscularity was diminished in comparison—and Tracy headed back to the makeup stand for a wardrobe change. Brian, it had to be Brian, could only be Brian, walked alongside her and I was struck by how appropriate they looked together, how right they seemed. They were so engrossed in their conversation that Tracy didn't notice me until she was in her chair and saw my reflection in the mirror.

"There you are!"

She held her hand out. I gave her the BlackBerry and she kissed me. A kiss I drew out for Brian's benefit. Her stylist cleared her bored throat. Tracy nodded in her direction.

"Right. A lot to do." I retreated and a blur of assistants touched and prodded her, handing her outfits, wiping at her face, brushing her hair. "Matt, this is Brian. Brian, Matt." She picked up her next bathing suit and disappeared behind a temporary changing screen.

"Nice to meet you, Matt," Brian said, holding out his hand. I took it, shaking it as firmly as I could, squaring my shoulders to try to close some of the inches of height between us.

"Same here. I hear a lot about you."

He smiled sheepishly. "Yeah, sorry about that. I guess it can get a little tedious if you're not in the thick of it."

It was only the fact of a man's life at stake that choked the riposte on my lips. I noted Abby, the client rep, listening to us with a slight frown. I suspected we were impeding the day's progress.

"Well, God's work and all that," I said.

"Exactly," he said. He seemed, to my great consternation,

quite decent—well mannered, respectful, even likable. Infected by my father's suspicious nature, I was certain he had to be hiding something.

Tracy emerged in a maroon one-piece open-backed swimsuit and sat in her chair.

"All good?" she asked.

There was a brief awkward silence. Neither Brian nor I knew what to say. The silence stretched on and I broke it, turning to the business at hand.

"Tracy, I need to talk to you."

"Sure, what's up?"

"Alone."

She looked up at me. This was an unusual request.

"Babe, we're all kind of right in the middle of things here. Can we do this later?"

I know how to deliver a line with consequence, and I did. "No. We can't."

The seriousness in my voice did the trick because she asked the stylist to give us a minute. Magenta sighed with irritation and stepped away. I turned to face Brian, who hadn't moved.

"Alone."

"Oh, of course. I'm sorry." He turned to Tracy. "I'll be in my car, making some calls." He touched her arm as he left.

Tracy turned her attention to me.

"That was rude."

"Does the vigorous defense of Ricky McCabe require him to touch you quite so much?"

I saw a smile fight to stay off her lips. "Are you . . . jealous . . . of Brian?"

"Of course not. Why the hell should I be jealous of a six-foot-two blond Superman?"

She found it in herself to be patient with me, threading her arms around my waist. "He's married. To an ex–Miss Universe or something. Has three gorgeous kids. He's living the dream. All of which is immaterial because I'm not available. So what are we talking about?"

What, indeed. The other suitor. The other man. The one I actually *was* jealous of. I took a steadying breath and asked her about the calls with my father. Her forbearance faded, replaced by something darker, sharper.

"You looked at my *phone*?"

"No! Well, sort of. Yes. I looked at your phone. I mean, not at first. I was in the car, it rang, I assumed it was Field Marshal Bettersea over there but then I saw it was my dad."

"Jesus, Matt. I can't believe you looked at my phone."

"I never have before. I never needed to, never thought of it." A half-truth, at best.

"You only had to ask. I don't have anything to hide from you."

"That's what I thought, too. Until I saw, what, a half dozen calls with my dad in two weeks? What the fuck did you two talk about for an hour? An *hour*?" I trailed off: "He doesn't *like* talking on the phone . . ."

"Well, he likes talking to *me*."

We sat in a long moment of silence, stewing. Tracy appeared to be torn. Abby continued to watch us with consternation but maintained a respectful distance. Finally, Tracy spoke, much of the anger gone from her voice, though a coolness remained. "He asked me not to tell you. We weren't talking about anything important, Matt. I should have told you. Most of the time I think he likes to hear me talk. He's just . . . I don't know, he's just lonely."

The word echoed in the space between us.

"Lonely," I repeated. "He's lonely." How dare she humanize the old bastard. "And the painting?"

"He's never brought it up."

"Never? Three million dollars and he's never brought it up."

"No, Matt. Never. I mentioned it once and he didn't want to talk about it."

I leaned against the table, trying to absorb all this new information. I couldn't put it together. It made no sense.

"So, he's lonely . . . okay . . . so you just talk to him? For hours and hours?"

She touched my arm as I'd seen Brian touch hers earlier. "Yeah. Because he's your father, you dope. Now can I get back to work?"

I nodded, dumbly, and she kissed my cheek and made her way back down to the beach, back to sinewy Antoine and his tats. Brian got out of his car and walked along beside her, showing her some paperwork. Abby came over and stood beside me, watching them, her nose twitching.

"I don't like that one, Matt," she said. "I don't like him one bit." I wanted to hug her, though I would only later learn how I had misread that remark.

As I watched Brian and Tracy recede toward the horizon, I felt ever more like that small, hunched figure on the edge of the *Budapest Street Scene*, all dark and furtive and leering, aside and apart from the action. Up to no good.

I T WAS RACHEL'S IDEA to visit the Kálmán bathers in the Norton Simon collection. She thought it might give me a better feel for the artist and his work. We agreed to meet on Saturday at the museum, another resplendent Southern California morning, and I walked through the jasmine-scented air thrilled, like a young boy on a date, which I suppose in some fashion I was. Rachel was waiting for me at the entrance, tickets in hand. It was, it turned out, a celebration. A date had been set to hear our case. Rachel was giddy at the speed of our progress, which she assured me was unprecedented.

"My treat," she said, taking my offered arm as we headed toward the galleries.

I took in the guards in each room, deflated, bored creatures. They were not in your league, Virgil, I can assure you. They were dilettantes without your sense of purpose, your barnacle-like scrutiny. I could, I think, have lifted a painting off the wall and they would have held the door for me. The crowds were no better than their chaperones, mostly retirees and students, the occasional couple, hands clasped. They all seem to read the information plaques before looking at the pictures, have you ever noticed that, Virgil? Oh, the place is pleasant enough, all marble floors, track lighting and oracular skylights. But there's something slightly unnatural about it all, isn't there? I watched a young man wearing a porkpie hat and a T-shirt for a band called the Kooks, as a young woman in tight jeans and spiked boots explained a sculpture to him. He nodded, the same dutiful nods glazed tour groups offer the docents who tell them what they should be noticing. Was he thinking about anything other than removing those jeans?

Rachel glided with familiarity through the galleries, slowing a bit as we passed through a hall of works by the Old Masters. Is it my imagination, or do people behave differently around them? The talking is softer, the mood respectful, or fearful, I'm not certain which. Perhaps the age or the subject matter is too distant, too far removed, and we are uncertain how to locate ourselves in relation to these works. One of us, it seems, doesn't belong here. I have never warmed to them, with their biblical tableaux and oppressive religiosity; or else their staid, bourgeois portraiture. Only the *nature morte*, with all its fussy verisimilitude, its glistening water droplets, appeals to me. But I prefer the indeterminate, shifting reality of Cézanne, his glorious mountain of quivering cubes, as riotous in its coloring as any of my mother's Christmas trees. Rachel, however, drifted among the artworks, unbowed, and when she spoke about the paintings, it was with a kind of love, a feeling deeper than whatever informs the obligatory chatter of the docents.

I know she spoke of many things, of the biblical scenes, of painterly technique, of impasto, of chiaroscuro, which she then connected in a line to the Kálmán bathers we'd come to see, but I wasn't listening, not fully. I was basking in the radiance of the art refracted through her reverence, and I remembered, in contrast, my first—and last—museum visit with Tracy. An international Van Gogh exhibition came through town, replete with the usual blockbuster crowds and ticket prices. Tracy paused in front of the greatest hits, watching me, I think, for cues on how to react, but she became overwhelmed and beat a hasty retreat to the café, where she took weary refuge in a double espresso. In contrast, the longer Rachel spent among the paintings, the more luminous she became.

I'd just about had my fill of Judas and Lazarus and John the Baptist when I strayed upon a large, disquieting canvas. An old man holds a knife to the throat of a young boy but an angel has stayed his hand. The three figures, joined by a ram, are shrouded in a forbidding darkness, although a distant, rising light appears to illuminate parts of each figure, including the bald dome of the patriarch, his back turned from what I now know to be his son.

"And you think your dad is trouble."

I looked at her blankly, missing the reference.

"Abraham? Isaac?" She regarded me with mild disbelief.

The tale began to come back to me. "It's about a sacrifice, right?" She raised an eyebrow and I ventured on, grinning. "And a goat. I definitely remember a goat."

"Oh, Matt," she said, smiling. The rebuke was gentle, indulgent. I listened as she walked me through the tale, chapter and verse. We moved on, but I was unable to shake the image of the father prepared to slay his son, and the son so docile in his fate. I understand only now how much I resented them both.

Walking on, we came to rest before a reclining Matisse nude. Our easy rapport gave way to awkward throat clearing, and I found myself unable to make eye contact with Rachel. Such a strange, childlike response! I glanced at her, and it seemed as though she'd flushed for just a moment. And then she surprised me with a gesture of such . . . I can only call it tenderness. She leaned forward and sniffed at the edge of the painting, as though sampling a fine Bordeaux. I found the gesture both charming and intimate—it was as though she were alone in the gallery. She exhaled sibilantly and drifted to the next painting. I stood before the odalisque, aware of my racing heart.

At that precise moment, a little boy raced into the open gallery and paused before a Giacometti. He pointed at the attenuated giant, shrieked with delight, and ran on. I envied that boy, Rachel. For a moment, at least, I wanted his freedom to express the sheer, unspeakable wonder of a previously unimagined form of beauty filling one's vision. I think if I had been given liberty to point at you and shriek with similar abandon, I just might have. Or not. I wonder these days about all I might have achieved if I hadn't always been waiting for permission to act.

Rachel guided me to the Kálmán and wandered away to look at nearby paintings, tactfully leaving me to contemplate the bathers. I still felt the pressure of her somewhere behind my eyes and so I forced myself to read the descriptive plaque in an attempt to focus. The card bore an audio guide graphic proclaiming its significance to the collection. The bathers were a recurring motif for Kálmán—he'd painted them both before and after *Budapest Street Scene*. This particular version had come afterward, about three years before Kálmán put a rusty Luger in his mouth, and was confiscated almost immediately and shown in Berlin with the other so-called degenerate art before being sold off for a pittance. The card assured me that the painting was restituted after the war and came to rest here legally. I turned my attention from the card to the bathers themselves.

The painting was full of dark hues, a gloomy work, so different from the bathers of Cézanne and of Picasso. Here, greens so dark they were nearly black slipped into actual blacks and oppressive blues. Three pale bathers—again, three figures— are grouped beneath some leafy trees, where they stand against an indistinct background, lit only by occasional feathers of color across their torsos. Under the glare of the spotlight reflecting on the glass protecting the canvas, I noted that, again, one of the three figures stood with his back turned to the viewer. The longer I looked, the more convinced I became of the similarities between these bathers and the street scene, and I puzzled over the timing, wondering whether this was Kálmán's prelapsarian view of the *Budapest Street Scene*. Or was this a return to the primitive in the wake of cataclysm? Probably neither. It was nothing more than a group of bathers.

I found Rachel standing in front of a small but striking seascape by a painter who was a contemporary of Kálmán's, who had suffered a similar fate despite trying to play nice with the Nazis. Her attention was fixed on the green, churning waves upon which a single red boat was being tossed. The painting exuded such foreboding that even now, more than a half century after its creation, I found myself rapt beside Rachel. Foamy whitecaps raged against a green-black sea, and the sinister movement of the waves felt so intense that I think we were both tempted to hold on to each other for support. This time, I had no difficulty looking at her, and in her eyes I saw a kind of fear tinged with excitement. It was the first of many times I wanted to kiss her, and although I did not act on the impulse, I allowed my hand to brush against hers, a hand fuller than Tracy's sleek metacarpals. The fleeting, almost accidental gesture felt shockingly intimate to me. Rachel neither pulled her hand away nor moved it to meet mine, which I chose to interpret as tacit encouragement. For if no means no, I have always taken anything short of no to mean maybe.

A STORY IN THE NEWSPAPER the other day caught my attention. A sculptor, en route to dedicate a memorial he had designed to commemorate a World War II massacre, was killed in a plane crash. What made the story poignant was that his father had been killed in the original massacre, so now the press made much of both generations being claimed by the same tragedy. In his last interview, the artist spoke about the difficulties of designing a monument to a father he'd never known, but I thought he'd gotten it wrong. Surely it was easier this way, the blank slate unencumbered by inconvenient reality. He was free to idealize, could imagine any father a son might wish for. I was touched by his expression of love and loss for a father he'd never known.

I was thinking of plane crashes as I waited for my father at baggage claim. I've often had lurid daydreams about being one of those people called in by airline personnel when the flight of a loved one has gone down. That these daydreams almost always accompanied my father's visits would seem to bear further examination. I didn't wish him dead. But I've watched the footage of these survivors, rent by grief, and have envied such deep feelings.

What I had instead was a world-class case of the hiccups. They started that morning, in the shower, and persisted throughout the day, resisting every folklore cure I threw at them. I waited at baggage claim, despite my father's insistence that I meet him curbside, and scanned the crowd when my phone chirped. An e-mail from Rachel asking me to call her for the latest update. I wanted nothing more than to bolt from the airport and fling myself into the sanctuary of her office. I had begun to type a reply when I heard his whistle.

Ever since I'd been a boy, we'd had a family whistle, a unique call that served to summon or locate us amid crowds, like a muezzin's call to worship. It was a lyrical knot of ascending and descending scales, a sort of musical sheepshank. I'd always appreciated the obvious good sense of the scheme but now, hearing his call, I felt like a dog being summoned by his master. I spotted his dyed black hair weaving its way toward me, through the crowd.

"I told you to wait outside."

"Hi, Dad." *Hic.* "I came in. Special occasion. Shoot me."

I moved forward uneasily to hug him, which he received, allowing his hand to brush my left shoulder. I know it was my imagination but it seemed I could still smell the paint from his shop clinging to him, though he had retired years earlier. He once explained to me it was the solvent content of the paint evaporating that caused the sour smells I associated with him, with my youth. I stepped back and took him in between hiccups as he scanned the conveyor for his suitcase. I hadn't seen him in at least a year, probably longer. He now had a wizened, elfin quality that I'd never noticed before. A malign elf, mind you. The kind that would steal your pot of gold while you slept and replace it with a bucket of steaming feces. Still, there was undeniable power, vitality in his sinewy muscles as he blocked my effort to reach his suitcase and hoisted it off the conveyor in a single, graceful motion. There was something formidable about him, about his adherence to adamantine standards that I could neither meet nor shake free of. Where my father was concerned, I was like one of those early Mercury rockets that struggled to slip gravity's fingers, only to plunge back burning into the sea.

"Come on, Dad. Let me help." *Hic.*

He looked at me, as though my hiccups indicated a failure of character or will. "Where's your car?"

I gestured to the parking structure across the street. "Outside."

"Let's go."

We stepped out of the terminal into that odd mixture of carbon monoxide and ocean breezes that always invigorates me whenever I return home. The sun was shimmering and the sky was cloudless, that deep Cézanne blue. I looked to my father, hoping for some kind of reaction, proud of myself for having chosen such a beautiful place to live. His gaze was fixed straight ahead, waiting for the DON'T WALK sign to release him.

"It's beautiful here, huh?" I prompted.

"It's an airport, Matt."

The light changed and as we crossed, I could see him struggle with the weight of his large metal suitcase, filled with toy cars. He bought it before wheels became ubiquitous and he was too cheap to replace it. He preferred to struggle with it, a marker of some deep well of virtue that his shiftless son could never understand. It drove me fucking crazy, Virgil.

"Dad, gimme the—*hic*—damn suitcase."

"I'm fine." His standard reply. He was always fine. What a blessing, I thought, to be fine so much of the time.

We stepped up on the curb and into the parking structure. I led him to where I thought I had parked but didn't see my car. I slowed and began to look around, uncertain, my stomach beginning to churn. My dad didn't say anything for a moment as I scanned the rows. Finally:

"Matt, what is it?"

I didn't answer. *Hic*. I stood on my tiptoes, looking over the tops of SUVs. I could feel the sweat dappling my forehead.

"Hang on."

"What? You don't remember where you parked?" His tone was thick with disgust, as though he had foretold this scenario, expected nothing less from me. My heart thudded. I could feel his gorge rising. I began to look more desperately, trying to keep the explosion at bay.

"I know I left it in this row . . ."

I tried to find the car, prayed it was stolen, as I felt his eyes heavy on my back. I did not need to turn to face him to register his contempt. Yes, a strong word, but, as usual, my old man stood there in judgment of his son. For this, he must have been thinking, I escaped the Communists? For a son who can't even remember where he's parked? Perhaps you think I judge him harshly, Virgil. But within a moment, he could no longer contain himself, and the outburst came, as expected.

"Goddammit, Matt. What the *hell* is wrong with you?" His voice rising.

I flinched, expecting a blow that didn't come. I continued looking down the aisles, clicking my alarm button in the air.

"Is your head so completely up your ass? Don't you pay attention to anything but yourself?" Shouting at me now, red-faced, drawing the stares of passersby.

I turned to face him, both mortified and furious. I wanted to tell him to shut the fuck up. That I'd made a goddamn mistake, that was all, as though he'd never made any himself. My father, as I have said, was prone to rages, so this one shouldn't have stood out. But I realized, as he set down the suitcase in a huff, the real reason for his anger: The suitcase had become too heavy for him. And I had seen his weakness. The greatest fear of the Santos men, I can attest. For an instant, my anger lifted and I felt sorry for my father.

My hiccups had stopped. I pressed the alarm button again and, at last, a confirming chirp issued far down the row.

WE DROVE IN SILENCE. My father offered a single approving grunt about my BMW, but after that there was nothing but the gentle whoosh of the AC and the rhythmic thump of the road beneath us. The only thing that broke the silence was an occasional clearing of the throat, both his and mine. It's a habit, a tic really, that emerges in times of stress, and I was shocked to find just how much we sounded like each other. It was as though I was standing atop the Grand Canyon, and each phlegmy, staccato burst was answered by its ancestral echo. Did my father feel as usurped as I felt dismayed? His features revealed nothing. He watched the boulevards pass with scant interest.

The car, I was sure, smelled of paint.

My phone rang. The car's display screen identified Tracy as the incoming caller. I let the call go to voice mail, unprepared to navigate a phone conversation with my father in earshot. We drove on for another moment before he spoke.

"You should have answered."

"We'll be seeing her soon."

"It's rude, Matt."

I thought about confronting my father right then and there. Don't laugh, Virgil, I really did. But the prospect of talking to him enervated me. I was preemptively spent. When I was a child, my father had seltzer delivered to the house. It was the only thing he liked to drink, and it was delivered in those old-style fountain bottles, metal heads affixed onto glass bodies. I was warned to treat them with care. The contents were under extreme pressure, and if I dropped a bottle I was assured it would explode. But I was drawn to them, to their crystalline colors, pale blues and greens and yellows, shades that seemed to exist nowhere else. (It was only many years later that I learned that these bottles were invented in 1829 by—wait for it—a Hungarian.) I dropped one, as predicted, and it shattered against the concrete step of our garage where they were stored. A piece of glass sliced through my shin, and, as my mother bandaged my cut, my father reprimanded me for not heeding his warnings— *Pay attention, Matt!* What I remember most, however, about these bottles was the sound they made when they were empty, an exhausted sigh of carbon dioxide, sputtering but final. I felt that same sputtering emptiness whenever I contemplated asking my father any of the questions that bedeviled me.

So we drove in silence. I glanced at his carry-on bag in the rearview, the one in which he always carried his most valuable toys. Although I no longer knew which pieces were nestled in there, I could still imagine them as if I had wrapped and packed them myself. The tissue paper, tattered and worn from years of reuse, wrapped carefully around the toy and then placed within a cocoon of bubble wrap. It was my own sacrament, wrapping and unwrapping his toys, preparing them for market. I conservatively estimated that I had performed the ritual thousands of times before moving to L.A., watching as cars of every make and size passed through my hands. I came to know the objects as if they were mine. But now, years later, they had all merged, indistinct in my memory. Only the space car stood apart.

A single piece of molded plastic, bubble-gum pink. A cheap friction wheel set on a single rusted axle. It resembled nothing so much as a giant, extraterrestrial sperm on wheels. My father read the disbelief on my face when he bought it for five dollars. Disbelief transformed into shock when he wrote a price of sixty-five dollars in his distinctive blocky scrawl on a tiny round adhesive sticker, which he affixed to the underside of the chassis.

"Really?" I said as he placed the toy on our display table.

"It will sell," he said. His usual maddening certainty.

"Sixty-five dollars? No way."

"Want to bet? If I don't sell it, I give you the sixty-five. If I do, you pay me." That was always how my father ended debate. Cash on the barrelhead, put your money where your mouth is. He knew I seldom had the courage or the means to take the bait. Just sixteen, I didn't have the money to bet, but I shook on it, I was that sure.

The space car attracted a surprising amount of attention. Well, it was surprising to me. To my father it was the universe acting in accordance with his grand scheme. Offers were made, some quite near his asking price. My father had once again demonstrated his ironclad grasp of his market. I began to look at my watch every few minutes in the hopes of running out the clock.

Finally, a voice on the PA announced that it was time for the dealers to begin breaking down their tables and packing their wares. I moved to grab the space car first but my father held my hand. There was always surprising violence coiled in those arms. It was only after I wrapped every other object on the table that I was permitted, to my relief, to wrap the space car.

On the drive home, failing to keep the smugness out of my voice, I said, "I believe you owe me sixty-five dollars."

"I do not."

I turned to look at my father, shocked and confused but not at all surprised. He was a master of the angles and I was a fool not to have seen it coming.

"But you didn't sell it. You said you would sell it for sixty-five dollars."

"I didn't say *when* I would sell it, did I?"

"No, but—"

"No buts. I *will* sell the car, and I *will* sell it for sixty-five dollars."

The evil genius of his plan sank in. I could never win this bet, it was open-ended in his favor.

"That's not fair." I sulked.

He turned to face me as though he were about to deliver the lesson of lessons. "Never bet if you can't afford to lose," he said. But what he surely meant was *Pay attention, Matt.*

In the months that followed, we attended show after show, and I packed and unpacked the pink space sperm dozens of times. The script played out without variation, interested buyers picking up the toy, examining it, making a modest offer, my father holding firm. I began to wonder whether he was dug in purely to punish me, or because he truly believed in the value of the car and refused to sell it for less. A bit of both, I suspect. Either way, I never stood a chance.

The months turned into years. Virgil, I cannot tell you how many times I packed and unpacked that fucking thing, how I grew to loathe the sight of it. Past the point where the sixty-five dollars would mean anything to me. I began to consider buying it myself, if only to spare me having to wrap the hideous thing one more time.

Of course, it happened, just as he said it would. One damp Sunday morning somewhere, maybe in Allentown, maybe in Hempstead, a young man—he would have been young, would have been male—scooped up the sperm car, clutched it close to his chest, and doled out the sixty-five dollars, all small bills and loose change, into my father's expectant hands. Yes, Hempstead. I'm quite sure.

He was never one to miss an "I told you so," my old man. And there was, to be sure, a gleam of self-satisfaction in his eyes as he stood at the table, holding the money. I pulled four twenties out of my battered wallet and handed them to him. He gave me back my fifteen dollars in the singles and change he'd received from his buyer, a gesture that seemed petty but probably struck him as entirely reasonable. The change sloshed around in my pocket all during the wordless drive home.

But when I awoke the next morning, the four twenties had been restored to my wallet. I never learned when, why, or how this happened. For all I knew, my mother replaced the money herself. That would be her style. But I allowed myself to believe he'd had a change of heart. It seemed important to accord him this small measure of humanity, for both of us.

WE MET TRACY for an early dinner at a neighborhood Chinese restaurant we frequented. My father was worried about jet lag after the flight from New York and wanted to get to bed, so we had the place to ourselves. He became the immediate center of the waitstaff's attention. They were delighted to meet Matt's father. You must be proud of your son's success. He's one of our favorite customers. It was excruciating for me. My father, however, transformed once again into Social Gabi, the creature I had glimpsed long ago at the Tower Club, and I marveled as he charmed them. More than once, Tracy looked at me with reproach, as if to say, "You see—he's not so bad."

He and Tracy fell into easy conversation, and while they

avoided saying anything of substance, it was clear that, on some level, the two of them had achieved an understanding. Whether they were programmed to get each other or whether their rapport had evolved over the life of their phone calls, I didn't know. They clasped hands as they spoke, exuding warmth, and I felt excluded, irritated. I felt them in cahoots against me. I was about to say something regrettable when my phone chimed. It was Rachel. I excused myself and stepped outside.

She was calling to tell me that a review panel had been convened on an expedited basis to hear our case. Something to do with a favor to the head of the firm, some sort of heavyweight connection. I don't understand how these things work, and have always been cheerfully oblivious to power and its machinations. What mattered was that I would have a chance to see her again.

We made an appointment for the following Thursday and I hung up and returned to the dinner table to find Tracy and my father in midconversation. Something had shifted in my absence, the energy at the table had changed.

"You're okay with this?" my father demanded of me as I sat back down.

I looked to Tracy. "I don't know. Am I?"

Tracy squirmed in her chair. "Ricky's appeal in Texas," she explained. "I want to go out there for it."

I wasn't seeing it yet. "Okay," I said. It seemed reasonable enough. I looked to my dad, waiting for more.

"It's not appropriate. With this Brian person? Are you nuts?" This last directed to me.

Virgil, was my father actually looking out for my interests? An unimaginable development. Even worse, the more I thought about it, the more I agreed with him. *Agreed with him.* I turned to face Tracy.

She flushed a bit, became flustered under the double-barreled Santos scrutiny. "Oh, come on, both of you. Brian is a friend. It's strictly professional. Matt knows that."

Inescapable Brian.

"So is it friends or is it professional?" My father, the pit bull. I felt myself growing angry, egged on by my father.

"Both! I mean, come on. Are you serious? You trust me, don't you, Matt?"

And there it was, the only question that mattered. We both knew it. I looked from my father to Tracy and back again, still irritated. "Of course," I answered. I faced my father. "It will be fine. He's a lawyer."

My dad swiveled his eyes over to me, taking me in for the first time since we'd sat down.

"Who called you?" he asked.

"Change in my call time."

He knew, I'm sure he did. So attuned was he to dissembling, a walking seismograph of lies. His expression, however, was inscrutable. Would he say something? Maybe later? Only to Tracy? At that moment, I decided that I had underestimated him as a cardplayer.

Tracy walked the two blocks home after encircling my father in a long and effusive farewell hug—I thought back to our own limp airport greeting—and I drove him to his hotel, where I agreed to pick him up early the next morning. Six a.m., he advised. Make sure you're on time.

"Good night," I said, as we idled in front of the hotel.

"Good night." He sat for a long moment. I was aware of his proximity, of his musty, elderly odor competing with his too-sweet cologne. So little space between us. Then: "Do not fuck this up, Matt."

"Fuck what up?"

"Pop the trunk."

I pressed the release and the trunk lid yawned heavenward. My father nodded to me and got out of the car. He hoisted his suitcase, and I watched him shuffle up the hotel steps. No bell-man came to greet him. I felt relief as he left, it's true. I was always relieved when we concluded any exchange, thrilled to get out reasonably whole. But this time there was something else. Curiosity about his admonition? Pity? Perhaps. An un-welcome stab of sorrow sliced my heart. But also familiarity. Recognition. And I didn't like it, Virgil. I did not like it at all.

M Y FATHER NEVER SAID "FUCK YOU," not directly. His way of saying it would go something like this: It's another Sunday, another toy show. I am a boy, maybe twelve, thirteen. Old enough to be distracted by girls but young enough to feel obligated to accompany my father to his early-morning toy fairs. A haggler in army surplus happens upon our table. I recognize his type at once. His dress is shabby, his hair unkempt, he's unshaven. He wears thick glasses and has bad teeth. He is someone who exists outside most social norms. He doesn't care what anyone thinks about him, and such people inflame my father. The haggler picks up a car to examine it and already my father is on edge, worried the piece will be damaged. The haggler turns it over for a long time, well past any meaningful examination, and my father's irritation grows. Finally, my father says, "Make an offer or put it down." The haggler looks at the price tag. Fifty dollars. "I'll give you ten," he says.

It's an insulting offer, though the haggler doesn't understand that. To him, it's a logical move. Nothing ventured, nothing gained, and it costs him nothing to ask. Or so he thinks. My father would be within his rights to say "fuck you."

"Sixty," my father counters.

The haggler looks at him with surprise. "It says fifty. You can't do that."

"Now it's sixty-five," my father says.

Rapt, I watch as the haggler contemplates his next move.

"Fifteen."

"Not for sale," my father says. He takes the car from his hand, wraps it up, and returns it to his bag.

Defeated, the haggler mutters "Asshole" and walks away. My father has delivered a classic Gabor Santos "fuck you" and it appears to satisfy him, though I'm left wondering, wouldn't it have been easier to just say what he was thinking? I feel a pang of pity for the haggler as he shuffles off. It's true, he's been a jerk, but he's such a wretch, he hardly seems responsible. For some reason, I think of him on the bus, going home, unloved and unknown, and I'm angry at my father for his rough treatment of this godforsaken creature.

I suppose my father had me pegged. No killer instinct.

I PICKED HIM UP at his hotel at the appointed time and drove him to Glendale, where the toy show was taking place at the Civic Auditorium. I planned only to drop him off and pick him up, but when we arrived it became clear that he expected me to fill my old role as his assistant. To my astonishment, I complied.

How can I account for this, Virgil? Was I afraid to turn him down, fearful of his displeasure, as though he could still punish me so late in the game? A little bit, I confess. But it was not primarily fear that drove me that day. This, at last, was familiar territory. Once again, I knew the part I was intended to play, had so internalized this character, this first great role, that I knew precisely how to step in and play him. My father understood, as good actors do. He'd picked up on my rhythms and responded in kind and, all at once, we found ourselves returned to the roles that made us famous, these earliest portrayals of ourselves.

We waited outside in the early-morning sun for the doors to open. He always insisted we arrive at least a half hour ahead of time, to ensure being among the first inside, where the best bargains hung in fragile equipoise, waiting to be claimed. My father eschewed the convivial chitchat of the other dealers. His focus was singular, his thoughts, if he had any, a mystery to me. I fidgeted, stepped from foot to foot, cleared my throat. Cracked my knuckles. Anything to pierce the monotony. My father looked over at me with disapproval, and I fell still.

At last the doors opened, and my father and I moved to his assigned table. He looked me over with concern.

"You remember how to do this?"

"Yes."

"Keep all the wrapping. Put the cars on top of their boxes."

"I know."

"Keep the fragile ones near the back."

"Dad. I know. I remember."

He nodded. "I'll be back."

He moved off, all business, leaving me alone with the empty table. I felt relief as he disappeared. I spread out his tablecloth, the same one I remembered, the yellow vinyl tacky to the touch from years of use. I set the suitcase on the chair and flipped open the lid. I had to admire the old man's skill at packing, even now. Row after row of snug, bubble-wrapped capsules. I pulled the first car out and unwrapped it. I tested my memory, identifying the toy without turning it over to read the bottom: a tin Bandai MG TF. I set it on the table, watchful headlights facing the aisle, and continued unwrapping the packages, careful to return all the wrapping to the suitcase. Even as I resented my father's presumption at dragging me along for the day,

I was soothed, gratified by the act of preparing the table. I opened up each tissue capsule, examined the piece, and sought to arrange it on the table in a way that would give my father pleasure. I felt entrusted with something once again, and for those moments, thoughts of Tracy, of Rachel, of the fate of *Budapest Street Scene*, all left me.

He returned to the table and handed me a cup of coffee and a bagel. The concession stand had opened.

"It's black. I didn't remember how you liked it."

It was a fucking cup of coffee, Virgil. Why did it make me feel like crying? "Black is fine," I said.

My father nodded and continued on his search for over-looked bargains. I settled in to watch the table. The doors opened to the public and the aisles filled with buyers. The tables around ours seemed to be doing brisker business, but I sold a few pieces for my father. When I was a boy, he would always cut me in for a percentage of the day's take, my "commission," he called it. I wondered if the old arrangement would still apply. My father hurried by, deposited a cache of newly bought toy cars in my arms without a word, and dove back into the crowd. As he turned from view, I caught a glint of perspiration above his lip.

Buyers continued to examine my father's wares, and some made offers lower than the sticker price. There was a time when I was empowered to accept certain offers, had developed a sense of what might not eat too far into my father's profits. He wasn't opposed to haggling on principle, and he understood it went with the territory. He just insisted it be done respectfully, and if he found the buyer sympathetic, he could be quite generous. But too much time had passed, and I had lost my confidence about what my father would or would not take. I shrugged more than once and said, "Come back later and ask my father.

It's his stuff." Even to offers a mere ten dollars below asking. The looks I received were impossible to decipher. Pity? Contempt? Mere annoyance?

My father was gone for what was beginning to feel like an unreasonably long time, and I sat there, my mood darkening. I had to pee. My back hurt. My feet were cold. I grew disgusted with myself, with the ease with which I'd slipped into my old, subordinate role. Irritation came and went, shaded into anger, familiar resentment, but then glided into something new. As I watched the buyers crowd the aisles, I became aware that they almost all traveled solo. Solitary collectors, spending a Sunday morning trolling the aisles of a Glendale auditorium. I felt a great sadness descend upon me. It seized me, squeezing my eyes, my throat. I suddenly wanted to get out of there, needed to get out. I didn't belong there. These were not my people.

My father finally reappeared, his arms laden with a second round of toys he had snatched up. He busied himself marking up the new prices and adding the toys to the table. He shook his head as he rearranged the cars I had set out, my positioning not finding the favor I'd hoped. I could see no improvement in his redesign. I tried to keep the pique out of my voice as I briefed him on the morning thus far, which pieces had sold. I handed over his cash and mentioned that a few offers had been made but I hadn't been comfortable accepting them without his approval, and had advised the buyers to come back and talk to him.

"Which pieces? What did they offer?"

I told him and he looked incredulous. "It was ten dollars. You didn't say yes?"

"I told them to come back."

"They won't come back."

"Of course they will."

"Ten dollars, Matt. What's wrong with you?"

My father's rebukes were always blunt but deadly. I bit down on the inside of my cheek.

"I need to pee. I'll be back."

Moments later, I returned to the table, having filled up my lungs with fresh air, but I could see from down the aisle that something was wrong. My father was enraged, his face a mask of darkness. I tasted metal. Before I could say anything, he was on me.

"The Meccano mail truck."

"What?"

"Where is it?"

"What are you talking about?"

"My Meccano mail truck. It's not on the table."

"I don't remember any mail truck, Dad. Are you sure—"

"Of course I am sure, Matt." His voice rose, drawing concerned glances.

"Dad, I'm sorry, I don't—"

"Were you paying attention the whole time? Your attention never wandered?"

I stood there, unsure what to say. Of course my attention wandered. Wanders.

"Jesus, Matt. Someone stole my Meccano. From right under your nose."

"You don't know that."

"It's not on the table. It's not in the suitcase. I packed it on Monday. Did it drive itself away?" Customers were backing away from our table now, my dad's voice carrying across the aisles.

"Maybe you didn't pack it. Maybe it's still in New York."

"Goddammit, Matt! Why can't you *ever* admit you fucked

up?" He was shaking with rage. "Be a man and don't blame me. That's a hundred dollars gone, a hundred dollars you owe me."

What happened next, Virgil, I can scarcely credit. How this was possible, where it came from, after all those years, I still can't say. But I felt something literally snap within me, a hard, dry crack deep in my chest. And for an instant, my rage had a voice, and it wasn't a role, it was sheer fury. I tore out my wallet, seized a hundred-dollar bill, and pressed it hard against his chest with my forefinger, my nose inches from his.

"Fuck. You."

The bill fluttered to the tabletop as I released my finger and stomped away.

IN THE END, I couldn't leave him there. I stormed out to my car, slammed the door, fired it up, got as far as the exit booth. The attendant waited for my ticket but I couldn't go through with it. So I backed up and returned to the auditorium exit and waited there—for how long? Two hours? Three?—until my father emerged dragging his suitcase. If he felt any surprise at the sight of me, it didn't show. I pressed the trunk release but did not get out. He loaded his suitcase, closed the trunk, and got into the car. We pulled away without a word.

The drive in from the airport had been silent, or so I had thought. But the drive back to LAX was much worse for its awful stillness, a frozen silence. It was eighty-three degrees outside and I was shivering. I drove like a maniac, speeding down the freeways. We arrived at the airport three hours before his flight.

"Just drop me at the curb," he said. His first words. I ignored him and drove into the parking structure. He said nothing.

I pulled into a spot and switched off the engine. The silence grew thicker. I turned to my father, who hadn't moved.

"Dad, why did you come here?"

"For the show." He continued looking straight ahead.

"The same show you've ignored every year for the last decade?"

"It's a big show, Matt."

"Yeah. Dad, just once, *please*—say what's on your mind. You're here about the painting, I know you are. Tracy's no cardplayer."

Did my father almost smile? I'm sure not. A nervous twitch, perhaps.

"What did you mean, when you said don't fuck this up?"

My father surprised me by laying his hand upon my knee. His pinky ring, gold with an oval onyx stone, gently rapped my kneecap.

"Mátyás . . ." he began, but the words failed him. "It's complicated."

"So uncomplicate it for me."

He turned to me and, with surprising gentleness, said, "If it was that easy, I would, *kisfiú*."

Kisfiú. How can I convey the effect of that one Hungarian word, Virgil? The unexpected tenderness of the word, literally "little boy," an affectionate nickname from father to son, one I'd heard often in childhood and despaired of ever hearing again. With one word, my father penetrated my rage and was briefly restored to me.

BOARDING PASS IN HAND, my father walked toward the security gates. I remembered something that I'd meant to ask.

"Hey, do you remember the space toy?"

"Hey is for horses."

"The space toy, the bet, do you remember?"

He nodded.

"The morning after I paid you, the money was back in my wallet. Did you do that? Or was it Mom?"

He thought for a moment. I could see his historical archive flip past his inner eye. He shook his head.

"I don't remember."

"Really?"

"I don't think it was me. It must have been your mother."

"I guess it must have been."

"Not a big deal, either way."

"No. Not a big deal, Dad."

We stopped at the security checkpoint. My father turned to face me.

"Well."

"Thanks for coming."

"It was good to see you."

"Safe trip."

He nodded. Then, as he turned to enter the checkpoint:

"Pushpushpush."

I stood there and waited until he was out of sight. I know it drove him crazy, the sentimentality of the gesture, and normally that would have been satisfaction enough. But there was something else keeping me there. At first I thought perhaps it was a desire to confirm with absolute certainty that the old bastard was safely out of my life again. Then I thought perhaps it was pity, not unlike the stab I'd felt the night before, watching him at his hotel. Something about his shrunken vitality haunted me. But the answer was simpler than that.

I was sad to see him go.

GOD RESTED ON THE SEVENTH DAY, we're told. No killer instinct. I learned from Rachel that He also bestowed on us conflicting directives to commemorate His day of rest. Exodus exhorts us to "remember the Sabbath day," whereas Deuteronomy commands that we "observe the Sabbath day." The nuances of those two words have kept the rabbis arguing for centuries. Rabbi Wolfe did not share their fascination, however, and shrugged when I asked her how one might parse the differences. "What do *you* think?" she countered, as a therapist might. As it happens, there is nothing for me to remember, as nothing was ever observed. Again, that telling vacancy. My parents never once lit a Sabbath candle. The notion of resting in any form, excepting our annual two-week vacations to somewhere sunny and cheap, usually Florida, was anathema to my father, who seemed tortured by everything that was transpiring in his absence. To give over an entire day every week to do nothing but sit with one's own thoughts? My father could have sooner breathed water.

This omission has come to sadden me, along with the rest of my lost Jewish childhood. Of the many doors the saga of *Budapest Street Scene* has opened for me, it is, for some reason, the idea of the Sabbath that most moves me, and not just because of that unforgettable evening with Rachel. I am fascinated by this notion of sanctified time. Time that is set aside, sacred, a space of quiet in which daily activities, material pursuits, the relentless, insistent connection of our lives might be stilled. This is the part of my denied birthright that I most long for. Yet it's too late in the game to start over, that much was clear to me as I sat with Rachel and her father, an outsider yet again.

Rachel's invitation came a week after my father left, at the end of one of our regular phone calls. Since our afternoon at the museum, we were finding more frequent, if trivial, reasons to be in touch. As often as not, the subject was Kálmán himself, some new tidbit I'd uncovered or something she had read. We had been discussing Kálmán's Judaism, and his suicide just hours ahead of the Nazis' entry to Budapest, and I became aware that it was one of the few times in our discussions that I had been faking it. Oh, I knew Kálmán front to back, could have played him in the miniseries by that point. But on the matter of his religion—no, not his, *ours* . . . but is that true, can I honestly claim that?—I fumbled, stammered, and simply agreed with Rachel wherever possible. A silence suffused the line, when she surprised me:

"Would you like to come to a Sabbath dinner?" she asked.

Picture me at a loss for words, Virgil. Is your imagination that good? She must have sensed something in my hesitation, because she hastened to add, "It's nothing fancy. Just my dad and me, at his house. It's kind of a ritual for us since my mother died."

Tracy had departed for Texas with Brian, and I'd been feeling aggrieved. I found myself thinking, why shouldn't I also enjoy the company of an attractive attorney? But I knew my lines, and recited them:

"Are you sure it's not an imposition? I wouldn't want to intrude."

"My father will enjoy the company. He's never happier than when he's educating someone."

"Educating?"

"Have you ever been to a Sabbath dinner?"

My silence was my reply.

"A Jew who barely knows Abraham from Isaac? Yeah, I'd say you could use an education, Matt."

RACHEL'S FATHER, Bernard—Bernie, he'd insisted—intimidated me, as I suppose all fathers must. I arrived, flowers in hand, shortly before sundown, it must have been before five, an hour at which I was unused to dining. Bernie, a retired litigator, quite fearsome in his day by all accounts, lived in an old Spanish duplex in the neighborhood where I'd gone mezuzah shopping. He owned the building, lived downstairs, and rented out the upstairs apartment. He would have preferred the top floor, he explained, but he was wheelchair bound, had been since a stroke on his sixty-eighth birthday. His health had continued to deteriorate and now, approaching seventy-five, he was essentially a prisoner in his own home. A nurse—Ingrid, worthless, he snorted—saw to his daily needs, but it was Rachel who attended to Sabbath dinner, and had done so since her mother died three years earlier. Rachel hadn't missed a Sabbath unless traveling for work, Bernie said with pride and, perhaps, a bit of territoriality.

"I used to go to temple religiously"—he shrugged at the pun, as though he somehow wasn't to blame for it—"but now . . ." He indicated the wheelchair. "Anyway, we've got candles, we've got bread, who needs to go out? Sabbath is for family."

Did I hear a trace of accusation in that last word? He scrutinized me, and I felt myself failing the first of many tests. He was such a contrast to my own father. Thick glasses had left permanent dents on the bridge of his nose. He had the frail, eggshell skull of an intellectual. But he burned, Virgil, he burned with a brightness that unnerved me. Is this, I wondered for the first time, what it was like to have God within? How diminished my father seemed to me in his shadow. Still, I thought back to Kálmán's painting, to my father edging his way out of the frame, and it was all too easy to imagine Bernie among those left behind, those consumed.

Rachel, who had been busy in the kitchen until now, chose this moment to appear in the doorway. We were unsure how to greet each other. Suddenly, the handshake of the office seemed too formal. At length, she leaned forward, offering her cheek, which I pecked. An awkward half-hug followed. I handed her the flowers, which she received graciously, disappearing to put them in water. My attention wandered around the sitting room. The furniture looked as though it had been in the family a long time, and the paint and carpet were worn, thin with age. The threadbare green shag was full of holes. Yet the fusty room felt inhabited, limned with echoes of family. I could remember no such room in my childhood home.

Rachel returned and invited me to join them as she stood with her father before a pair of candles in dull bronze candlesticks on a silver tray. Bernie handed me a kippah—from his nephew Ari's bar mitzvah, he explained—which I set on my head, and I was back in temple with my grandfather. As Rachel lit the candles, she explained this needed to be done before the commencement of the Sabbath, since the lighting of fire was prohibited.

Once the candles were lit, Rachel set down the burning match on the tray, and she waved toward herself three times, as though beckoning a tired and frightened animal to approach. I was unprepared for the quiet, intense openness the invitation conveyed. She then covered her eyes and said the prayer, one I had never heard before. I maintained a respectful distance as I watched. It felt like I was intruding on some act of great intimacy. For the first of many times that evening, I was aware how out of place I was, and yet I wanted nothing more than to take my place beside them. Rachel and Bernie finished their prayer, exchanged a kiss on the cheek, and turned to me. A framed reproduction of a Chagall dominated the far wall where I stood. Rachel joined me in front of it. It was an image I'd seen many times before. A woman stands in the corner of a small apartment room, holding a modest bouquet of flowers. A man in a green shirt rises over her like a parade float, his head twisted back as if his neck is made of rubber, and kisses the woman. His eyes are closed but hers, I noticed, are open with what appears to be surprise.

"It's one of my favorites," she said. "We've had it forever."

I nodded, speechless around her. In truth, the awkwardness I felt never dissipated, not to this day. I did not know where to sit, how to behave, what role if any I was expected to play. Following Rachel to the dining room, I hovered near the table until Bernie invited me to sit. He rolled up to his place at the head of the table. Rachel and I sat on either side of him along the battered rectangle. As Rachel brought out prayer books to place on the table, she spoke about the review panel that had been convened, about the makeup of its members and—

"Rachel, please," Bernie interrupted.

She nodded and smiled. "Sorry, Dad."

Bernie turned to me. "We don't discuss work matters on the Sabbath."

"We can talk about it tomorrow," Rachel said to me.

"Yes," Bernie sighed, "Saturdays she works. But Friday nights, she's mine."

I nodded my understanding. Did he blame me? Was he challenging me? I settled in and listened as they opened their prayer books—Rachel opened mine to the right page—and then they began to sing. Despite the reedy thinness of Bernie's weak voice, the contrast with Rachel's lilting contralto was not unpleasant. As I listened, I had a feeling, mistaken, as I would later find out, that I was listening to ancient music, tunes that had traversed the centuries. They are, in fact, twentieth-century creations, but they are still, I find, redolent of something. Of tradition? Or devotion? Of struggle and sustenance? Perhaps it's merely the language that gives it the patina of the ancient. I watched Bernie as he sang with his eyes closed, thumping the table with his fist with surprising force, keeping time to the music. Rachel sang from the prayer book, and I sat there, mute, the page a welter of indecipherable symbols to me. And yet, I felt my eyes fill. I could not fathom this response, Virgil. Tears? Me? Over prayers? The lengths I would go to deny my irreligious father. I could think of no other explanation than delayed youthful rebellion for this sudden display of religious fervor. Bernie opened one eye and allowed it to fall on me as I fumbled with the pages of the prayer book, trying to find my place.

"*Eishet Chayil*," he said. "Usually the husband's prayer to his wife. But for Rachel, I say it." Bernie took Rachel's hand, a bit wistfully, it seemed, and recited the Hebrew from memory. Rachel's eyes briefly flitted in my direction, and she blushed. As Bernie concluded the prayer, he kissed his daughter's hands. "Her value is indeed far beyond pearls."

"Yes, it is," I agreed, to all of our surprise.

I watched Bernie and Rachel kiss their prayer books as they set them aside. It felt absurd for me to follow suit, and it felt absurd for me not to. I brushed the musty book against my lips.

"Come on," said Rachel. "Time to wash our hands."

I followed them to the sink and watched as they removed their rings and then poured water from a bronze jug over each hand, twice on the right, then twice on the left. I followed, marveling at how foreign something as familiar as washing my hands could feel.

It was over the first course of matzo ball soup that Bernie exposed me. You know the moment, you've seen it before. A scene not unlike this one:

"Your parents are survivors, Matt?" he'd ask between slurps.

Rachel would blanch. "Dad!"

"No, it's okay," I'd say, impressed. "Yes. My dad. How did you know?"

Bernie would have shrugged. "Your first Sabbath dinner. And from the way you handle a prayer book, I'm thinking you didn't receive a Jewish education. More often than not, especially with Jews your age, it's survivor parents. They don't want to be reminded, you know?"

I would have nodded, sadly. Something deep would have collapsed within me, Virgil, as if a lifelong house of cards had been flicked to the ground by this wheelchair-bound senior. That's how it's supposed to go, right?

"Was he in the camps?"

I'd shake my head. "Hungary," I'd say.

"Budapest?"

"Yes."

Bernie would have nodded, as though he understood it all.

"You're lucky. Did your father ever tell you about those times?"

A wild urge to laugh. A dozen responses would careen through my mind. "No, sir."

"Well, don't wait until it's too late." Replete with kind eyes.

Hah, there you are, snickering again. Those wise eyes of yours, Virgil. You know nothing of the sort transpired. How soothing such gentle schmaltz might have felt. What is it in me that seeks such platitudes, craves their comforting simplicity? But it didn't happen like that at all. It never happens like that.

Take two. Marker. Speed. And . . . action.

It began innocently enough, as he asked me a series of conversational questions. And yet, all along, they seemed a formality, as though he already knew the answers. He had a disconcerting habit of answering himself, as though the truth were a private joke that he and I enjoyed—"But, of course, you'd have to have been bar mitzvahed to know that"—and I began to see what a sly, formidable attorney he must have been, polite beyond reproach but devastating. At least he saved me the embarrassment of having to answer "No" time and time again. Well, Hebrew is such a difficult language to master . . . A young man must have his Saturdays free . . . Being Jewish doesn't mean the same thing to any two Jews. The questions deepened, and although my embarrassment became evident, Bernie persisted, gentle, relentless. A kindly battering ram.

"Do you celebrate the high holidays?" He dismissed them with a wave of the hand. "Tickets are expensive, the synagogue is crowded. What about God? Do you believe in the big guy, at least? He comes in handy on bumpy airplane flights, I've found."

I felt very much like a slow-witted criminal being interrogated by a brilliant detective. I shook my head, looked to Rachel, as though I might find the answers in her eyes. She seemed uncomfortable, embarrassed on my behalf.

"I don't know." Had I never before considered so fundamental a question?

"That's honest. How about the soul, Matt? Any spark of the divine within? Or are we just meat and bones?"

Rachel had had enough and spoke up.

"Dad. Matt's our guest. It's Shabbos."

Bernie exhaled, and the litigator deflated back into the invalid. "So it is. Forgive me. Fathers," he said. "You know how it is," he said. I did, indeed. All too fucking well.

OVER THE MAIN COURSE of roast chicken with wild rice, Rachel and Bernie engaged each other in a conversation on some fine point of Talmudic interpretation. Something about what they called Oral Torah and something else called Malbim, and questions about justification for halachic interpretation. It was nothing I had any hope of following, though Rachel made generous albeit unsuccessful efforts to include me. But I was fascinated despite my feeling of exclusion, so different from the exclusion I'd felt with Tracy and my father. They had traded in comforting small talk, but here I was missing something of weight, and not just from the moment at hand but from my entire life. I watched this father and his daughter, bound by faith and devotion. Unlike that afternoon in the museum, I now found myself listening to Rachel. Consuming her every word, digesting it, turning it over, looking for nuance, mining anything I could from it. I have always been good at appearing to listen when, in fact, I am merely waiting for my next turn to speak. But here, I was so thoroughly left behind that I knew no next turn was coming, and so I was free to truly listen, and it was in those moments, in that examination of Torah, that I think I began to fall in love, and not just with Rachel.

We sat there for hours, Virgil, and I was never bored, not once. Not even watching them pray. I so wanted to understand what they were saying, what they were asking for, what they were feeling. They seemed rapt, transported, their eyes closed, bobbing ever so slightly as they offered themselves up to God, who, I assumed, was only too happy to receive them. My phone vibrated in my pocket. I ignored it and sat there, isolated, conspicuously the Other. See me, the Creature, all fangs and humps and cloven feet, the beast of fairy tales.

After several minutes, Rachel concluded her prayer and held her finger to her lips. Her father had drifted off to sleep at the table. I helped her clear the plates, and we tiptoed around Bernie, his baritone rumbling reminding me of Tracy's own rattling snores. I paused to look at my phone. A missed call from Tracy, and a voice mail. I slipped the phone back in my pocket and stood beside Rachel, helping her load the dishwasher. I cannot remember any time a chore has brought me such pleasure. I closed the dishwasher door and Rachel took my hands and washed and dried them. I felt the floor fall away as she patted my hands dry, felt my body begin to lift from the ground. She indicated I should follow her and we stepped into the sitting room, where we could whisper freely.

"I'll need to put him to bed, he's out for the night. He'll be sorry he didn't say good night."

"I don't think he liked me very much."

"He's a father. You're a man. He's not supposed to like you."

We stood for a moment, before the Chagall, in silence.

"So? Your first Sabbath dinner. What did you think?"

I looked from Rachel to the painting before us. She could read the answer to her question in my eyes, I was quite certain, and so there was only one thing left for me, for us.

Virgil, I kissed her.

WHEN I GOT BACK to my car I played the terse message from Tracy. As expected, the Texas Supreme Court had denied Ricky McCabe's appeal. We had all moved one step closer to the end.

IN THE WINTER OF 1939, Ágnes Kálmán left her husband. Her departure followed a ban on travel for Jews and the revocation of membership in all official organizations. Kálmán did not much mind the loss of travel. He'd been turning inward, away from the West, since his return from Paris and was happy to stay in Budapest. But the loss of his teaching position created unbearable financial strain. This newly constrained life, amid the terror of growing waves of anti-Semitism, caused Kálmán to relapse into his addictions, and by the time he was found delirious, feverish, half-naked on the *Váci utca* in the early hours of a freezing February morning, poor Ágnes had already returned to the Hungarian countryside, where she would be murdered sometime in April 1944.

I think often about the rupture in their marriage. I wonder what changed in those last months, what would have become of them both if she had had the strength to stay on, if he had had the will to resist his addictions. It often seems to me that the stories of our lives are too easily reduced to single moments of decision, whether to stay or to leave. I suppose the Clash had it right, after all, but the wisdom of punk notwithstanding, I am consumed with this question.

I built sand castles as a child. I always placed my damp, crumbling battlements close to the shoreline. For it wasn't the pleasure of building that drew me back again and again. I rushed through the construction, my final product much like my familiar film-set facades. I would retreat to the rocks and sit there, shivering with anticipation, as the waves crept in and consumed my creation. There was a thrill, almost erotic, in watching how all evidence of my handiwork could be washed away, devoured by sizzling foam until not a trace remained. I was reassured by how completely my tracks could be made to disappear. Then I set about building another castle in its place, anticipating the next in an endless series of erasures.

TRACY HAD NOT YET RETURNED from her Texas sojourn with Brian when Rachel called me the following afternoon to express regret. She blamed the wine, though we both knew she'd had barely a glass. It was irresponsible, unforgivable, really. You are my client, it can't happen again. I told her about the mezuzah. All of it, from her office to Sabbath night. I think perhaps she thought me a bit mad but she was moved, I could hear it, a thickening in her voice, like desire but purer, like honey, even as she insisted that the kiss would never happen again. Promise me you won't do that again, she pleaded. I made no such promise. The misdirection of it would have been second nature days earlier. But it felt trivial and false following our Sabbath eve, and so I said, No, no, I cannot make that promise. I guess I'll have to fire you. We laughed, at last. Was that all she wanted, all we needed? That laugh, that release?

Such clarity and such confusion residing on the head of the same pin, Virgil.

Before we hung up, I asked her a question, one that had troubled me since the night before.

"Rachel, do you think . . . is it . . . I don't know, is it too late?" I hesitated, fumbling.

"Too late for what?"

I was almost ashamed to answer.

"For me, I guess?"

She was silent for a moment.

"Oh, Matt."

Oh, Matt. How often I would hear this particular construction in the weeks ahead. I tried to make my peace with this dismissal, then she surprised me.

"Why on earth would you think that? It's never too late."

This golden thread of hope stayed with me all day, echoed in my brain and buzzed through my hours on the set. Despite my assurances to the director, my performances had continued to slip, and I could no longer even be accused of phoning it in. Try as I might, I found it impossible to stay engaged, and everything exploded when I stood there, stony and silent, following the director's bark of "Action!"

The line was mine, I knew, but I could not remember it. I held up my hand.

"Sorry. Line?"

The script supervisor glanced down at her bound script and robotically intoned:

"'That's just a bit more reality than mankind can bear, boys.'"

I nodded.

"Just keep rolling," the director said. I took a steadying breath.

"That's just . . ." I stopped speaking, stood there in frozen silence.

I could not remember any of my lines. Nothing, not even with the prompt from the script supervisor. It had all washed away and every time I tried to remember a line, I could only hear the echo of Rachel's whispered, fervent prayers.

At this point, the director, as the kids say, lost his shit. He had been patient enough with me in the weeks leading to this moment, the dozens of tiny lapses and flat performances. But now he unleashed his full fury and shrieked obscenity after obscenity, lamenting wasted money, missed opportunities, calling me a hack. I stood there and took it all in with surprising equanimity. This only served to enrage him further. I thought he was about to take a swing at me when I said to him, "For fuck's sake, Derek, it's just a shitty TV show. Get a grip." It all suddenly felt so trivial, so insulting, to pretend that I cared about what we were doing. Which was when Derek did, in fact, punch me with surprising force and accuracy, and the first assistant director wisely wrapped the day's production.

I think back now to that punch, Virgil. How it set me free. How much did it matter, does it matter, that Derek was a six-foot, blond-haired, blue-eyed Aryan sort? Or do I just remember him that way? Perhaps he was short, balding, and hairy-chested. My faith in my recall is shaken. I think, at moments like these, that I remember nothing, that my life is merely a script, a tale told, revised on the fly in a desperate attempt to retain the teller's fading interest.

I WAS IN MY CAR, driving aimlessly, my cheek throbbing, when the phone rang. My agent, Simon. I pressed answer and his voice filled the car. I felt sorry for him. He'd never been less than exemplary, had launched my unlikely career and kept it aloft. Every call brought good news, a bigger role, a better offer. He'd never made a call to me like this before.

"How bad?" I asked. Simon's protracted silence gave me an indication.

Finally. "I'm sorry, Matt. They fired you. It's all over social media."

Simon went on to detail the show's frustration with me over the last few months, relaying the particulars of the network's case against me. Derek wasn't alone, the producers were also fed up. I had cost the show too much and was being written out. Plane crash, Simon was told. I tried not to laugh.

I laughed.

I DROVE FOR HOURS, Los Angeles's twisting freeways and long, open streets being well suited to aimless wandering. At least, I thought I had been wandering, but I once again pulled up in front of Solomon's emporium of Judaica. Unlike my meek and quivering first visit, I strode into the store, acknowledged the surly boy at the register, and selected the sleek bronze mezuzah I'd been drawn to the last time. I paid for it and left the store, eager to return home and test its magic.

I ARRIVED just as the sun was vanishing behind the hills to find several boxes on my doorstep containing the contents of my trailer. I couldn't help being impressed by the studio's ruthless efficiency. I felt the mezuzah pressing against my leg in my pocket. I opened the door, kicked the boxes inside, and fired up my laptop.

I navigated to a popular gossip blog. The post headline said C-LIST MELTDOWN. Fucking bloggers. Not even my name? Parasites, Virgil. If you'd like to put your dusty nightstick to good use, first let's kill all the bloggers. A grainy cell phone video showed Derek screaming at me, then throwing his punch. I was gratified to have stayed on my feet.

I suppose I should have cared more. But I took a mental inventory and found I cared about many things, about Rachel, about the mezuzah in my pocket, even about *Budapest Street Scene*, about Tracy, and, very possibly, though not conclusively, about my father. But about this, no. I did not care. That much was clear to me.

I have never been good with my hands. As a child, it was my rickety model airplanes. As an adult, I avoided anything that required a sharp eye and steady hand. I kept a minimal supply of tools, not much more than a few screwdrivers, a hammer, and pliers. I would think with shame of the macho assortment of tools cultivated by other men and sensed one more deformity, one more measure of unmanliness to confirm my father's disappointment. I remember his workshop in the basement of our home, wall-mounted pegboards arrayed with tools of every conceivable size and purpose. Last year, I bought a bookcase and Tracy insisted on building it. "If you do it, it will collapse in the first breeze," she said.

This, however, was a job that only I could do, and so I pulled the small plastic orange toolbox from under the sink and set to work at the front door. I took unusual care, sketching out a line with a ruler, a hypotenuse of an otherwise invisible right triangle, and predrilling holes in the doorframe. I felt intense gratification with each turn of the screw, the grain of the wood offering pleasant resistance to each twist. I, who had spent my entire life standing around saying things, now felt the visceral pleasure of doing something. The screw crunched satisfyingly into place and I slid the mezuzah into position along the pencil mark I had made, and fastened the bottom.

I stepped back and admired my handiwork. My heart was beating hard as I reached my finger out once more, as I had seen Rachel do in her office. I traced a line along the mezuzah and was startled to feel its whispered reply—a mere murmur, but something there. Inarguable. Palpable. As that tiny flare sighed into life, a taxi pulled up and discharged Tracy, roller bag clattering along behind her.

She smiled a weak smile as she approached me. I was taken aback by how pale and drawn she looked. Raccoon circles beneath her bloodshot eyes. She fell into my arms and hugged me tightly.

"Hey," I whispered in her ear. I was consumed by guilt, relieved to have my face hidden.

"Hi," she sighed. "What a nightmare."

I nodded. "I'm so sorry."

She shrugged her thanks. "Anything exciting happen here?"

Where could I possibly begin? I had gotten as far as a falsetto "Um . . ." when she raised her head from my shoulder and noticed the mezuzah.

"What's this?" she asked, stepping around for a closer look.

"It's a mezuzah. You know. For doorways."

She looked from me to the mezuzah and back again, momentarily perplexed. Then she nodded, picked up her bag, and headed inside.

"Okay," she said with a bemused smile, and stepped through the door. I followed her in as she paused before the boxes.

"What are these?"

More explaining. I sighed and told her of the day's events, showed her the blog posting and the video. She sank into her chair, exhausted, and I watched for a reaction. Finally, she spoke:

"I never liked that director." She touched my arm. "You okay?"

Again a wave of guilt. I debated telling her, but the thought of so unprecedented a display of Santos honesty reared its head, only to scurry back into its hole like a cold February groundhog.

"Yeah," I said. "You?"

She shrugged.

"It was a long shot. But . . ." She trailed off, rubbing her eyes and taking in the boxes. "Shit, before this is all over we might both be looking for work."

I looked at her with curiosity. She rarely swore.

"Abby chewed on me for thirty straight minutes. Harvest Moon isn't happy with my work for Ricky. I guess they sell a lot of bathing suits in Texas. They're making some noise."

"Oh, for fuck's sake. Really?" I remembered Abby's dark mien on the beach.

She shrugged. "It'll be all right."

Tracy was exhausted, so tired she skipped her nightly ritual of cleansing creams. I followed her up the stairs, carrying her suitcase. I set it in the corner of our bedroom and watched her glide fully clothed into bed. I was about to leave her when she mumbled something.

"Oh. Present . . . side pocket."

Tracy always brought me home a small present from each of her many trips. They were usually silly trinkets, standard airport gift shop fare—shot glasses and paperweights and teddy bears—but it was another of our rituals, one Tracy had adopted from her parents. I reached into the side pouch of her roller bag and pulled out a tennis ball–sized snow globe bearing the legend REMEMBER THE ALAMO around a miniature model of the doomed fort. An absurd, tacky keepsake and yet I was moved and assailed by guilt again. I kissed her forehead and headed back down to the living room to attend to the boxes still scattered across the entryway. I spent the next hour returning my books to their shelves, except for one of my illustrated Kálmán biographies. I dropped onto the couch and settled in, opening the book to its gallery of photographic plates. There was a grainy picture of Kálmán at his bar mitzvah, posed with his family. I was struck by the *Mitteleuropa* sternness of the tableau, no smiles, no physical contact, just four serious, erect figures. Perhaps this is mere indulgence, but it seemed to me there was something present in young Ervin's eyes that the cold distance of his family could neither apprehend nor extinguish. Did he already know how different he was from those around him? It saddened me as it hadn't before, looking at this young boy, knowing that within only a few decades, he would die by his own hand. I realized that I was angry at his father for failing to protect him from what was gathering to consume them all.

I sat there on the couch, surrounded by my books, until a sodden sleep overtook me. I slept fitfully that night, in scattershot repose, and dreamt that a raven was tearing at my throat. I wrestled with it, could feel its sinewy wings fighting my grasp as it plunged its bloody beak again and again into my neck. I pleaded wordlessly with its angry, forbidding eyes for it to stop. I awoke terrified before dawn, my neck raw from what must have been my own frenzied scratching.

AND THEN, ALL AT ONCE, with almost obscene ease, *Budapest Street Scene* was mine. Well, nominally mine. Possessives, I have learned, cause us no end of trouble. Tracy was mine, I was hers. My lawyer. My faith. My father. In spite of which, all these chasms remain.

Still, for the moment, at least, it appeared that my ship had arrived. I am aware of how unlikely that sounds, absent years of motions and appeals and legal maneuvering, the painting moldering in a vault deep in the bowels of the National Gallery. Instead, the panel had reviewed the evidence, found it convincing, and, in the face of no counterclaims, ordered the immediate transfer of *Budapest Street Scene* to me. A day after Tracy left for a ten-day location shoot in Bali, Rachel e-mailed me the panel's decision. I could not make any sense of the welter of legal counterpoint that passes for English. The point, she exclaimed over a celebratory drink later that evening, was that the painting was on its way to Los Angeles, would be here within the week, and was mine to do with as I pleased. Given its value, she added, the firm would be happy to store it in their vault until I had made any decisions regarding its disposition.

"There's still a lot of paperwork and the tax implications are a whole other matter but Matt . . . we did it. It's yours."

We did it.

I did nothing, of course, and I knew it. You surely knew it as well, Rachel. I was a beneficiary of circumstance and connections. Nothing more. You were so pleased that night in the bar, champagne between us, proud of your hard work. I listened to you, tried hard to share your enthusiasm, but couldn't escape a feeling of incompleteness. There were still too many questions, old ones and new ones. How could I, who knew so little about my father, his father, their lost worlds, take meaningful ownership of this object? Something tugged at me as we sat there. Perhaps I understood that our time together was going to come to an end. All of the above, no doubt. And so I nursed my champagne, lost in the trail of disappearing bubbles.

We did not kiss good night that evening, though I believe we both wanted to. Go home, you smiled. Sleep it off.

THE NEXT DAY, I woke with the dawn and I tried to call my father to tell him the news. He did not answer, which was not unusual. I left a message asking him to call me back. Then I tried my mother, but her answering machine reminded me she was away on her Pyrénées retreat, disconnected from all communication for the rest of the month. Tracy was several time zones away, so I texted her the news. I then sat back, at a loss for what to do with myself. I had worked steadily since coming to L.A., had never not had a job or not known where my next job was coming from. Simon had warned me it might be a while before I was welcome to audition again. I should expect a half-life, a fallow stretch. I looked helplessly around the empty house, another unfamiliar condition. Even with her frequent travel, I had come to value the reliability of Tracy's presence. The sheer physical fact of her being had always been enough to get me through the day. Did I inherit my extravagant standards from the old man?

Inherit. See what I did there, Virgil?

I BURNED TO TALK TO MY FATHER. How unfamiliar that felt. Normally, I would have been pleased, relieved, to get his answering machine, able to discharge my filial duties without any actual interaction. Now, each time his machine answered, I plunged into disappointment. My first few messages had been polite, urgent: Dad, call me, please, I have news. As the days wore on, they became more clipped. I could hear the dejection in my voice. Me again. Call. I stopped leaving messages altogether, though I continued to call. Did I feel any worry, any dark premonition? No. None at all. My father would often ignore me for weeks on end. I would simply have to wait the old bastard out and stew in my urgency. I didn't even know what it was I would say to him when we spoke. Would I gloat? Share a victory lap?

Tracy's return call, on the other hand, filled me with relief. She was overjoyed, of course, thrilled not for the money but for the symbol of the thing, of its return to the family. She asked me if I wanted her to come back, but I told her there was nothing to be done for a few weeks. I told her that the proceeds could be used toward McCabe's defense fund. She thanked me dutifully.

Have you heard from my father, I asked her before saying goodbye. She hadn't.

I NORMALLY TOOK GREAT, SENSUAL PLEASURE in my Saturdays, a morning of late breakfasts and farmers markets, a satisfyingly untethered state. But now, without a job, the mornings blurred together, bleak and purposeless. I found myself thinking about Rachel, wondering where she was, what she was doing. It occurred to me that she would likely be at temple this morning, and quite unexpectedly, I gathered myself up and headed to the synagogue she and Bernie had mentioned over Sabbath dinner. I parked a few streets away to ensure I wouldn't be seen driving up, and walked the last few blocks. I got as far as the threshold, close enough to hear the voices within, the music that had so moved me at Bernie's, drifting my way. But the building emanated something that held me at bay. Though I realize now it was not the building at all, it was me. For just as I felt that the painting had not been earned, I somehow felt unfit to step inside. I imagined every covered head swiveling toward me, one giant furrowed brow of disapproval connecting them all. I believed Rachel would have taken me in, cleared the way for me. But I wasn't sure. She would have had, I think, every reason to doubt my motives.

She never got the chance. My nerve collapsed like a trailer in a tornado, and I headed back to my car.

I RETURNED HOME to find a missed call on the caller ID. My father, and his maddening habit of never leaving a message. I redialed him and when he didn't answer, something unhinged in me. I left the message I would come to regret. I said I was tired of his evasions and I didn't understand why he couldn't simply be honest with me about himself, about our family. I said it was not hard to understand why my mother left him. I said there was more to life than a cellar full of toy cars, and that his obsessions were just a substitute for human interactions. I said that it was not I who risked fucking things up, it was he.

So, whether or not he chose to call me back, this painting was now in our family, such as it is. Mazel tov, I said. And with that, I hung up on the old man.

Quoth the actor, nevermore.

IN 1941, Kálmán destroyed a number of his paintings, some thirty-five canvases in all. Many of these were early works or preparatory sketches, which have led some to believe that he was burnishing his legacy, trying to craft a narrative of a talent that emerged fully formed. But several mature canvases were thrown to the flames as well, and as racial laws continued to tighten in Hungary, others have taken this as a precursor to his suicide, ensuring his work would not fall into unworthy hands. He was, we know, relieved that *Budapest Street Scene* was long ago sold to the Weisz family, to spare him the horrible decision about its fate. As he wrote in a letter dated August 12, 1941, to his friend and dealer János Gati, "I am certain these paintings will mark me among certain types as a degenerate or worse, but I am pleased they are in the world and hope they will remain safe from the pyre. I know I could not bear to extinguish them."

I found it hard to imagine, find it hard, still, that Kálmán would have been pleased to see his masterpiece fall into my hands, but there I stood, at last, with Rachel, a few days after I'd scurried like a rat from her temple. We were ushered into a massive vault, its gaping door hanging open obscenely. An armed guard sat on a stool outside the portcullis. Rachel pulled open a large, flat drawer—I thought of a mortuary slab—and we lifted out *Budapest Street Scene* and propped it against the wall, where we could examine it. I was surprised at how light, how insubstantial something so valuable felt.

We stood back and stared at the painting. It was in the same gilt frame that had accompanied it across the ocean and decades. It was like the afternoon in the museum all over again. We were speechless. But this time, when I took Rachel's hand, she grasped it, and we stood there together, taking in the sixth and final version of Ervin Kálmán's *Budapest Street Scene*.

"It's smaller than I thought it would be," I said.

She nodded.

"And the colors . . ."

"Yeah. Very. So . . ."

We stood before the painting then as I stand before it now, but how different the moments are. Here tonight I am reconciled, in my fashion, but there, as we stood together, I was almost dizzy with the weight of it. It seemed a focal point upon which so many feelings and thoughts converged. I remembered the words of the Jew-hating poet, *At the still point of the turning world . . . / . . . there the dance is / . . . Where past and future are gathered*. In the figures I saw my father. In the colors I saw Rachel, whose warmth I felt radiating beside me. In the tableau I saw the approaching war, its specters and wraiths. In the ridges of the brushstrokes I saw Kálmán, broken, dead, and gone. I saw too much, more than I could digest, and I swooned before it all like the weak-kneed heroine of a gothic romance. Rachel steadied me, and before I knew it, we were kissing once again, but in earnest this time, and I felt promise flow through me, through her, through the painting. Unlike the public announcement of that first boulevard kiss with Tracy, this kiss was private, full of intention, and I thought again of the mezuzah and all it foretold.

But two things happened that disrupted my fleeting hopefulness.

First, Rabbi Diana Wolfe of Temple Beth Israel of Chicago

filed a claim of ownership for *Budapest Street Scene*, which was followed by an injunction to stay the transfer of the painting to me. And then, that very day—Hashem's black sense of humor at work—my father had his fourth, and final, heart attack.

Part Two

THE SECOND OF MY TWO CHILDHOOD MEMORIES of Judaism comes three years after my temple outing with my grandfather, during a visit to Miami with my mother. My father, always disinclined to visit family in general and hers in particular, remained behind. We had gone together to the Jewish cemetery to visit her father's grave, and had brought her mother along. She was my last surviving grandparent, now long gone, our tribe dwindled. She was a sour, miserable woman, incapable of taking pleasure in anything, including her grandson. Her lips perpetually pursed so that even when she smiled she frowned. The family legend was that she literally nagged my grandfather to death, and I never saw anything to make me doubt the story's plausibility.

Still, as she aged, her edge dulled and her anger transformed into a sort of cartoonish despair, mawkish tears its primary currency. They were in ample evidence on this warm afternoon, as she busied herself cleaning my grandfather's black granite headstone with little cups of water ferried to and from a nearby drinking fountain. She fussed with the stones that had been set on the grave, arranging and rearranging them, and prodding my mother and me to add our own. I was fascinated by her performance, a borscht-belt parody of grief. My mother watched impassively, a scowl edging onto her face, hardness in her eyes, and muttered to me, "If she had given him that kind of care while he was here, he might still be alive." With that, she turned and left my grandmother to her work, and I stood there for a confused moment, unsure whom I was meant to attend, before hurrying off after my mother.

Virgil has silently placed a box of Kleenex at my elbow. It's possible my sniffling has been irritating, and the gesture is more rebuke than kindness. But we've been through a lot together, and this evening is far from over. He is watching me with renewed interest, leaning almost rakishly in the doorway, more virgule than Virgil. He senses a dramatic turn approaching.

My father's condition, the doctors were reporting, was critical. The heart attack had been major, and now other organs had begun to fail. Infection was filling his lungs with fluid, and he was not expected to survive more than a day or two. Perhaps only hours. They urged me to hurry to New York, while there was still time, to say what needed to be said. A day or two. When a lifetime hadn't been enough.

As I rushed to pack and catch a midmorning flight, Tracy called from Bali. She'd already arranged a ticket and insisted that she meet me there. I told her that I loved her for offering but that she was unlikely to get there in time. It took some persuading. I wanted this moment to myself, my private reckoning, but I had Tracy's deep affection for my father to reckon with. In the end, she reluctantly agreed to stay where she was. Did I detect the slightest layer of relief in her voice? Looking back, I'm sure it was there, and I'm sure that I missed it.

I was in the taxi, en route to the airport, when Rachel called with the details about Rabbi Wolfe. Apparently news coverage of my case had reached her in Chicago, where she led a large congregation, and she was able to connect the image

He beckons me to his bedside. Open the drawer, he says, voice barely audible. I slide the industrial metal nightstand open. A hundred-dollar bill sits amid tissues, rubber gloves, and cookie wrappers. Take it, he says. I look at him, confused. I was wrong. You were right. I left the Meccano at home. I look at the money but there's no satisfaction in it for me, only ineffable sorrow.

My father has never before said to me "I was wrong."

With all that remains unsaid, the words jam up like a rush-hour freeway, and I can barely think of what to say.

"Thank you," I whisper. My father looks at me with curiosity.

"What for?"

I shrug and mumble, "For giving me life."

We sit in silence until I blurt, "I'm sorry about that message I left."

"Vat message?"

Such relief. "Never mind. Dad . . . the painting. It's . . . ours. It's ours now." I do not mention Rabbi Wolfe.

His eyes grow distant. "The painting . . . My street, where I grew up in Pest, it was named for a painter . . . *Székely Bertalan utca*. Street. Father knew him."

"I . . . I didn't know that."

I don't know anything. And now, it's too late. The man lies dying before me and he takes his stories with him.

And then he startles me again. "I'm proud of you, *kisfiú*."

I clamp my jaw but still my eyes run. His eyes close and he drifts into sleep.

IT SEEMS LIKE MY LAST ESSENTIAL DUTY. I resolve to sit here, at his side, in this stiff chair, until the end. I lean forward and whisper in his ear. *It's okay to let go. There's no need to keep fighting. You've done enough.*

A nurse comes in to check on him. I am startled to see her tear-filled eyes. She pats his hand and whispers to me that my father is a good man. What has she seen in him, I wonder, to prompt such tenderness? What does she know about him that I don't?

In the distance, the quiet of the night is punctuated by beeps and whirrs of medical equipment, and a woman wails "No more!" Startled awake, my father looks around the room and commands: "Stop the credit cards." Then he turns his head slightly in my direction and drifts back into sleep. I watch his eyebrows rise as though his dream is surprising. His body heaves with the effort of breathing, his lips purse as if trying to coax a note from a defective trumpet.

DESPITE MY BEST EFFORTS, I eventually doze off in the chair and fall into a light, dreamless sleep. I don't know how long I've been out when the nurse touches my shoulder and wakes me with a simple "He's gone."

I rub my eyes and leap out of my chair, disbelieving, and approach his bed with trepidation. It's my first time with a corpse. I hang back for a moment, as though his condition might be contagious. A dull fascination overcomes me, crowding out the guilt I feel over missing his passing. He has been switched off. Everything that I knew to be my father is lost. I feel light-headed as I lean over and draw my cheek gently across his stubble. He is cold, so cold, and it's the coldness that finally makes me weep. Father. Dad. Daddy . . .

I T WAS JUST AFTER DAWN when I arrived at my childhood home. The taxi wheezed off into the still Queens morning and I stood in the driveway, taking in the simple two-story brick house on a corner lot. My father bought my mother out after the divorce, simultaneously underwriting her Paris escape and ensuring he did not have to pack up his thousands of model cars. Signs of neglect were everywhere. Overgrown grass. Chipped flagstone. Peeling paint like patches of eczema. Rust-covered siding.

I entered through the back door, an old habit, the front door having been reserved for guests and distant relations. I found the spare key, still under the geranium pot, and I slid it into the lock, propping the screen door open with my roller bag. The house was so still, something newly sepulchral to the place. I stood in the kitchen, exhausted, and listened to myself breathing. I left my bag right there on the red linoleum and walked toward the living room. I passed my childhood room along the way, and despite my fatigue, I poked my head inside. The room had been repurposed as an office for my father. Childish things had been put away. There was nothing, not even photos of family. I found myself wondering if there was anything at all in the house that once belonged to me, that could attest to my place in this family.

I called Tracy, got her voice mail, and left her a message

telling her what had happened, that I was fine. I also called my mother, still unreachable at her Pyrénées painting retreat, and left the same message. I grabbed a blanket from the linen closet and went into the living room. I cracked open a window to allow the spring breeze to caress the curtains. I kicked my shoes off and stretched out on the couch. To take to my father's bed would have been more Oedipal than I could bear. I closed my eyes and thought about him, in his frigid repose beneath the hospital. I thought about him going into the void alone and I began to weep again, and that is how I fell asleep, the morning light streaming into the living room.

MY PHONE RANG in the early afternoon, rousing me from my slumber. As I sat up, massaging the ache in my neck, Rachel informed me that Rabbi Wolfe's stay had been granted. It was, as she said, a whole new thing now. The rabbi's filing with the court claimed that her grandparents had purchased the painting legally from the Weisz family, although the only evidence Rabbi Wolfe had was an entry referring to the painting in her family's ledgers. The original bill of sale had been lost. But references to the work appeared in family journals and letters throughout the 1940s and '50s, which she hoped would support her claim. This was enough to convince a judge that a second look was warranted before any final decisions were made.

"Maybe I should go see her?" I wondered. Mostly looking for a reason to be elsewhere.

"Oh no, Matt. That's a terrible idea. That's why you've retained me. Leave any conversations to me, please."

"You don't think it's worthwhile to just sort of take her temperature? See what she's like?"

"No," she said with startling firmness. "Please. I need you to *promise* me you won't do that. I mean it."

Rachel, it turned out, had learned something else. Rabbi Wolfe had terminal cancer, and was not expected to survive the year. The news distressed Rachel. She was all attorney again, at least for the moment, and wanted me to understand that she had always believed in me, in my claim, but if information came to light that swung the weight of evidence toward Rabbi Wolfe, it would be a struggle for her to argue my case. I told her I understood, and I offered her a chance to abandon my case then and there. Even in my addled state, it was, we both knew, a test. I wanted her to refuse me, to stay on, as though that affirmed a deeper commitment to me. She did as I hoped, and then asked about my father.

He died, I said. The words felt foreign, as though I were trying out the idea, or talking about someone else.

Rachel was silent for a moment and then her sorrowful sigh filled the line. "I'm sorry, Matt," she said. Was she, I wondered, thinking about her own father, his precious remaining time? No, I think not. There was, is, something about Rachel, about her capacity to erase the boundaries of her heart that leaves me ever so slightly in awe to this day. She made me promise to check in with her each day until I got back to L.A.

I should have cared more about her news, but I didn't. All I cared about at the moment was going downstairs, into the basement, to see my father's collection. As I traversed the hallway, I passed the nook that held my father's answering machine, and I saw the counter set to zero. My message was no longer there. Was he bluffing to spare me, cagey cardplayer to the end?

I opened the basement door and walked down the dozen

steps into the dark, musty space. A damp smell filled the air, mold probably. I flipped on the light at the foot of the stairs, and I was startled by a jowly old man in a shimmering golden helmet who eyeballed me from the shadows. In an instant, I remembered the painting, this reproduction of Rembrandt's *The Man with the Golden Helmet* that my father had hung here, I always imagined, to scare me away. As a boy, I spent many nights in bed, my bladder full, too scared to enter the painting's field of vision. My father was proud of the cheap reproduction, though I learned later that it had been found not to be a Rembrandt but rather the work of one of his students.

I inhaled sharply and took in what my father had wrought. It never ceased to amaze me and, perhaps, frighten me, with its familiar mania. Four interconnected rooms, each with floor-to-ceiling cabinets like you'd see at a jeweler's. Every shelf, every nook, every inch jammed to overflowing with row upon row of toy cars. Twenty nearly identical roadsters might be grouped together, with only minute variations in color and detail to differentiate them. Looming over them, a large model, perhaps one of the 1:8 scale custom-built cars my father commissioned. One wall had been reserved for a row of bookcases, shelves sagging with automotive books and memorabilia. I wandered through each of the rooms, turning on lights, wiping away layers of dust with my sleeve. Here was a life's labor, his one concrete expression of self. I thought about how I had derided him, but I've begun to see that perhaps there is something hopeful about the collector, striving toward an elusive completeness, forging ahead long after other, lesser men have packed it in.

As I took in the various toys, remembering this show or that where the piece had been acquired, it began to dawn on me that all this, as the patriarchs like to say, would be mine.

On the one hand, I couldn't imagine my father leaving this to me. But he surely would not have left it to my mother. And in the end, isn't that what fathers do? Pass their worldly possessions on to their sons? Whether or not I would come to possess *Budapest Street Scene*, I was now custodian of my father's collection of molded plastic and die-cast tin.

The prospect irked me. I could not, it's true, imagine myself maintaining his collection, but neither could I see myself dismantling it, selling it off. Why hadn't he talked to me about it, given me some indication of his wishes? I became irritated with him all over again. Then I noticed a toy that had beguiled me as a child. It was a large, red '67 Corvette, substantial and rendered with remarkable verisimilitude. The parts all articulated, moving in concert on axles and crankshafts. It was a toy I had longed to play with, to roll along the floor, but like all the rest, it was forbidden. Now I slid open the display cabinet and carefully hoisted out the car. I sat down on the warping linoleum tile, flecked with water stains, and began to roll the car along the floor.

HOW LONG I SAT THERE PLAYING—yes, playing, Virgil; can you picture it?—I cannot say, but when my phone rang I answered expecting either Rachel, Tracy, or, for an instant, my father. How many times in the days, even weeks, ahead I would briefly forget that he was gone. Tenses confuse me, as you can see. No tense more so, perhaps, than the first-person present. To be. I am. I was surprised to be greeted by Rabbi Wolfe. Her attorney had advised her not to call me directly, but she'd learned of my father's death and wanted to express her condolences. *Baruch dayan emet*, Blessed be the one true judge, I later learned. She also apologized for what she called "the unfortunate timing of all this." She reminded me that death was not, in and of it-self, a tragedy. And I oughtta know, she said. At least, I think she said it. She said other things, too, words intended to soothe, but although they were sage and appropriate her manner was brusque, brittle. Perhaps it was the husky rasp of her voice, more thorns than roses. A smoker, surely. The life, she said, signing off. We think of the life, remember the deeds. We cel-ebrate as we mourn. She invited me to visit her synagogue in Chicago and said goodbye.

NOW I STAND HERE ALONE in the stillest and darkest moment of the night, with this strange painting and my strange story, tired and aching, and I can only think about all I have squandered, the astonishing lack of care with which I have blundered through life. So much beyond recovery, things that can never be restored, truths devoured by time, by neglect. The essence of a man. The street outside is deserted. There's not a sound to be heard, not a move, a creak, a hiss. Even Virgil has deserted me, off doing heaven knows what, dozing in a storage room, perhaps. The darkness is complete, without and within, as though the sun has collapsed upon itself. Neither Rachel's honey nor Tracy's gleam can illuminate this darkness. Is this how Rabbi Wolfe will experience the death that stalks her, as implacable night? Is this how my father quit this world? How far they all seem from me now, how impenetrable, re-moved from everything I am, standing here in this dark, still room with a painting. His painting. My painting. Whose fuck-ing painting?

In 1944, Ervin Laszlo Kálmán put a gun in his mouth and killed himself. Coward or realist? What would my father say, who also fled, in his fashion? There must have been a moment when I wanted to know more, needed to know more? Was the desire so mercilessly brief that I missed it?

In the half-light, the auction house has begun to take on the outlines of a temple. Melodrama, epiphany, or sleep deprivation, I cannot say, but the rows of chairs resemble pews, the framed posters of prior auctions throb like stained glass, and the curtains blocking off the offices suggest an ark. I again hear Rachel's whispered prayers whipping through my ears like a desert wind, hear the not-so-ancient tunes drifting from the temple, and I feel the presence of something in this room. Is it my father? Is it God? I know You're here. Show Yourself. The light shifts and all is again as it was, nobody here but us chickens. Don't mind me, I'll sit here alone in the dark.

The life, Rabbi Wolfe said. The deeds. These are the facts of my father's life, as I know them: He was born in Budapest. He left it twice, once for London in his childhood, only to return two years later, and once for New York. He married my mother when he was twenty-seven and they had me when he was thirty-five. He was a commercial painter and a cardplayer and a collector of vintage toy automobiles, and a Hungarian Jew. He was my father. Just the fucking facts. It would take a journey to the other side of the world for me to learn the rest.

THERE WERE FIVE OF THEM in all, wedged into a small apartment that appeared to have been in the family's hands since the Communist days. Cheaply furnished, groaning with belongings, so insistently foreign it seemed to me. My father's first, second, and third cousins filled the room, the Lowenheims and Ujvaris I'd only read about, in the flesh, though not a Santos in sight. My relatives sat in a semicircle facing me, as though I were some alien specimen that had washed ashore and was now drawing their scholarly attention. Or was it worry? Did they all appear just a little bit worried? As they offered their condolences on my loss, I glanced across the room to Rachel for comfort, but found none in her jet-lagged eyes. Beyond the window, the sun baked the sweltering, muggy city. I shivered at the sight of it, even as another cool beverage was pressed into my hands.

Rachel had persuaded me to submit my claim to arbitration. "Matt, this woman is dying," she'd said little more than a week earlier, as I drove away from the funeral parlor. "This might be your only chance at a swift resolution. In the courts, this could drag out for years, and then you'll have to deal with her estate, and all its competing interests."

The trip to Budapest was also her idea, to see if we could find evidence to explain how my family had come into possession of the painting to begin with, the one conspicuous hole in our case. The courts liked nothing better than original documents, she explained, and perhaps if we traveled to the source, we might uncover something useful. I agreed—New York was already halfway there—and so we found ourselves on a Saturday afternoon, the day after landing in Budapest, surrounded by my Hungarian relatives.

Tibor had the best English and did the translating. Paunchy and gray, he had a silky accent that bore traces of the years he'd spent in Berlin on government business, back when that evoked something glamorous and sinister. A pompous man, he reveled in his role as interlocutor, though without him, I would have been lost. Despite my childhood visit to the Balaton sleepaway camp, I find Hungarian impenetrable. It eludes me, defies my attempts to form even its most rudimentary sounds. It's as alien to me as Hebrew, though without the music. What language, I wonder, did my father think in? His English was serviceable if heavily accented, a touch of Bela Lugosi, though I like to imagine that he dreamed in his native tongue, the familiar sounds of his childhood language perhaps giving him some fleeting nocturnal comfort. He never seemed to mind my inability to learn it—it was useful for keeping secrets—but I wonder if he was perhaps a different man in Hungarian, more like the man I saw at the Tower Club; lighter, more at ease with himself. Like an aria transposed to another key.

I tried to discern anything of him in the faces of those around me. The ridge of an eyebrow or contour of a chin. But there was that apartness again, something so separate in these people that I was reminded of the furtive figure in *Budapest Street Scene* planning his escape. Eszter, the elderly white-haired matriarch, asked Tibor a question in Hungarian. There was a smile embedded between her round cheeks, and at first I mistrusted it but soon came to see it was genuine. She seemed truly delighted to meet me. Although she still exuded that strange layer of worry. She grasped my hand when I sat down, and it remained there, sweaty, firm. Despite her frailty and age—she must have been in her late eighties—there was a vitality in her every syllable in which I finally recognized something of my father. Tibor translated for me as his elfin wife, Kati, shuttled beverages in and out of the sitting room.

"She wants to know if you have been to the Oscars." He pronounced it *bean*.

Rachel suppressed a smile. I shook my head. "Not yet," I answered.

Eszter's mother, Dora, the oldest living woman I had ever seen—she was believed to be 102—dozed in her chair, mouth wide-open. Wisps of a mustache adorned her lip, and in her denture-less pucker I saw my father's deathbed visage. I asked about any memories they might have of him. Tibor made a show of remembering, the sort of man who trafficked in ostentatious gestures. I learned of my father's sole, reluctant visit to his homeland. He'd left at the first opportunity in 1956, and waited until the wall came down to set foot on Hungarian soil again. He refused to return as long as the Communists remained in power. Apparently, it had been an uneasy visit for all, my father oddly American in his affect, restless, eager to leave almost as soon as he'd arrived. It was only when he visited his parents' graves that he became still, ceased struggling against the pressures of memory. He'd missed the death of his father. She saw the regret in his eyes, Eszter insisted, as he lay the stones on the simple markers.

Rachel asked all the right legal questions about how the painting came into the family's possession, anything about documents left behind, letters, journals, that sort of thing, to little avail. The consensus was that it had simply appeared in the apartment without fanfare early in 1944. Vague promises were made to rifle safe-deposit boxes and dig through long-closed drawers. It went on for hours, the endless, guttural gibberish, the vain searching for clues, the sweetness, the smiles. They were kind, solicitous, and they drove me mad. I wanted out, Virgil. They offered every imaginable kind of help, but there was really just one thing I wanted.

"I would like to see my father's apartment. From his boyhood."

"Of course," Tibor said, as though the question needn't have been asked. "We will take you there."

MY FATHER'S CHILDHOOD HOME. What I saw that afternoon . . . It was all . . .

But first. Unfinished business. I've lost the script again, something that's been happening with alarming frequency these days. Simon tries to convince me that the relative quiet on the work front—few auditions, fewer callbacks, no offers— is the fallout from my on-set black eye, but I've begun to wonder if something hasn't permanently shifted in me, and somehow the casting directors around town can feel it, too.

It's a bit hard to credit. I've been working for my entire adult life, and can't imagine it just stopping. I do confess a mild irritation watching my parts go to others, my less talented competition. (Oh, not *him*. Really?) And there are practicalities to consider. Food. Shelter. BMW payments. But finally, this change, alleged, hinted at, is not, I think, complete. It's begun, yes, the shapes are shifting, but I haven't yet been delivered to . . . To where?

To where the story ends?

Fuck, Virgil. This is exhausting. Anyway, the script. Before Rachel and I made our way to Budapest, there was some pressing business left to resolve in New York. I had to lay the old man to rest, in body at least. I found a funeral parlor close to the hospital and presented myself to make the necessary arrangements.

"What sort of a service did you have in mind?"

I sat in the plush carpeted funeral parlor, irritated with my father, even in death. He'd never discussed it with me, had given me no indication at all of his wishes. Perhaps the old bastard just intended to go on forever, imagining that if he didn't concede the inevitability of his demise, he would somehow outsmart it. I didn't even know whom to invite, who might care or be bothered to attend. I thought my mother might know more, though I don't know why, so thoroughly had she excised him from her life.

I shrugged. The funeral director, a fellow named Glide, delivered his well-rehearsed options to me, and the whole thing felt rather businesslike—two from column a, one from column b—and in the end, we settled on a cremation without a funeral service. I struggled with the historical resonance of the choice but could not imagine my father being lowered into the earth in a box. I envisioned soil of any fertility vomiting him back up into the sunlight.

"And would you like for us to have the remains interred or returned?"

Part of me would have liked to have outsourced the problem of his remains. To have the funeral house set his urn in a niche somewhere was not without its appeal. But the last shards of inconvenient filial duty kicked in, and I said I would take possession of the remains when I passed back through New York on my way home from Budapest, without the slightest idea of what I would do with them.

I STOOD IN FRONT of a covered mirror in my father's hallway. I covered it because I couldn't bear the sight of myself, couldn't stomach my resemblance to my father, which seemed to have sharpened with his passing. But I told myself, and Rachel, that I was trying to honor custom. She had called to discuss travel arrangements.

"Shiva—there's something I'm supposed to do with mirrors, right?"

"You're supposed to cover them. You're also supposed to tear a garment."

I looked at the James Perse crewneck I was wearing. I had no intention of tearing it.

"What's the point of that?"

"Which? The mirror or the clothes?"

"Both, I guess."

"Well, it's complicated. There are a number of reasons, some symbolic, some practical. It's not one thing. It's never just one thing."

I sighed. "Yeah, complicated."

We finished our call with a plan to meet in Budapest the following week. All brisk efficiency, she had already sketched out a full three days: interviews with relatives, a visit to the National Gallery to meet with their Kálmán expert, and even a lead on our Arrow Cross betrayer Halasz. I half listened when she got into the case's particulars. I focused, instead, on how good it felt to talk to her, how her voice carried in it that mysterious ancient music, notes of faith that I believed could restore me. I think she sensed this because she inquired with genuine tenderness how I was holding up.

I'm fine, Rachel. I'm always fine.

I LOGGED INTO MY FATHER'S E-MAIL to set his auto-reply with news of his death. He was always careless with passwords, had used the same one—littletoycarz—for everything for as long as I could remember. To my surprise, his inbox already contained more than thirty condolence e-mails. How had word spread so quickly? The funeral parlor? My mother? To this day, I have no idea.

I hurried through them at first, just scanning to see if I recognized the senders. Then I sat back and began to read.

Gabi will be missed. He was a true gentleman. Klara and Dezső

He was? By what standard?

Such courage! He lived his life on his own terms and was an inspiration to me. Viktor

Yes, he was an obstinate, rigid bastard.

Also buried in there somewhere: *Will you be selling his collection?* I deleted that one.

For more than an hour I read on, taking in these memories of my father from his contemporaries. I couldn't reconcile the picture they painted with the man I'd known. *Classy. Generous. Charming. A straight shooter. A good man.*

I could only chuckle and think, *You obviously didn't know him like I did.*

And then a darker, more troubling thought announced itself.

What if *I* was the one who didn't know *him?* What made

172

me think my impressions were the accurate ones? After all, the numbers were against me, thirty-seven to one. I sat back in my chair, deflated. How ungenerous had I been all these years? How wrong had I gotten the old man?

One evening when I was fifteen, my father and I were walking back to his car from a shopping trip to a neighborhood mall. It was a winter night, slushy and cold. The icy night air pierced my wool coat. It hurt to inhale. As we hurried up the street toward the parking lot a young man intercepted us, bearing some kind of religious literature. Before he could utter more than a few words, my father cut him off. *Not interested.* A forceful parry. Something about the handouts had disturbed my father—Jews for Jesus? Moonies, perhaps? His anger was whiter than seemed warranted. I apologized to the young man with a glance, forever ashamed of my father's hotheadedness. The fellow, thinking I had communicated interest in his wares, tried to slip me a brochure while my father waited for the light to change.

My father erupted. Yahweh's wrath. Shouting, he stepped between us and shoved the youngster, who lost his footing on the icy pavement and fell on his ass. I lowered my eyes as the light changed and my father charged across the intersection, hauling me along in his wake. Whenever I thought about that moment, I would shudder with embarrassment at his overreaction. Now I wondered, would these correspondents have seen it differently? A loving, protective father, shielding his son?

My phone chimed. A text from Tracy, wanting to know how I was doing. She was taking my father's death harder than I was. She had tearfully offered to come to Budapest with me, and part of me wanted her to, very much. But she had several Harvest Moon shoots lined up, more or less back-to-back, and I pointed out that one of us needed to be working. Now I texted that I was wrapping things up in New York, that I was as good as I could be under the circumstances, and that I missed her and loved her. All true, and yet once again, that strange carnival barker emptiness haunted me.

I set the phone aside and resumed reading the e-mails. I was struck by the repetitions, the banal language of consolation. Are the options for offering comfort really so paltry, or did it just reflect the linguistic shortcomings of the e-mailers, most of whom were not native to English? However well intended, a tedium set in: *We're so sorry. I wish there was something I could say. I know how you feel, I lost a parent, too. You are in my thoughts and prayers. Please tell me if I can do anything to help.* And so on until I choked on all the good intentions and shut the computer down. I closed my eyes and, for the briefest of moments, I saw my father's paint-flecked pants, a storm of blues and whites and pinks, the cloth hardened beneath the layers.

VIRGIL IS SNORING somewhere around here. I've lost track of his movements but I can hear his dry rumble. It reminds me of Tracy, rattling through the hallways like an unattended popcorn popper. Let's liven things up with a complication. Perhaps it will rouse you, as it roused something in me. Indulge me these last few hours, Virgil. It will all be over soon enough.

There was one more thing to do before I departed for Budapest, before I was ushered into the clutches of family. Despite my promise to Rachel, I took a flight to Chicago. I did not tell her, and the omission rattled me with guilt. I viewed the trip as a necessary bit of opposition research, though I wasn't even sure I would speak to Rabbi Wolfe when I arrived. Still, I determined that it would be helpful to know a bit more about my adversary.

I remember the steaming, pouring rain. Between the heat, the humidity, and the downpour, I felt like I was venturing into the Amazon as I dove into my rental car, which had been started and defogged for me. I punched the address of Temple Beth Israel into the GPS. It was an urban congregation, just steps from the lake. A touch under twenty miles. I followed my robotic narrator's instructions and drove carefully out of the airport, worried about hydroplaning. Driving to temple on a Friday night. I know, Virgil. I know.

Chicago, that somber city, whipped past me in a sodden, windy blur. I could sense the large, dark lake hovering just outside my window, though it was invisible to me. I could not manage to balance the temperature inside the car, either too cold and foggy or sweltering and damp. It chilled me, and I thought of my father's awful chill as he lay still on the hospital bed. *You have arrived at your destination*, my vehicle informed me with what seemed like a sneer.

At first I thought I had been delivered to the wrong location. The synagogue looked jarringly modern to me, sandstone with casement windows, more like a university research library than a house of worship. A flight of exterior stairs saw-toothed their way along the perimeter wall, and it was only when I saw the gold-inlaid Hebrew lettering over the doorframe that I switched the car off. For a moment I thought of Rachel and considered restarting the car and returning to the airport. It wasn't too late, not yet.

Instead, I hurried across the street, jogged up the stairs, and rushed inside. I would like to say some deepening sense of self enabled me to bound into the lobby. It was the deluge, nothing more, that prevented any dithering.

The lobby was carpeted, climate-controlled, and inviting. Wood-paneled walls with plaques identifying generous donors. The cantor's muffled song throbbed behind two massive closed doors. A well-heeled middle-aged couple in the lobby had been whispering when I entered. They stopped and looked at me briefly with ill-concealed hostility. They took their conversation down a side corridor. I'm sure they were merely vexed at the interruption, but it seemed they knew I did not belong.

I patted my hair dry and grabbed a kippah from a conveniently placed wooden box and eased the door open. I found myself squinting against the radiance of the temple. It was a soaring, modern space, built in a triangular frame with the pulpit at its apex. The room was full of sharp edges and hard angles. The ark looked like a space capsule. There were perhaps two or three hundred prosperous-looking people gathered, bent over prayer books. I wondered what *Béla-bácsi* would make of these modern, American Jews, and of his grandson, setting foot, at last, into a temple for the first time since that childhood visit decades ago. I marveled, Grandpa, at the unexpected familiarity of it all. Do I have you to thank for that?

I slid into a bench near the back. In front of me, a beautiful baby boy slept in his mother's arms. His lush black hair shone thick and curly, and his limbs had all gone slack. He might have been dead except for the complete serenity on his face and the gentle rise and fall of his chest. He was so tiny, not more than six months old. Yet he slept, safe and secure in his mother's arms. I envied him, Virgil. How I envied him. His mother's eyes never left the rabbi, who now, finally, drew my attention.

I don't know what I expected to find. Frailty, weakness, my fallback handbook of Hollywood clichés and types. I was taken aback by her blunt vitality. Thick-limbed, she had short, gray hair that bobbed only about a foot over the lectern. The graveled voice was as I remembered it from our brief phone call. She closed her prayer book, removed her glasses, and began her sermon, which concerned itself—serendipitously? Inspired divinely?—with the role of community and its importance in Judaism. She muddled her way through with neither style nor wit, a plodding presence at the pulpit. It was hard to believe she had so central a role in the spiritual deliverance of so many. Perhaps this was where her illness had taken its toll. Yet for all my estrangement from my faith, and for all the dryness of her delivery, I found myself nodding as she spoke, semi-listening as I studied my fellow worshippers. I was surprised at how casually dressed many of them were. There were blue jeans in evidence, many open-necked shirts, and even the occasional pair of sneakers. Gone was the dark-suited severity of my grandfather's temple. There were more children and teenagers than I'd expected, bright-eyed and engaged. As I listened to Rabbi Wolfe, as I began to relax, my feeling of otherness began to lift and—I know it's all illusion, Virgil, but illusion is what I do—I felt the room begin to warm toward me. My muscles unclenched, my shoulders dropped, and, more or less at the very moment that Rabbi Wolfe said "Do not separate yourself from the community," the room began to feel familiar to me. I believed that I could have been in any temple in any city anywhere in the world, and these faces would have been known to me. And as I scrutinized Rabbi Wolfe from the rear of the temple, I wondered not whether the painting was mine or hers, but whether there was a deeper claim to be laid, a claim beyond mere ownership, a claim of worthiness. Whether or not *Budapest Street Scene* actually belonged to her, I had a strange sense that she was entitled to it. Though she was, in some ways, a performer, too; but look at the value of her lifetime role, against the dozens of nameless, faceless hats I've worn.

Rabbi Wolfe ended her sermon and introduced a vocal sextet, young girls, perhaps thirteen or so. I looked at the six of them, dark-eyed, lovely, and as they opened their mouths I felt the breath briefly leave my body, so beautiful were the sounds they made. I didn't know the song, another modern ditty all gussied up to sound ancient, I expect, but it soared into the golden space of the temple, sung by these six who smiled beatifically with the realization, I think, that they were part of something indelible. I turned to look at my fellow congregants, to watch them watching. Some of them smiled at me, at the surprising dampness around my eyes. I felt as though I'd stepped through a door that had been held open on my behalf.

All at once, I wanted to see Rachel. To tell her. To share the moment with her. I felt so foolish for not having gone inside her synagogue in Los Angeles, for having missed this opportunity. I wanted her to know what I was feeling. Yes, to have her approval, of course, to have her see she was right, I was not so far gone after all. But I couldn't tell her. The impulse behind the trip would have undermined me.

My mind flitted to Tracy, and all I have kept from her. Had kept. Again those damned tenses. I tried to imagine her in this room, taking it all in as she had taken in the Van Goghs, a little tired, a little mystified. I wondered how she would fare with every eye trained upon her flaxen beauty. Though it's fair to say she has always stood out in any room she enters, it now seemed clear that more than Ricky McCabe had begun to separate us.

These long, dark tunnels. They all look so much alike.

A new note began to creep into my darkening interior melody, so vivid a counterpoint to the angelic tones rising from the stage before me. For all at once, I was angry with my parents, furious at my denied birthright. Yes, I was here now; yes, I felt warm in the room but there was no escaping the truth: that I was an outsider. All the years of study and devotion that marked the lives around me, whereas I had nothing to clutch but my blankness. My fists hardened into white-knuckled blocks and I muttered "Fuck" to myself, to my parents. To my emptiness. I was appalled as soon as the word passed my lips, but the comment went unheard. Or did it? You heard, didn't You? You up there. In Your house.

The six girls onstage continued to sing, these beautiful

young treasures, containing infinite and varied futures. But now, unbidden, all I could see were their young corpses lying in an open grave somewhere in Poland. Or Russia. Or bobbing in the Danube. I looked back down at the sleeping boy in front of me, certain in the knowledge that he, too, would have perished, that his safety was nothing more than an illusion. No parent could have saved him. No parent can.

I was assaulted by the kaleidoscope of faces, of these girls, this boy, my dead father in the hospital, Rachel's understanding eyes, Kálmán's devastated street, until, at last, I hurried out of the temple, found the bathroom, and threw up my in-flight snacks.

IT WOULD HAVE BEEN EASY enough for me to disappear among the crowd streaming from the building. But something in me would not relent, some strange force sent me back into the temple at the service's end, so that I could insert myself in line and greet the rabbi. I can't imagine what I thought I had to gain, what knowledge might be transferred to me in the course of a simple handshake. I watched her as I neared, and now I saw something of the toll her illness was taking. She was weak, trying to keep her interactions as brief as possible, limited to a friendly "*Shabbat shalom*," though I sensed friendliness did not come easily to her in the best of times. She bent down stiffly to greet the children, the first betrayal of any physical discomfort. She knew a good many congregants by name. I felt my heart speed up as I neared her, as the foolishness of my idea became clear. What if she recognized me? Though I am not, as I have said, famous, nor is my face entirely unknown. The news coverage she had seen would have included a grainy photo or two, and the riches of the Internet would have been just a few clicks away. What a foolish impulse, Virgil.

She did not seem to recognize me. There was, perhaps, the tiniest hesitation as she took my hand, though I may have imagined it to soothe my ruffled ego. How dare she not recognize me, I thought, as she *Shabbat-shalomed* me like I was just another wealthy Chicago *macher*. I wanted a sign, Virgil. Yes, a sign. Divine inspiration, a twinge in the gut, something, anything to tell me what I was meant to do next. Instead, her fingers released me, without so much as a backward glance. And yet, as I left the synagogue, I felt her eyes on my back, though I looked over my shoulder twice, and each time found her consumed with her greetings.

Another day, another walk-on to add to my résumé, albeit one, unlike the rest of my oeuvre, that would return to haunt me.

VIRGIL IS OFF SOMEWHERE talking on his cell phone. I can't make out what he is saying, his conversation is muffled by the walls separating us. But the timbre of his voice is not at all what I expected. I assumed he'd have a sonorous basso profundo to match his Falstaffian girth. Instead, there's a reediness to his nattering, and I'm suddenly alive to a new dimension of my hitherto silent comrade. Whom can he be talking to so urgently at this late hour? A lover, surely. What do they discuss with such intensity at two-thirty in the morning? The dim contours of a life outside the auction house begin to emerge from the mists, and I am curious to know more. I am aware of the silent, shattered cell phone in my own pocket, heavy and still.

I return my attention to *Budapest Street Scene*. I'm feeling renewed, a second (or is it third? Fourth?) wind upon me, and I am drawn to the *Andrássy út* facades, the sight of which casts me back to that first day in Budapest and revives all the disappointment that I experienced as I strolled down the actual boulevard.

Rachel and I had arrived midafternoon on a Friday, a week to the day after my Chicago sojourn. We checked in to our hotel, a turn-of-the-century landmark recently restored to its full Belle Époque grandeur. The lobby was rich with gilt and Russian mafia. I was restless, anxious. An amorphous foreboding had settled on me, almost from the moment I'd cleared passport control, and I wanted to take a walk. Rachel was ragged with jet lag and begged off, opting for a short nap in her room. We agreed to meet in two hours in the lobby and then head off to Kálmán's studio, where we would meet with its curators.

As I set out along the steamy boulevard, I called Tracy to check in, let her know I'd arrived safely. I imagined we'd talk about McCabe, whose emergency appeal to the Supreme Court was being prepared, but she surprised me.

"Your lawyer is an attractive woman."

Ah, Google, slayer of secrets.

"Yes, I suppose she is."

"I thought you said your lawyer was a 'he.'"

"Did I? Maybe you misheard. Or maybe you were thinking about Brian." When in doubt, deflect. "Anyway, it's all very professional. Just like you and Brian."

In truth, after all the Brian business, I was flattered that she still cared. We talked for a few more moments, and I laid out the agenda of the next few days, a slew of interviews with family members and Kálmán experts. I told her that I missed her, that I couldn't wait to see her back in L.A., and that I was hoping we'd each have good news to share.

I strolled along a leafy side street, lined with listless, gray buildings. Exposed brick was visible everywhere beneath torn stucco, yet no building was without a satellite dish. I noticed strange divots in many of the buildings, near windows. Tibor later informed me these pockmarks were bullet holes, scars of war, of revolution. The farther I walked, the bleaker I felt. The sun could not penetrate the narrow streets. The whole city seemed coated with soot. Bored, surly young men on bicycles fingering cell phones, collected in driveways and alleys. The women all dressed like reality-show extras, stuffed into cheap and revealing dresses. A tremendous sadness gripped me, a heaviness that deepened as I walked.

I continued along aimlessly, or so I told myself, but in truth I was drawn toward the *Andrássy út*. There were, perhaps, other more logical starting points. My father's childhood home, for one. But I wasn't ready to face that, not yet, not alone. Instead, the place I was pulled toward was *that* corner of *that* street, the vantage point from which Kálmán had seen what he had seen, in order to paint what he would paint.

I turned onto the *Andrássy út* and exhaled as the street widened into a wide, sunny boulevard. Budapest's Champs-Élysées, they call it, though the French would probably disavow any relation to this poor bastard cousin. I strolled past the Opera House, a hulking pile of stone squatting on a city block, all columns and spires and looming statues. The soaring eaves illuminated from within like sunken, baleful eyes. I shuddered under its scrutiny and hurried on. At last, I arrived at the facade that, according to several of my Kálmán textbooks, was the actual location of *Budapest Street Scene*. The presumed actual location. The generally agreed upon but unconfirmed actual location. The scholars, in fact, had no idea what the fuck they were talking about. One of my books reproduced a black-and-white photograph of the intersection from roughly the same period as the painting, and there are familiar aspects, not least of which are the cobbled archways. It's comforting to accept their truth, but it's one possible narrative, a best guess, and one impossible to confirm since that street had been obliterated. I stood there throbbing with disappointment. Another past erased, unconfirmable, unconfrontable. A bad omen for the trip, I decided, though I never have believed in omens, even as I dread them. My feet ached, fatigue swept over me, and my thoughts briefly turned to Rachel asleep in her—

Virgil has fallen silent. He has either resolved his dilemma, or he has given up. Those are the only choices, after all.

RACHEL ARRANGED FOR A CAR to take us into the Buda foothills, to Kálmán's home and studio, which had been converted into a museum. Despite Kálmán's international reputation, the museum had a ramshackle feel to it, the obvious good intentions of the curators hobbled by lack of funds. A suite of seven large rooms, including a working reproduction of his studio, opened onto a desiccated courtyard garden bathed in late-afternoon sunshine. The smell of age, a slow rot, hung about the place. While Rachel was busy talking with the director, their hushed, urgent whispers echoing in the courtyard, I wandered around, taking in the digs, which were brighter than I'd expected, given the darkness of Kálmán's output. A slide projector threw an image of *Budapest Street Scene* against one of the bare, whitewashed walls, a spectral reminder of our purpose. I perused the framed black-and-white photos and documents. It was a touching, homespun presentation, lacking finesse or a sense of occasion. There were no other visitors present, and Irma, the lethargic bespectacled intern, advised me in broken English that weeks went by without anyone stopping in. It saddened me to see Kálmán so neglected in his own land, and I imagined him here, veronal-addled, painting feverishly, especially in those last days, trying to finish his canvases to the sounds of his neighbors being carted away. There was so little time left, he must have known. Might those last days have been more profitably spent arranging an escape? Doing as my father did, getting while the getting was good? Or was it already too late?

Why didn't he stop painting and make his escape? Instead, he worked. Making do. And then he was dead.

Rachel's goodbye to the museum director ended my reverie. She took my arm and guided me to the door. Outside, on the street, she smiled. They tend to be conservative in these matters, she explained, especially since Kálmán was a popular target of forgers, so they've got liability every time they weigh in. But, she went on, they were aware of the provenance of this particular version of *Budapest Street Scene* and, having reviewed the file with Rachel, concurred that our claim appeared stronger than Rabbi Wolfe's. They would sign an affidavit to that effect.

"So what's next?" I asked her.

"That's it for today. I'm off the clock," she said.

"What do you want to do?" I asked.

THE DOHÁNY STREET SYNAGOGUE—the largest one in Europe— didn't look much like a temple, with its strange Ottoman- flavored spires. I don't think I'd have been surprised to hear a muezzin's call. The taxi deposited us in front of a fenced-in graveyard that ran along the building's flank. How many times, I wondered, had those faded tombstones been desecrated? A single file of people was moving through a metal detector. Virgil, how inadequate you would have felt, how much less of a man in the shadow of the armed uniformed policeman who stood by while his partner, a bearded fireplug in a kippah and polo shirt, greeted the worshippers. We approached and I craned my neck to see past the line, to the space within.

"Is this the entrance to services?" I asked.

"Why?" English. A relief.

"It's Friday."

"And?"

"It's the Sabbath."

"And?" I wondered whether he was a petty tyrant or merely yanking me around, some Friday fun with the tourists.

"I am here for services."

"Where are you from?"

"L.A."

"What was the last Jewish holiday?"

"Passover." Even I knew that one.

"Shavuot," he corrected me. "What's the next?"

I didn't know the answer, so to spare Rachel the need to rescue me, I pivoted. "Do I need to pass an entrance exam to go to shul?"

"I don't know you. I have never seen your face before."

I explained that I was trying to follow in my Hungarian father's footsteps and that he could search our bags if he wanted to reassure himself.

"I am just trying to protect my people," he said with a trace of apology.

I held his gaze for a moment, then replied: "I *am* your people."

Hah. I wish. What would Rachel have made of me if I'd replied with such certainty? In truth, I only thought of the riposte the following morning, as I was still fuming over my mistreatment, though I think the scene is better in my version. At the same time, I couldn't escape a feeling of sadness that such measures were required to keep his people safe and, more pointedly, that I was so obviously not one of them.

Rachel finally interceded and spoke to him in Hebrew.

Once again that terrible feeling of exclusion as he nodded and dismissed me with a final shrug, insisting we remain for the whole service. He perused our passports, checked our bags, and waved us in.

"No pictures," he said. Then he returned to greet more familiar arrivals.

A WROUGHT-IRON BALCONY encircled the space, and stained-glass windows allowed the fading evening light to enter. Dark polished pews, vaulted ceilings, and illuminated archways, gilded Hebrew lettering. I took in the beautiful interior and turned to Rachel.

"Wow," I whispered. "How did this survive the war?"

"It didn't."

The sparse, elderly crowd looked even thinner and older in the cavernous emptiness, a stark contrast to Rabbi Wolfe's robust and prosperous Chicago congregation. Fewer than forty people scattered through the first dozen pews, leaving row upon empty row stretching back toward the doorway, where we now stood. Rachel pulled a lace head covering from her bag and fastened it to her hair with a bobby pin. She looked at me expectantly. I was, of course, unprepared. I searched the entryway for a supply of guest headgear without success, and shrugged at her when a sixty-something who bore a striking resemblance to Saul Bellow handed me a temporary. I'd expected one of the felt, silk-lined kippot of my youth. This one felt disposable, like a piece of vacuum cleaner filter. He insisted I return it at the end of the service.

Rachel took a seat near the rear, in a pew on the left. I started to slide in beside her when she stopped me and pointed to the center pews. I hadn't noticed that the men and women were seated separately. Disappointed, I slid in across the aisle from her and felt exhaustion settle over me. This had been a mistake. But we were here, we were committed. I dug in and pulled the prayer book out, hoping for some kind of refuge or guidance from the printed page. This time, however, the bilingual prayer book was in Hebrew and Hungarian. I set it back, envying Rachel, who had kissed it and found her place in its pages.

Twenty minutes into the service, everyone in the room turned to face the rear of the temple. Why? I didn't know, still don't, but I have been overwhelmed by how much there is to know about being a Jew. At any rate, see me there, standing terrified. Because my comfortable position hiding in the back of the congregation has now been promoted to the front, and I'm certain I will miss the moment when I'm supposed to turn back. I will be left facing the rear alone, exposed in my ignorance. I perspire and strain my peripheral vision looking for movement, waiting for a telltale rustle of clothes to alert me. Which it finally does. I turn, not quite seamlessly with the room, but not completely out of step either.

The cantor takes the stage and begins to sing. I am transported. The song—*Hashkiveinu*, Rachel later tells me—seizes me. Perhaps it's just the jet lag, but I am newly aware, intimately aware, of death and loss and eternity and my family, all lost to me now, this journey, this long journey, and the music continues and the cantor closes his eyes and reaches into himself to infuse the words with knowledge and wisdom and history and, above all, soul. I try to hide my tears from Rachel, but I know she sees them, I can feel her eyes upon me, and I want him to finish, to stop singing, because it's too much, more than I can bear, here in the land of my dead father.

At length he concludes, and finally, as I wipe my eyes, a

moment I recognize. The wine is being poured. Trays are loaded up with the kind of white plastic cups one uses in a dentist's office. My poor jet-lagged stomach heaves at the notion, the sickly sweet taste clear in my memory, but I can see no way to refuse. A few rows before me, a senior in a white windbreaker vigorously dumps one cup into a second, then inspects the double shot. My thoughts cannot help but return to *Béla-bácsi* as I turn to Rachel and raise the cup toward her in a manner I hope she'll find charming, but as I toss the wine back, her expression tells me I have not achieved the desired effect. The wine remains unconsumed in every cup but mine. I consider spitting it back into the cup. Instead, I swallow it, shuddering at the sweetness. A lengthy prayer follows, during which I do my best to hide my empty cup from view. When, at last, the congregation drinks, I follow suit, a heathen mime. The empties are collected and the service comes to an end, and the congregation, released, turns in toward itself, shaking hands, embracing, wishing one another a good Sabbath.

Why do I feel so sad, so excluded, when the men turn to shake each other's hands? It seems a childish, almost petulant response. After all, this is a congregation. These people see each other every week. I am, as the pit bull out front observed, an outsider. I shouldn't take it personally. But for neither the first nor last time, I contemplate the high price of my father's spiritual indifference, as well as my own. Did he ever, in all the years he lived here, set foot within? Perhaps accompany his father to this service? I look around and some of the faces are old enough that I allow myself to believe that perhaps one among them might remember him, might have a story to tell me, if only I weren't so obviously apart. I think of my father trudging with his suitcase into his hotel.

And then Saul Bellow extends his hand to me. I think he's

asking for his kippah back, but there's a smile on his face as he shakes his head and says, "*Shabbat shalom.*" I grasp the hand and for a moment it seems as though I will not be able to release it.

I turn to look at Rachel across the aisle. There is something so beautiful about her in this moment. That sense of home I felt in her office amplified. That sense of belonging I felt in Chicago with the dial turned up to eleven. Everything is so foreign, the language, the people, the time zone, as I sway, hobbled by too little sleep. Yet I cannot deny the power of this, this third time that I have stood among other Jews and felt at home. But beneath it all ticks the threat of discovery. To be seen as a fraud, a performer, again. Buzzed on Manischewitz, I surrender to Rachel as she eases us into a waiting taxi.

H AVE YOU EVER HAD A MANISCHEWITZ HANGOVER, Virgil? I think not, by the look of you. Just as well. I wish no such misfortune upon so stalwart a companion. There was something about this particular brew, an excess of sugars, even in such small quantity, that held me in its mephitic grasp as I stumbled through the National Gallery the following afternoon.

More experts. More authentication. The third stop of the day. I was, I am ashamed to admit, already bored. Rachel introduced me to the museum's Kálmán experts, and they fell into an abstruse conversation about provenance, from which I quickly excused myself. Why don't you browse the galleries, she suggested, as a weary mother might dispense with a restless child. The Kálmán collection is superb, she reminded me. One of the conservators glanced at me with ill-concealed distaste. He had tobacco-stained teeth and fingers, and a thin ladder of hair pressed across his skull. He no doubt saw me as a usurper, laying claim to riches that rightfully belonged in his galleries, so I smiled my best Unthreatening Second Banana smile (stars similarly hate being usurped) and excused myself.

I wandered through galleries that were surprisingly modern, a contrast with the building's neoclassical exterior. Here were the same blond wood floors I'd seen at the Norton Simon; the same bored guards, your Hungarian cousins, Virgil; even

the same kissing teenagers who were, if anything, more fla-
grant in their gropings. The Kálmáns were afforded a place of
honor, a dedicated gallery in a prime location. But the museum's enthusiasm for its treasures was unreciprocated. The
gallery was empty with the exception of an unpleasant docent
with a bulbous nose jutting from her creased face.

Despite my diligent research into the man and his art, I was
unprepared for the explosion of color that greeted me. I had
become so used to *Budapest Street Scene* and its darkened palette that I was dazzled by the raucous, vibrant hues that shone
out from the room's many gilt frames. Kálmán the colorist had
drunk deeply at the well of the fauves, and everywhere I turned,
electrifying shades greeted me. Some were almost garish, arti-
ficial; others were almost bottomless pools of color into which
my poor hungover eyes swam.

And yet, contrary to Rachel's endorsement, the gallery's
offerings seemed a humble assortment of second-rate works
from an artist considered a national treasure, and one of the
few Hungarians with an international following. I expect
the rest had been snapped up by eager collectors around the
world. From the sampling that remained, the highlight was a
canvas of *csárdás* dancers. The docent's nose wandered into
view and advised me these traditional dancers were a favorite
subject of Kálmán's. Her educational brief fulfilled, her nose
moved abruptly away to leave me with the painting.

It bears some superficial resemblance to *Budapest Street
Scene* in terms of composition, of framing. Again, three characters, all female this time. But where *Budapest Street Scene* is
a frozen moment just prior to an escape, a mad dash, in which
you can feel the tension waiting to be released, as when the
hammer of a pistol is drawn back, these dancers are all bright,
kinetic colors. Oranges, yellows, and light reds swirl against

light green and pale blue backdrops, suggesting something of sunrises against the horizon. It was hard to believe these were the work of the same artist, and I marveled at the mind that could contain such multitudes. For a moment I heard the music of the *csárdás*, which I can remember playing on the radio that one afternoon I visited the Tower Club with my father. Or if it wasn't, it should have been. I felt my chest constrict, and was about to leave the gallery when I noticed an empty space on the wall, bearing the trace outline of a painting. A work on loan, presumably, or in the lab for restoration, but I felt as though the rightful spot for *Budapest Street Scene* was announcing itself to me.

I roamed the adjacent galleries, all filled with minor paintings by unknown Hungarian artists, and I was struck by how Hungary always seemed to lumber a decade or so behind the rest of the world. All the great movements found their way to Budapest eventually, just later. Pointillism in 1912, blue period portraits in 1913, cubist forays in 1925. It was as if those who remained were fated to be also-rans, their country an eternal backwater. I felt a grudging gratitude to my father for choosing to plant his mediocrity in more fertile soil. I was about to head back to look for Rachel when I noticed a side gallery labeled "Székely, Bertalan." The painter after whom my father's street was named. He'd mentioned it in the hospital. On his deathbed. How melodramatic that word feels. And yet it discomposes me. I was headed to that very street later in the day. Convergences, Virgil. Mark them. They infect this tale.

What a contrast this gallery was. If the previous galleries had depicted a Hungary limping to keep up with the currents of the art world, this gallery was an unabashed tribute to a style of romantic painting long gone. Traditional compositions on classic themes. Székely was partial to nudes. A luxuriant Leda and the Swan. A painting of what I presumed was a geisha. I looked at these idealized figures and remembered Matisse's reclining odalisque, that electrifying moment with Rachel. Could these polite, restrained nudes evoke the same response? It seemed unlikely.

I was drawn to a self-portrait, a shockingly handsome, idealized self. It's possible he was, in fact, so beautiful a specimen; I've never seen an actual photograph to argue otherwise. But as the actor knows, self-images are the most unreliable visages of all. Still, there was something about the sheer romanticism of his portrait, of the outer beauty implying an inner transcendence that actually took my breath away, and I remained staring at it for an indecent interval. The more I looked, the deeper I looked, the stranger I began to feel. It was as though he and I had become locked in a staring contest, each daring the other to look away.

Hours later, it seemed, Rachel touched my elbow. It was time to go.

WE SAT IN THE TAXI for several minutes, lost in our thoughts. The throb of my hangover was now replaced with the echo of the irruption I'd experienced in the galleries. Rachel stared out the fogged window at the gray Danube racing past, chin in hand. She exhaled as though she'd been holding her breath since we left the museum.

"They're not going to help," she said.

I was surprised, though I shouldn't have been. Everything had been going our way for so long, the setback was probably inevitable. This is another trait of my father's, this waiting for an unseen shoe to drop. I once mentioned the Concorde to him, how I wanted to fly it despite my own fear of flying. It had never crashed, after all. "It's due," was all my father said. When a Concorde disintegrated at Charles de Gaulle Airport a few years later, he began our phone call with the words "I told you." He would have seen this turn coming.

"Why not?"

She couldn't say for sure. The stated reason was that the documents were inconclusive, particularly with respect to the journey from my family to the Yuhaus collection. But she detected another agenda at work, probably some desire to lay claim to the painting themselves. She shrugged. It didn't matter. It would have helped, she said, but it wasn't fatal to our claim—provided that they did not side with Rabbi Wolfe, though she felt they treated both claims with equal disapproval. We would just have to see what turned up from my family.

AND SO THAT ENDLESS LUNCH with my relatives, the unwanted beverages, the stifling, airless good cheer. Eszter's worry. Once the proceedings wound down, Tibor ferried us across Styx to my father's childhood home in his Peugeot.

"This is it," Tibor said. I was surprised how quickly we were upon the place, how without ceremony it rose up before us, though why I persist in expecting, what—trumpets? Fireworks? I should sort out my propensity for the dramatic. The building was a shabby two-story beige square around a courtyard, the paint peeling off in patches the size of bedsheets. The bars over the windows made the whole thing feel like a prison, which is no doubt how my father experienced it. I wondered what he'd make of the graffiti on the door and walls, unimaginable in his time. I sat in the car for a moment, taking it in.

"Would you like me to wait here?" Rachel asked. Tibor was already out of the car, walking to the building, no niceties of privacy for him. I shook my head and took her hand. She let me, an answering pressure. I was briefly ashamed of my clammy palm, aware of my racing heartbeat. We made our way to the front door of the building, which Tibor had already nudged open. He walked in as though he belonged there, and Rachel and I followed hesitantly through a short corridor of saffron walls and faded checkerboard tiles underfoot, lined with mailboxes and trash cans. We emerged in a small courtyard, where Tibor whispered to me, "Time stops here." For once, his portent matched the occasion.

The ground-floor units huddled around a cracked, uneven concrete slab with a small, lifeless garden languishing in the middle of the courtyard. Even at the height of summer, the plot was bare. Empty rows suggested the presence of a long-gone herb garden. A single evergreen jutted bravely past the roofline. The garden was encircled by chipped black wrought-iron bars. The apartment facades, rising three stories around us, were painted in different shades of yellow. The whole place felt smothered by neglect. Dizziness washed over me, a feeling that I might faint, so close was I at last to something palpable about my father, something we had never shared but shared now, here, as I stood in the presence of his ghost.

It will not speak. Then I will follow it.

To my right, a dark, dank stairwell, with a serpentine staircase twisting from view. Tibor nodded. First apartment, second floor, he said. I indicated he should wait and entered the stairwell alone. My footfall disturbed a black cat—yes, Virgil; really—that bolted into the courtyard as I made my way up, past the crumbling walls, gripping the rusted handrail. At last I came to rest in front of my father's apartment door. Two thick lacquered brown halves, a square brass doorknob in the middle of the right half, and two opaque strips of ochre windows, covered with bars. No name. Nothing to indicate its current occupant. I stood there staring at the door for a long moment, expecting . . . expecting what? I really did expect *something*, it wasn't just the usual pose. I wanted to feel my father.

I thought about knocking but to what end? My Hungarian was insufficient to the task, and I did not want to reengage Tibor. Not that I would have known what to say. I still don't. So I walked out instead, onto the narrow walkway that overlooked the courtyard, where I watched Rachel bent over, petting the cat that had surrendered itself to her attentions. I imagined my father, running around as a child, ducking into stairwells, playing in the garden, trying to sneak home after a long night out. I remembered a story he told me after my first beating by bullies, about a night he'd gotten so thoroughly beaten up by a group of local toughs that his mother initially refused to let him into the apartment, failing to recognize her own son. It had been years since I last thought of that. How many other submerged memories were lying in wait, ready to be tripped to life? How much more did I know than I thought? Rachel turned to look up at me and smiled.

Our eyes held the moment longer than either of us was prepared for. Then I imagined the courtyard filled with the Arrow Cross, looking for Jews. Saw Rachel being dragged away. I shook myself clear and was about to return to her when I heard a woman's voice:

"You are the son, yes? Gabi's son? From America?"

I turned to the source of the sound, an emaciated, white-haired woman in her seventies, leaning on a chipped walking stick. I nodded.

"You look exactly like him," she said. I recoiled at the thought of any resemblance between us.

"Did you know my father?"

She smiled. "Oh yes. When he was your age. Would you like to come in?"

WE SENT TIBOR AWAY, told him we'd take a cab to the hotel. The woman's name was Klara. She'd lived in the same apartment her entire life, knew my father through childhood and his teen years. I looked at an old black-and-white photo she handed me while she made some tea. I was shocked. My dad was handsome, dashing like Székely's self-portrait. He wore a brown leather jacket, and a flashy metallic wristwatch. I was most struck by his rakish ease as he leaned on the handlebars of a motorcycle, a lit cigarette propped between his lips.

"He smoked?" I asked plaintively. "I didn't know he smoked . . ." I looked at Rachel, confused and lost. Klara limped into the room and served us a meager tea from a cracked, grimy set of cups. As shabby and forlorn as the courtyard had been, I was unprepared for the stark poverty of the post-Soviet collapse. The apartment was crumbling around us as we sat. Huge, jagged cracks ran along the walls in all directions, like a network of varicose veins. The furniture was broken and wobbly and the upholstery stank of age.

Klara took the photo back and stood there regarding him, hand on her hip.

"It was a prop, he liked how it looked in the photo." She shook her head. "We all knew he didn't belong here. Look at him. How could a man like this live in a Communist country?" She sighed and returned the photo carefully to a drawer. The reverence of her action told me they'd been lovers. She sank into an easy chair and began to talk about my father, telling us stories. How he'd had "many friends"—her surprising words—and yet, though he was popular, he was not intimate with anyone. She told us a story about a night at a jazz bar when their group had been seated at a table with a large column obstructing the view. You were expected to tip to upgrade your table. My father saw through it and refused to pay. He planted himself and waited, until he was eventually shuttled away in exasperation from the moneymaking table. That was his way: break the system, wait the bastards out.

"He liked to drive fast, you know," she said, "but when he had to stop, he put his arm out like so." She extended her right arm out across the torso of an imagined passenger. I gave an involuntary cry.

"Matt, are you all right?" Rachel asked.

"I . . . Yeah. Fine." I addressed myself to Klara by way of explanation for my outburst. "He did that to me, too. When I was a boy."

Rachel asked Klara a few questions about *Budapest Street Scene*. It was a long shot, we both knew, and she shook her head sadly, unable to recall anything about the painting.

"I was very sorry to learn Gabi had died. I hope you don't mind if I tell you that I have thought about your father every day of my life. I have always missed him but I was pleased he found life in America." The kindness in her voice, her obvious love for him squeezed at my throat.

"Your father used to brag about you," Klara added.

That broke the spell. I laughed. "Really? My father bragged? Gabor Szantos."

"Just a minute," she said.

She left the table for a few moments and returned with an envelope from which she withdrew a glossy eight-by-ten color photo, which she set on the table before me.

"Go on. It won't bite."

Klara was wrong. It bit deeply, Virgil. It was a cast photo

from my short-lived cable sensation. I picked it up warily, as though it were a summons. In thick, black magic marker, someone had scrawled *To Klara, Best wishes, Matt Santos* across the photo. It wasn't my father's handwriting. I could recognize his blocky, angular scrawl anywhere. But it wasn't mine, either. As I held the photo in my hand, wondering how my father had come by it, whom he'd employed to forge my autograph, I couldn't escape the single crushing truth of the image: my father, for reasons known only to himself—ego? Pride? Shame?—was unwilling or unable to ask me to sign a simple photo for him.

I gave Klara a thousand U.S. dollars. My father, tight as he was, would have approved. It was his kind of gesture. She refused it at first, then wept and hugged me. It was all the currency I was carrying but she needed it far more than I did, and her compassion for my father cried out for some kind of acknowledgment. The money would last her the year. She offered to give me the photo but I told her to keep it.

Documentary evidence, Rachel had said. The courts love documentary evidence. I can't yet speak to what it does for sons.

WE ENDED THE AFTERNOON at Memento Park, a graveyard of Soviet-era statues outside the city limits. Rachel was solicitous toward me during the bus ride out there, her hand having taken up more or less permanent residence in mine. She wanted, I think, to talk, to ask me questions about what I was feeling. I should have liked that, had she asked. If only I could pluck one from the welter of throbs in my head and heart and assign language to it. Instead we sat in a soothing silence as the city fell away and we traveled along highways that looked like any highway in any country, but for the undecipherable billboards for unknown products.

As the ride wore on, Rachel apologized for dragging me so far out of our way, though in truth I was enjoying the quiet moments beside her. She hadn't grasped just how far it was, but she'd seen photos and it was the one thing she wanted to see while here. She also thought I might enjoy it, thought the kitsch of the place might banish some of the day's ghosts. At length we reached our destination, nearly missing the poorly marked entrance, and receiving no prompts from the bus driver, who must have known where we were headed.

As the air-conditioned bus belched away, we trudged in the blazing heat across a large lot of sun-bleached gravel. We approached a bizarre Doric facade, suggesting the outlines of a Greek temple but with two arches on either side of the entrance, one containing a towering granite statue of Lenin, the other of Marx and Engels. We seemed to walk toward it for a long time during which it came no closer, and then all at once we were upon it. The monoliths seemed to sag in the humidity, and waves of heat rose from the desultory husk of a Trabi, the monoxide-belching workhorse that was once the People's Car. A young woman with a buzz cut and a pierced eyebrow sold us two tickets from behind her window, never once setting down her mobile phone.

We bypassed the souvenirs, Stalin hip flasks and CDs of Soviet marches, and wandered out onto the grounds, which were about the size of a football field. Out from under the shade of the entry building, we were again assaulted by the heat. It was unbearable, Virgil, there wasn't another person in the place. Perspiring, we soldiered out into the open. More blanched gravel, punctuated by occasional patches of dead grass, the whole affair ringed by low, bare trees, with spindly branches. The massive statues dotted the perimeter, rising up from what could reasonably be mistaken for a postapocalyptic landscape, the remains of a war that was never fought.

They had names, the Martyrs Monument, the Soviet Heroic Memorial, though it scarcely seemed to matter what they were called. The labels seemed like afterthoughts, unnecessary in the shadow of such monstrous grandiosity. Here were Stalin's gleaming warriors and workers, rushing toward a future that has ceased to exist. A pair of massive bronze boots set atop a two-story concrete foundation looked comic and forlorn, long relieved of the towering Stalin that once filled them. (I would only learn later that the boots were a copy, the originals long lost.) Another enormous figure, a worker, I think, struck me as especially sorrowful. His knees buckling, he reached for the sky as he fell. Or was he rising?

Rachel broke our silence.

"I can't decide if this is funny or creepy or sad."

I shrugged. "A little of each?" She nodded.

We continued to wander, and I paused before a striking pair of bronze hands encircling an umber sphere that floated just within its grasp. Rachel continued on, briefly disappearing from view, but I was mesmerized by the object. If one looked past the megalomaniacal subtext, it was almost possible to apprehend a strange beauty in these statues, like the ugly beauty of the Kálmán painting. If you divorced them from their context, their meaning, saw them as objects only. Can you do that, I wonder?

Klara was right. How could my father ever have stayed, have lived among objects such as these? With his leather jacket and outsized ambitions. The Eastern Bloc was too small to contain him. I've gotten nearly everything wrong, Virgil. I judged my father for the way he left his own father, the way he insistently sought out his own life, but he was a survivor. It is the only reason—the only one—that I am standing here, right now, in this place. The only reason I was able to make my own journey westward.

Rachel appeared with four small cups of water. She'd found a drinking fountain. She poured the lukewarm water on my arms, on my neck, let it trickle down my back. I shivered and then did the same for her, gently pouring water along her freckled shoulders. Rachel must have sensed something shift within me, because she took the empty cups and whispered, "You seem lost, Matt."

I turned to face her, letting her read what was in my eyes. "This has all been . . . It's a lot, you know? A lot to take in."

She nodded. "Listen, there's something I've been meaning to ask you. I should have asked it weeks ago."

I nodded, inviting her to proceed, not without a frisson of dread.

"The painting. Do you really believe it's yours?"

I FEEL THE WEIGHT OF HER EYES upon me, sense all that is riding on my answer, and I know I cannot fumble this one. It's so hot. Can't think clearly. What can it really mean, to be "mine"? Such a loaded question.

"I really don't know. I'd like it to be. And not for the money." I look up at the floating sphere. "I just want to feel . . ." I trail off, embarrassed. *I just want to feel.* But she seems satisfied with the answer, because she threads her arm through mine as we walk on. I feel the water where it's run down her forearm, sinking through my shirt.

"The thing that I can't figure out . . . well, it's just . . . my dad. You know? He grabbed at every angle. He would have been all over this. I know it. I know *him.*"

Then she says it to me, the words I didn't know I was waiting for. The words I have needed to hear all along.

"Matt. Do not make the mistake of assuming that because
you know what someone will *do*, that you know who they *are*."

And she kisses me. And then, to my surprise, despite the
heat, despite my guilt, despite everything in the air that day, I
gently pull her into a copse of dead trees, hike up her long
dress, and—

CAN WE REALLY HAVE BEHAVED AS I REMEMBER IT, Virgil, there
in that furnace, among the stone, among the steel? The place
was deserted, to be sure, the ticket taker undoubtedly still
glued to her phone; and there were any number of hidden cor-
ners. My memories of Rachel, turned away from me, hands on
the massive calf of a charging soldier, offering herself to me,
crying out despite the unbearable heat, are undeniable. There
was an electricity, an illicit madness, and perhaps a sort of des-
peration that briefly overtook us both, discarding all our normal cautions as we fell on each other as two people amid a
dead or dying world. Under the watchful eyes of these discarded behemoths, my lawyer and I rutted like dogs. Of course
it happened. And yet.

Do not make the mistake of assuming that because you
know what someone will *do*, you know who they *are*.

Just a few months later, as we were to lay the old man to
rest, Tracy would say those identical words to me—not a paraphrase, but word for word—and that cannot be possible. They
cannot both have said this to me in precisely the same way. I'm
sure it happened, yet those few hours with Rachel have the
quality of a dream misremembered. So brief, so inscrutable
this window of intimacy, of honesty.

We raced past the ticket seller to catch the last bus back, and something in her eyes told me she knew what we'd gotten up to out there, and that we probably weren't the first. By the time we arrived at our hotel it was dark, hotter still if that was possible, and we retreated to the air-conditioned safety of my room. Amid the awkward fumbling, the tussle with our desires and our good sense, she noticed the blank sheet on the writing desk, creased, bare but for the single word *Dad*, the list I'd begun but never finished. She asked about it, so I told her. She looked at me with such pity. "Oh, Matt."

R ACHEL SPENT THE FOLLOWING MORNING VOMITING in my bathroom. Something had come over her, perhaps it was the sour cream–rich Hungarian cuisine or maybe something deeper, regret over our performance in the park. Her piteous groans as she slid back under the covers did not invite inquiry. She waved me off, urged me to go out and make something of my last day in Budapest. I ventured once more, map in hand, into the blistering heat, though a storm now threatened, promising relief from the relentless humidity. One of Rachel's investigators (yes, her firm used investigators, which seemed to me both quaint and sinister) had come up with the address where Ferenc Halasz, our deceased Arrow Cross instigator, had last lived in Budapest, and I wanted to see it.

Halasz had lived on a broad, tree-lined street near what was now called Heroes' Square. Town houses stood shoulder to shoulder, low gates encasing modest patches of grass. I stood in front of his building, a reddish-brown three-story structure with an untended lawn. I wanted something, was feeling confrontational, and finally walked up the five steps to the button on the door, which now bore the name ORBAN. More than sixty years had passed since Halasz traded my grandfather his life for a painting. This was a fool's errand but my anger was growing, roiling like those green seas I saw with Rachel that day at the Norton Simon.

To my surprise, I rang the bell. I had no plan, did not know what to say or do, but it didn't matter. No one answered. For some reason, the silence provoked me, and I rang again and again, longer and harder, and then I began to bang on the door, harder and harder, and the knocking became pounding, obscenity laced, and then I began kicking the door, which didn't budge an inch, bored beneath my blows. I paused in my shrieking to catch my breath. I was drawing attention from passersby when I noticed a mottled old face—man or woman? Impossible to tell—peering out through a tattered lace curtain next door, and although it's nothing more than melodramatic fancy, I was sure he/she/it was snarling at me. She, a crone, surely. Had she known Halasz? She was about the right age. What did she remember, the bitch? The lace billowed and when it settled, the space in the window was empty. I turned and looked up and down the street and suddenly every elderly face was suspect. A pensioner—do they call them that here?—hobbled by, hunched over a string shopping bag filled with canned goods. He wouldn't make eye contact with me, and although it was probably nothing more than an advanced case of osteoporosis, I was convinced it was guilt that stooped him.

I surrendered to the futility of my errand and decided it was time to move on, lest someone call the police or make other mischief for me. I felt so defeated, Virgil. Halasz is dead and in the ground and any evidence of his time here is long since swept away. His was an age of tanks and pistols and telegrams and mine is an age of cell phones and broadband. This house—this street, this place—may throb with interred guilt, with accusation, but I am too late. There are pages of the past that are lost forever, never to be rewritten or recovered.

——————

TWO HOURS LATER, the effects of my outburst still pulsing within me, I struggled to find Kálmán's headstone. A layer of gray clouds had settled in overhead, the rain imminent, the wind gusting. Still, I didn't mind meandering down the peaceful, tree-lined lanes that could have been a city park but for the wildness of the place, overrun with untended flora. I thought back to Kálmán's bathers at the Norton Simon. A profusion of grays, more than I had imagined possible, shaded the landscape, impressing a damp but welcoming sadness upon my heart. I only rarely encountered another mourner—is that what I was as well, a mourner?—and I found the quiet restorative, briefly silencing that angry buzz that had plagued me since we'd arrived.

The Kozma Street Cemetery was enormous and not well mapped out. I had a grave-site location that I'd found online, but it took ages to find the corresponding spot. The headstones were by and large well tended, though a few were so old that they had begun to crumble, the inscriptions long ago worn away as though by the tide. Between Hungarian and Hebrew, they were unreadable to me regardless of their condition. I passed flowers and stone-laden markers, and I thought with shame about my father's ashes, languishing in a New York mortician's office, waiting to be collected.

I finally found Kálmán's grave huddled in semidisgrace with the other suicides, in a section set off from the main part of the cemetery, just a few yards along from a pale blue art nouveau tomb that looked like the entrance to a carnival ride. His stone was black, highly polished, with gold letters. His name. Dates. A Star of David. And the Hungarian word *festőművész*. I looked the word up later. Painter—*festő*. With connotations of an artist—*művész*. An abundance of flowers suggested a regular stream of visitors, more it seemed than frequented his galleries. I stared at the headstone for a long time, hoping for some wisdom, and then I actually spoke to it.

"So, I've got your painting. What now?"

I thought of the decomposed remains beneath the stone, the life that had once animated those bones, the sentience that had directed his brushstrokes, and *Budapest Street Scene* never felt less mine. Unsurprisingly, Kálmán offered no wisdom, no guidance. I took a photo of the headstone with my phone to show Rachel.

It took me another thirty minutes stumbling around to find the Szantos gravestones. Béla and Lily. My grandparents. Order of operations, eh, Virgil? There would have been no body beneath Lily's stone, her bullet-riddled corpse having been swept along the Danube with countless others. It pained me to think of poor *Béla-bácsi* alone in this place, and I wondered, as I scanned the horizon, the tombstones like soldiers on the march, how many other markers ending in 1944 sat over empty graves. The date stung no less than it had in my study, as I examined the family tree. I touched Béla's fading granite headstone, and felt a tightness in my chest as I remembered our evening in synagogue. I placed the stones on his grave, as I had seen my mother's mother do years ago, without knowing why. Rachel would explain it later, although, as with so much of Jewish tradition, there appeared to be no clear-cut answer, with possibilities ranging from the permanence of stones (as opposed to the fleeting lives of flowers) to a method for helping keep souls weighted in place. I had no knowledge of any of this at the time, just a desire to make some form of tribute to my grandfather. I contemplated placing a smoldering cigar on the edge of the headstone and imagined a conversation between Kálmán and my grandfather, whiling away eternity in the ground, arguing about art. Their styles could not have been more different and in life they would not have had the remotest interest in each other, and yet, for some reason, it pleased me to think they might enjoy each other's company, their talk frequently turning to serious affairs.

The afternoon's long shadows were beginning to stretch toward me. A light rain started to fall. As I left the cemetery, I saw a pair of young workmen halfheartedly scrubbing away at a swastika that had been painted on a headstone. I could only make out one of the Hungarian words scrawled beneath it: zsidó. Jew.

LUCK OF THE FUCKING DRAW, Virgil. Had I made the decision to return to the hotel after the cemetery, none of what came next would have befallen me. And yet, months later, I cannot shake the feeling of Yahweh's rough justice.

Tibor had told me about a Holocaust memorial on the Danube, sixty bronze pairs of shoes left on the embankment where many of the murders had taken place. The last light was fading, but this seemed like a fitting cap to the day. I planned only to stay a few moments, and then return to look in on Rachel. I still break out into a cold sweat when I remember, when I think about how easily I could have turned away.

The memorial was difficult to locate. There were no signs or markers that I could find, and it was along an embankment separated from the city streets by a busy, fast-moving highway. The two access points to cross the road were equally distant in opposite directions from the memorial itself. It was as though having reluctantly allowed this confrontation with the past, the city was determined to keep it from view. They were going to make you work for it. I was tired, impatient, and eschewed the distant crosswalks, waited for a break in traffic—not easy to see around a blind curve—and ran across, narrowly avoiding being hit by a speeding Volkswagen full of raucous teenagers.

Once safely on the other side, I walked across a wide field of gray, cracked cobblestones, toward a concrete ledge that marked the edge of the embankment and the beginning of the Danube. The rain was now steady, though not heavy, and after the oppressive heat of the day, it was a relief. From a distance, the shoes looked like flies stuck on paper. A handful of tourists lingered beneath umbrellas over the strange sight, these abandoned objects, unexplained save for a single plaque, rendered in Hebrew and in English: TO THE MEMORY OF THE VICTIMS SHOT INTO THE DANUBE BY ARROW CROSS MILITIAMEN IN 1944–45. The word "Jews" nowhere in evidence. It was easy to imagine they'd been left behind by a group of midnight swimmers who had not yet returned to collect them. Until you approached them up close and saw the stones nestled inside, where a child's foot was supposed to fit. Memorial candles flickered plangently, housed beneath glass to protect them from the wind and rain. The detail of the sculptures was admirable, and despite the permanence of the bronze, the shoes all appeared worn and neglected. Men's loafers beside women's boots beside children's slippers. I stood there alone, light-headed, breathing heavily. The sounds of the city, of the traffic racing past behind me, fell away, as did the rain, despite the angry winds whipping off the river and racing unchecked through the wide-open river walk.

I bent over to set a stone in a woman's shoe for my grandmother—how natural the gesture was becoming—when I noticed a flight of stairs, leading down, away from the memorial, toward the river. I straightened up to the sight of a pair of tourists, pausing for a photo op. A heavyset, middle-aged couple. I thought I heard a word or two of German but I hardly trust myself on that score anymore. He held the camera as she posed, smiling for the photo. It was that idiot grin that undid me. Could she be so unaware of where she was standing? Or, perhaps worse, was she aware? Either way, I needed to escape them, lest my need for confrontation, simmering again, get the better of me. So I took the stairs down, away from the shoes, to the Danube.

I felt uneasy as I walked down, already sensing . . . well, dammit, it must be said, sensing the presence of death. I knew this was a bad place, marked by time, but I had turned away from too much already. I tottered down a dozen or so steps of cracked stone—there was no handrail, nothing to grip along the way. The stairs were littered with cigarette butts and the odd patch of grass and weeds struggling between the cracks. The walls of the embankment rose around me until I reached the bottom, a landing level with the river. I was now invisible to anyone on my side of the Danube, could only be seen from the Buda side. I felt confined, as in a prison cell. There were no safety railings. No warning sign. The landing was completely exposed. It would have been a simple matter of a single step— or push—to be borne away by the current. The platform was wet, scattered with muddy puddles, water lapping up and over at my feet. I was impressed by the speed of the current, and re-volted by the ugly brown-gray color of the water, no romantic Blue Danube here.

Standing there, it was as though I were no longer myself. I imagined, instead, being—literally—in the shoes of the people murdered here, imagined their terror, their disbelief that their lives were coming to an end at the hands of their neighbors, their classmates, their coworkers. Not Germans, not outsiders. The people they saw in the street every day. The Fat General from the Tower Club, come to murder his countrymen. And women. And children. Could they see beyond the disbelief of what their world had become to understand that their last sight would be this ugly, cold river roaring past? I saw my grandmother among them. Bound to her neighbors by wire or rope, the brief pop of a pistol, and then the weight pulling them over, into the water, dragging them away.

My father's mother. Murdered. Right here, steps from his home. His remoteness, his anger, these made a new kind of sense as I stood there, trembling. Had he ever come to this spot, I wondered? No need. He'd lived it. I always thought my father an unreflective man. Perhaps Tracy's more generous estimation of his nature had been right all along. All at once, I yearned to speak to her. Wanted to be restored to the present. But I didn't call. How could I have explained all this in a single phone call? I didn't know where to begin. The sun had disappeared from view and the storm seethed. The last of the day's warmth faded and I became aware once again of the chilling rain. Later, I decided. I would talk to her later. Will you see to it that that's what it says on my headstone, Virgil? *Here lies Mathias Santos. If only . . . later.*

And then she called me. Right then. Right there. As if she knew. I answered immediately, gratefully. She asked me about our progress, wanted to hear if I was doing all right, but I could hear at once that something was wrong.

"What happened, Tracy?"

"It's over," she said. "They turned us down." Her voice was barren. There was a dullness in her tone, an awful distant stillness. I could hear in the burred edges of her words that she'd done her crying earlier. Standing there by the rushing bloody river, I experienced a convergence of death, my lost family now conjoined with the certain death that awaited Ricky McCabe. She told me he would be executed as planned in just under two months.

I thought again of Tracy watching that video that night, of McCabe's whispered plea: *"Please don't let me die."* She had taken his words to heart, had tried so hard, had done all that could possibly be done, and now she had come to the end of things. I remembered with shame the way I had pressed her in the kitchen, and we stood in long silence together there in the rain, knowing that words, for once, would not do. My poor, fallen Tracy. We were six thousand miles and five time zones apart, and I had just slept with another woman, and yet in those silent moments I felt us bonded, grounded in death, loss, and disappointment.

These thoughts must have infected my voice with something, a flatness maybe, because when at length I whispered, "I'm so sorry," Tracy's surprising response was a terse "Really?"

"What? Of course I am. What do you think?"

"I don't know. I'm just angry. I'm sorry."

Was she right? Was part of me relieved? Hopeful that I would have her attention again, at last? It seemed easy enough to blame my indiscretion with Rachel on her benign neglect, all those hours on the case, all that time away with Brian.

"You think I want him to die?"

"No, of course not. Don't be an idiot, Matt."

"Then what? I wasn't enough of a true believer? I was always behind you."

"But that's just it, Matt. True believer? I don't know what you believe in at all, half the time. I mean, I love you but I swear to God, some days it's like the world doesn't exist beyond the tip of your nose. That's no way to live." She paused. "I can't live like that. I don't *want* to live like that."

This time it was my turn to pause.

"Are you sleeping with Brian?"

"Oh, for fuck's sake, Matt. Grow up."

My phone began to beep, warning of a low battery. I began to speak quickly, trying to get it all in.

"Look, whatever you think, I'm sorry. I really am. I *know* this mattered to you and I know it's a person's life, for god's sake. I'm not an animal. But I tell you, if you want the truth, I've never understood why. Why you keep putting this in front of everything else. Tracy? Tracy? Are you there?"

The line was dead. I had no idea how much she'd heard, what she'd taken in. I wasn't going to get an answer, not today. But at least I'd asked.

I returned to the embankment, climbed back up the stairs in a daze, squinting against the darkness and the rain-streaked glare of the passing headlights. The storm had become a deluge. I was about to leave when I passed them, two thick goons— that's the only word for them really. Let's give them jackboots and shaved heads, though my memory of what follows is shattered, so they might have been wearing soccer outfits and sneakers for all I know. I remember jewelry. Bracelets and rings. And that sickly sweet aftershave, far too much of it. It was the idiotic guffawing that drew my attention, as they crouched before their handiwork, shoving each other playfully as though they'd chucked a water balloon instead of done what they'd done, which was to fill several of the shoes with raw, bloodied pigs' feet. Cars passed by but took no notice.

As my feet carried me toward them I knew that I would confront them. And although they were bigger and stronger and greater in number, it would not be a performance. I didn't care, for once, who was watching or wasn't. I shoved the one closest to me, and he toppled into his friend and for a moment they were both on the wet ground, surprised and confused, something almost comic about their disarray. I used the moment to scoop the gelatinous pigs' feet out of the shoes and hurl them into the river. I turned to face them as they got to their feet. I might have sworn at them, but I don't remember. I do remember getting in one respectably solid blow to the taller of the two—I felt the satisfying crunch of a tooth breaking beneath my fist—and then they set upon me.

THE FIRST BLOW takes me by surprise, the sharpness of it, the sudden eclipsing focus on a single point of pain, the explosion as a fortissimo fist crashes into my cheekbone. Then the punch to my stomach, which temporarily blinds me to the world, all sensation sailing from me except for the inability to breathe, to stand. Those two blows I remember best, but after that a numbness quickly sets in as I fall to the wet cobbles. In the instant before the boots—yes, jackboots, they must have been—begin their dance, I give myself over to the pain, electrified by the notion that in some measure I have invited this. And in the space of an instant, two memories crowd my brain. Another toy show with my father, this one a small one, in the conference room of a Pennsylvania roadside motel. I am a little boy, watching through the window as a German shorthaired pointer races toward its master. The happy animal has not perceived the closed glass sliding door between them, and I watch with horror as the dog shatters the giant window and limps, yelping and bleeding, into his arms. I am heartbroken and run sobbing into my father's arms, astounded at this fundamental failure to protect. Then, a final leap, I am older, playing in the front yard of our family's home. My father is walking our vizsla without a leash across the street. I am excited to see the dog, who has now spotted me and races in my direction, when a car rounds the corner and hits him. I watch in horror as he rolls over two or three times, then leaps up and races into my arms, shaking but with nothing more than a skinned patch on his forehead. My father's fury is incandescent, as he blames me for distracting the dog and causing the accident. He rages until he is spent, and then he stalks off, leaving me with a trembling dog. The last thing I remember amid the dulling pain and the downpour is the spreading warmth of my urine as a final gray draws across my vision and I slip into a welcoming oblivion.

THAT NIGHT, IN MY HOSPITAL BED . . . *raise us* . . . as I slipped in and out of consciousness . . . *shield us* . . . I thought I heard a woman singing. The music . . . *set us aright* . . . that had haunted me so . . . *remove us from foe* . . . at the synagogue. What had Rachel called it? . . . *Your wings shelter* . . . On alternating waves of pain and narcotics, I was buoyed by the quiet melody, barely more than a whisper. Was I hearing things? It seemed so close, so real—and I was borne along . . . *protect and rescue us* . . . into sleep.

Amein.

THEY TOLD ME I WAS LUCKY, VIRGIL. That still amuses me. Lucky. Well, perhaps when one considers how it might have turned out. No internal organs damaged. A few cracked ribs but nothing broken. Nothing that a week in bed and a few fistfuls of Vicodin couldn't set right.

I awoke shortly before dawn to find Rachel slumped in an armchair, asleep. How had they located her, I wondered. For a moment, I thought of my last visit to my father's bedside, asleep in that stiff-backed chair as he died. I let my eyes wander across the primitive hospital room. An iron-framed bed, the white paint chipped along the headboard. The equipment, a collection of 1970s castoffs, rattled and buzzed. Wires and tubes were held into place by scotch tape and yarn. There was no call button in evidence. It felt more like an interrogation chamber than a place of healing.

"Hey," I said, loudly enough to wake Rachel. Her eyes opened and she leapt out of the chair and took my hand, aghast. I must have been quite a sight, though I hadn't seen a mirror yet. "You look terrible, Matt." Again I remembered my father arriving home after his beating, unrecognized by his mother. I imagined Rachel was looking at me in similar disbelief now. "I've been so worried. What happened?"

I shrugged. Shrugging hurt.

"Forgot to bring my stunt double."

She didn't smile. "The police are here, they've been waiting to talk to you."

I nodded. "Yeah, okay. Just give me a minute, please?"

"Sure. I'll go tell them." She kissed my forehead and headed out but paused at the door to turn back. I was surprised to see her eyes filling with tears. "Why would anyone do this to you, Matt?"

I thought of my father, what he would say. Because I was due, Rachel.

LIEUTENANT COLONEL ISTVAN ALMASY had been assigned my case, and seemed inconvenienced by this fact. I was surprised to find someone of his rank handling what seemed like a garden-variety case of ass-kicking and said so. He nodded his large head in dolorous agreement, muttering, "Yes, just so," but apparently being an American television actor was enough to warrant the attention of the higher-ups. I also assumed that the anti-Semitic dimension would have lent the case some urgency, but Almasy waved away any attempt I made to suggest I'd fallen prey to a pair of Hungarian Jew haters.

"So you push them first," he said, jotting perfunctory notes in a small, worn leather notebook. I held his gaze as well as I could given the amount of drugs in my system. Everything about the man was square, blocky. A square head, a square nose, a square mouth. Even his bored gray eyes seemed square, if such a thing were possible. He reeked of smoked meats. I explained that yes, I did push them first, but only after I'd witnessed them desecrating the memorial.

"Yes, yes, you push. Then they beat you." That was the only thing he wrote down. He held out his hand. "Passport."

Rachel reached into my bedside drawer, withdrew my passport, and handed it to him. As he thumbed through its contents, he asked, "They steal from you?"

I didn't know. I looked to Rachel. She shook her head.

"He had his money and wallet and phone when he was found," she explained. "That's how they located me."

I glanced at my phone on the nightstand. Cracks spiderwebbed across the crystal display. He nodded his square head as I tried to describe my assailants but he wrote nothing down. I finished recounting the evening's events and sat back to wait for his response. He remained quiet for so long that I thought he hadn't been listening, that his thoughts had wandered to the soccer match he was probably missing.

"We have here many hooligans, it is sad. One should not provoke them. They are probably university students, drinking, making bad prank. Very hard to find."

With that, he flipped his notebook shut and rose to leave.

"You may return to United States. We will tell you if we find anything."

Rachel stepped in front of the departing officer.

"This was not a 'prank,' sir. He was beaten up by a pair of neo-Nazis defacing a Jewish memorial."

Lieutenant Colonel Istvan Almasy's composure never wavered, as he addressed us quietly, evenly, which was all the more chilling for its calmness.

"You are lies. Hungary completely safe for Jews. You start fight, then come to police." He stepped around Rachel. "Go home. Go back to *America*," the last word a sneer. The final "Jew" unspoken.

He tossed my passport onto my bed and glided out of my room, Rachel pursuing him. For a moment, I could just make out her raised voice in the hallway and then she returned. Furious.

I shared her fury. "I want to go home."

She nodded. "Of course you do. We'll give it a day or two and then—"

I shook my head. "No. Tonight. As planned. Is today Monday?" I sat up in bed and swung my feet out onto the cold hospital linoleum. I felt liquid, vibrating, like the rippling surface of a lake when a stone has been thrown in. It was unpleasant but not intolerable. Rachel rushed to my side, concerned, and tried to ease me back into bed but I grabbed her hand.

"I'm leaving. Right now. Not one more minute in this place."

I tore myself free from wires and tubes and hobbled out, leaning on Rachel, over the pro forma protests of the hospital staff, who must have been happy to be rid of us.

WE AGREED that Rachel would return to the hotel to collect our belongings, and I would take a cab to say goodbye to my relatives. In the car leaving the hospital, Rachel surprised me.

"I hope you don't mind, I did contact your fiancée. I thought she should know what was happening."

"Of course," I said, trying to keep any uneasiness out of my voice. "What did she say?"

"She wanted to come right away."

Of course she did. I felt a wave of remorse announce itself through the nausea.

Rachel nodded. "I told her it wasn't worth it, that we'd be back soon—I didn't realize how soon—and that I would keep her posted until you woke up. You should probably call her."

I looked at my watch.

"It's too late in L.A. I'll text her that I will be on the flight tonight."

"Sure," she said. We drove in silence for a moment. Then I asked:

"Was it . . . weird for you? Talking to her?"

She spoke so softly I could hardly hear her. "All of this has been weird for me."

She said this almost precisely as we drove past the embankment, past the shoes. My cosmically stage-managed life. We rode on in silence.

KATI ANSWERED THE DOOR. I had arrived just as they were settling down to dinner. I could see Tibor at their cluttered dining room table, head lowered reverently over his cell phone, which he fingered with the dexterity of a safecracker. Would my father have been driven to leave Hungary had the Internet been available to him? The world was the same everywhere now. The economies of the West available at the tap of an icon. Why would he leave? Just sit back and let the world come to you.

Kati recoiled at the sight of me. As I started to apologize for coming unannounced she grabbed my elbow and ushered me inside. She was surprisingly forceful for such a sprite. The smell of onions and peppers sautéing threw me back to my childhood kitchen.

"What happened to you?"

At the urgency in her voice, Tibor looked up and blanched. For a moment, I considered not telling them. Making up a less disturbing version of events. A barroom mishap or a shakedown for my wallet.

I told them the truth. Too many stories have been lost to time, this would not be one of them. Did I see fear in their eyes? Did they have a dawning sense of the truth of the place where they lived? I think so. And I felt saddened and a little worried to leave them here, to their fates. As I imagine my father must have done, as I hope he did. Kati implored me to stay for dinner. Eszter was on her way. I thought of that smile, that worried look, and said my goodbyes.

Despite my weakened state, I insisted, over Tibor's protests, on walking back to the hotel, which wasn't far. There was an appealing symmetry: the journey began with a solo constitutional, and now ended the same way. But how thoroughly my eyes had been transformed by these few days. I limped down the narrow streets, avoiding the riverbanks, soreness reverberating in every pore. An appalling sadness choked me as I wandered. And the sounds. I cannot explain it, Virgil, but the shards of Hungarian conversation that filled my ear as people strolled past made me queasy. I was physically repelled by the voiced palatal plosive, the guttural yawps, the endlessly rolled *r*'s. It eludes me, any rational explanation for this extreme response, although I sense it has to do with the me I might have become had my father remained. I felt trapped, even though my flight was only hours away. How irresistible it must have felt when that brief window of escape flew open for him.

Right now. Not one more minute. I understood him, Virgil, as never before.

HOME. It was good to be back in Los Angeles again—and how like home it truly felt, more than ever before—even though my career and my personal life were in disarray. Both required my attention but as summer slouched past, I settled into a carefree daily life, all the more remarkable for how disconnected from the magnitude of events it seemed. The arbitration was upon me and I loafed, the weeks following Budapest an intoxicating blur. Indolence, it seemed, suited me. So much for "pushpush-push." In contrast, my mother's postcard from the Pyrénées boasted of productivity in paradise, but I was too content to feel my usual shame.

I had missed the spiced metal smell of the ocean, missed the gentle curves of the coast highway where the glass-flecked green and blue sheet shoulders up against pale, windswept beaches. Despite the fiendish aches and soreness, I spent weeks perched on the same bench, staring out upon scalloped teal. Tracy worried that it was a malaise, a depression born of trauma, that compelled my ocean-side vigil, but that wasn't it. On the day before I was to leave for Chicago for the arbitration hearing—it was early August by now—I took my father along, sat there with him at my side, the lid of his urn rattling slightly in the wind. What a strange picture we must have made. A boy and his dad. I found him an oddly companionable presence in this form. It wasn't that he'd been silenced, awarding me a definitive upper hand. Rather, he seemed settled. I would tip open the lid and look at the dust that filled the urn and lose myself in his monochromatic stillness. I did think about chucking him into the Pacific right then and there, remembering what he said about the "Ruskis" in Big Sur. I thought he might enjoy it here, dissolving slowly, ecstatically, into the roiling foam.

Instead, I bundled him under my arm and limped back to my car. I decided he deserved to see how the story, his story, ended.

RACHEL AND I HAD PARTED awkwardly in New York. What a pair we were, hobbling together through baggage claim, I bruised and stiff, she pale and wobbly. She was connecting through to Los Angeles, whereas I had a stopover for the day to collect my father's remains. We fumbled and avoided eye contact in the manner of those who have shared a life-altering experience only to find themselves back in their unaltered lives. Lots of "well"s and "so"s, until we finally performed the time-honored handshake-cheek-kiss two-step. Even now it astounds me. Not seventy-two hours after our tryst in the park, we were shaking hands, like we'd just concluded a mildly successful business deal. Which I suppose we had. Or were about to.

Neither of us could think of anything else to say or do, and so we said goodbye, agreed to get in touch in L.A. in a few days, and walked in opposite directions. I cleared customs without incident and a larcenous cabdriver took me to collect my old man. The following day I was home, deposited so neatly back at the beginning of things. To my great surprise, Tracy was waiting for me at the airport.

Even in normal times, this would have been no small thing. Between her modeling career and my film and television work, we have spent much of our relationship on separate airplanes, and have never gone in for the airport drop-off or pickup routine, not even during our most ardent beginnings. In the wake of our phone call at the river, she was the last person I expected to see bathed in the sickly fluorescent lights of baggage claim, frowning in the distance, sidestepping roller bags. As I approached, she covered her mouth in dismay at the sight of me—Rachel hadn't prepared her for how bad I looked. Her face softened a few degrees and she approached me gingerly, as though afraid I might bolt. She reached out to touch my cheek.

"My god, your face . . ." Words failed her.

"It looks worse than it feels. Really."

"It looks *terrible*."

I put my arms around her waist and she allowed me to draw her close. "Yeah, terrible is about right. I'm surprised to see you. Aren't you supposed to be off Harvest Mooning somewhere?"

She shrugged. "Abby fired me," she said. "It's okay."

"Shit. I'm sorry, Tracy. About McCabe, all of it. I really am."

I had no desire to revisit the stuff of our last conversation, at least not yet, and neither did she. Instead, we held each other for a long moment there in the airport, bodies skittering around us, the sights and sounds fading away as we sat in our bubble of grief and loss and guilt, until she registered the urn I was carrying. Her eyes filled with an immense sorrow as she touched my arm and laid a hand on the lid, and I was awash in all the things I loved and missed about her. I loved the way she loved my father, the way I was unable to love him. I hadn't credited, until the moment of this simple touch upon his remains, how similar they had been, superficial reticence masking unknowable depths. She had loved him for us both because I couldn't.

I remember the first time I took her to New York to meet my father. He was solicitous of her in a manner that betrayed his approval, though he'd never admit it to me. She sealed the deal when he showed her his car collection and she failed to commit the unpardonable sin so many before her had: she did not inquire after its value. I would watch in dread, wincing as my unwitting friends all made that fatal error, only to be rebuked by my father. We don't discuss such things in this house. Tracy never asked and that alone would have secured her Most Favored status.

As she drove me home, I remembered those lines from high school, "the end of all our exploring / Will be to arrive where we started / And know the place for the first time." This life Tracy and I had carved out for ourselves, against the odds and despite recent events, was warm and pleasant and I felt a fool for being so restless. We left my suitcase in the hallway and went straight to the bedroom, where she settled me between the sheets and then crawled in behind me. We lay there together, exhausted, grateful for the silence, a pair of clothed spoons. My back to her, she fingered my hair, and I packed away my confusion and my guilt and my shame to be examined at a later date. For the moment, there was only gratitude, compassion, love. For the moment, Virgil, I felt safe again.

The rhythm of Tracy's gentle stroking of my hair slowed. "I can't believe Abby fired you over McCabe," I said. "I'm so sorry." The fingers stopped.

"It wasn't because of McCabe. It's because I came home now. For you."

Moments later, Tracy's snores rumbled through the sheets

like an approaching thunderstorm. I knew that I would have to tell her everything and that I could never tell her everything. I listened, instead, to the snores, each one distinct in its own musicality, their coarse timbre as strangely beautiful as Kálmán's ugly paintings, and I allowed myself to be carried into sleep upon their vibrations.

TO MY SURPRISE, in the weeks following my return, I was briefly in demand again as an actor. Being an actual hate-crime victim suddenly made me irresistible to the Industry. Whatever the reason, I didn't question it, and I auditioned tirelessly and with aplomb. Oh, I still found it all trivial. But I needed to be busy, to fill the weeks leading up to the arbitration with some kind of purpose, if only to prevent my thoughts from devouring me. It was breathtaking, the speed with which Tracy and I resumed the contours of our earlier life, even as my infidelity pressed upon my chest. Twice I nearly told her. Once we were enjoying a stroll down the side streets of our neighborhood at dusk, and once we were having dinner back at the sushi restaurant where we'd had our first date. Both times my nerve failed. Both times I wondered whether, by my remaining silent, the relationship might survive. It seemed we were both eager to return to our comforts, to what had been, so we conspired in this last coproduction.

It was weeks before Rachel and I spoke again. Were we parrying, I wonder, circling to see who would call first? Or was there, as she insisted via the occasional, terse e-mail, nothing new to report? Her time was consumed preparing for the arbitration. All that paper, so much of it, flowing endlessly from her desk to my inbox and back to her again. I stopped looking at it, it meant nothing to me. My case had taken an unhappy turn for her, and I was quite sure I knew the cause. It came out, at last, one evening over a cocktail at a fashionable Beverly Hills hotel bar, full of black glass and sharp angles, when we both felt we could defer our reckoning no longer. It took little prompting for her to unload.

"It's a terrible thing we did, Matt," she said, dipping her finger in her gin. "So unethical for so many reasons. Honestly, I would quit this case right now if I could."

"That would make me sad. And it would raise a lot of questions."

This irritated her. "What's wrong with that? Why are you so scared of questions?"

Her bluntness startled me but she apologized.

"Have you told her?"

I shook my head.

"Are you going to?"

"Honestly, I don't know. I'm trying to figure out what to do."

She nodded with sympathy and I changed the subject. "How's Bernie?"

She smiled at the mention of her father. "Good, thanks. The same. Eternal."

"What does he think about the case?"

"He's on your side. He believes in restitution. I tell you, he'd probably disown me if he knew what we did." I watched her fiddle with her drink. Her sense of herself, her belief in her rectitude had been undermined. A heaviness had settled on her, such a pointed contrast to the evanescence I had witnessed that first day in her office. She looked tired, her eyes ringed with regret. I felt as though I had ruined something fragile and beautiful.

"You know," she said, "sometimes I feel like what happened to you in Budapest was my fault. I was the one who dragged you there. And if we hadn't behaved that way in the park . . ."

"Restitution?" I asked. She shrugged.

"It's possible."

"Rachel. I got beat up because I picked a fight with two Neanderthals who were bigger and stronger than I am."

"Now you sound like Colonel Almasy."

"Yeah, well. Broken clocks. Et cetera."

Rachel took my hand, raised it to her lips. The gesture surprised me until I realized it was a goodbye kiss.

"Listen, Matt. I've never been 'that woman' and, barn doors notwithstanding, I don't want to start," she said, setting my hand back down on the bar. She stood up to leave. "If you figure out your relationship with Tracy, let me know. But until that time, let's stick to business, okay?"

It was a reasonable request. I nodded.

"See you in Chicago," she said as she left the bar.

I watched her go with a deep sorrow, coupled with relief. In all our time together, it was the only thing you got wrong, Rachel. I'm not scared of questions. I can ask them for days. It's the answers that cause all the trouble.

RABBI WOLFE WAS TOO SICK to travel, and so we agreed to hold the arbitration hearing on her turf. Tracy accompanied me. The conference room was lushly padded, like a cabin aboard a private jet, and sat high above the Magnificent Mile, with cloudless views of the Sears Tower and the dazzling blue of the great lake beyond. The city gleamed with the humid buoyancy of late summer and seemed altogether more welcoming this time.

Rachel introduced herself to Tracy, shook her hand, the first of several moments I had been dreading for days. I hadn't told Tracy about Budapest, nor had we returned to our rocky phone conversation at the side of the river. I was sick with guilt, and I suspect Tracy felt her own share in the wake of my beating, and we both simply hoped that a little benign inattention might set things, if not right, then at least familiar again. They exchanged friendly hellos, and Rachel began to arrange papers as we were pointed to the coffee. Even with all the briefs that had already been submitted, forests of paper littered the conference table.

Then there was the judge. I shall call him Judge Handlebar, and not out of any great disrespect but because it simply feels right. It's the way I've made my choices as an actor, never one for elaborate backstories. He was interchangeable, after all, his seat could have been filled by any competent jurist. The only thing that made any kind of impression on me was his elaborately lacquered handlebar mustache. Mostly white with streaks of brown and orange, it gave him the mien of a cartoon character and told me that he was prone to the theatrical. Which I supposed might favorably dispose him to my claim— we performers must stick together. I thought of my father's unprepossessing pencil mustache.

We were arranging piles of paper like stones upon graves, when a wraith appeared before us. Rabbi Wolfe and her lawyer. I was shocked at the sight of her. In the months since I'd crept into her synagogue, she had withered. Her cheeks were hollowed out like an ill-fitting mask and she struggled to hold her head upright. Her clothes no longer fit her, she rattled loose within them. Only the rawness of her hands remained as she took my hand by way of greeting. Did I note a flare of recognition in her eyes? If she remembered me, she gave no impression of it, another crafty cardplayer. I was introduced to her lawyer, Gawain something-or-other (yes, I know, bear with me, it hardly matters now), to whom I was immediately and inexplicably drawn. He was around my age, but seemed decades deeper. His thinning blond hair conferred an unexpected gravitas, and although he was my nominal adversary, he had a kind and gentle manner and, oddly, I wanted him to like me. Such strange footing for this enterprise. But it had all stopped seeming real to me and I felt, for a moment, as I did in my hospital bed in Budapest, drifting from one state to another, the distant notes of the *Hashkiveinu* in my ears.

Judge Handlebar cleared his throat and then the dance began, all bits of business, pockets of busy, papers turned in, statements made, questions answered. The plot moved forward and I was barely in the room. It made no difference, I knew the particulars of our claim all too well, and the bits of

Rabbi Wolfe's claim that drifted in seemed thin and circumstantial: a substantial family collection, a sacked gallery, and then years of gaps in the provenance reduced to a half-dozen ledger entries: "ELK/BSS." It all unfolded around me, reduced to a kind of buzzing as I kept glancing from Tracy to Rachel to Rabbi Wolfe, wondering when the whole thing would come down around me, as I knew it must. And the painting. Oh yes, right. Something to do with that. Restitution. The word kept flying around the room, penetrating my haze, and I thought of my father's ashes, languishing at home. We were spoken to, Rabbi Wolfe and I, at least I seem to remember that we were, each given our moment in the spotlight, asked questions by both parties, and even Judge Handlebar roused himself to clarify a point here or there. It was all very gentle and civilized, Rachel deferential to Rabbi Wolfe's condition, and her lawyer solicitous of my own recent traumas. The beating, my dead father. I wished I'd brought him. What would Judge Handlebar have made of that? Oh, why don't you ask the old man himself, then *wham*, remains on the conference table as though I were throwing down a winning hand at a high-stakes poker game.

We took a break for lunch. Rachel, Tracy, and I. It was unbearable, worse than being trussed up in my hospital bed. A quick sandwich in a loud lobby café, soggy brown salads on wet serving trays. To my astonishment, Tracy and Rachel seemed to get on. Is it always this way, when the gods wish to destroy? What should I have preferred? Arid silence? There were, I was coming to understand, no good outcomes. My only thought throughout that endless meal was of green model paint soaking its way through the fabric of my pants, my knees damp and sticky.

Then back to the conference room, the second act, perfunctory and limp, as though the playwright had run out of ideas. Closing statements, notable for an absence of passion, and as quickly as it had begun, it was finished, Judge Handlebar announcing he'd take a few days to absorb the material. I wasn't sure Rabbi Wolfe had the days to spare.

We were collecting our papers and were about to leave, spent by the day's effort, when Rabbi Wolfe approached, her troubled eyes upon me.

"I'm sorry, but it's been bothering me since you came in. Have we met?"

There it was. I could have lied, Virgil. Perhaps I should have. The performance would have been effortless, instinctive, perhaps even the truth after a fashion, so deeply would I have convinced myself of its veracity. I am certain I could have made Rabbi Wolfe doubt the memory of her own senses.

I felt Tracy's eyes upon us. Or were they Rachel's? No more half-truths. I nodded.

"Yes. Briefly. We shook hands."

"In my temple. Yes, I thought so."

I did not have to face Rachel to see the surprise on her face. "You went to Chicago? When?"

"Just after my father died."

"But why?" Who asked that? Rachel? Tracy? Or Rabbi Wolfe? Perhaps they said it together, like some angry Greek chorus.

I shrugged. "To lay eyes on you. To see who I was dealing with, I guess."

Rabbi Wolfe nodded, satisfied, it seemed, and shuffled out of the conference room. Rachel waited until she was gone to speak.

"I asked you not to go, Matt. You promised me you wouldn't."

I turned to face her. I could feel Tracy's gaze, insistent on me, on us.

"I know. You did."

"I wanted this to be clean, honorable. No sneaking around. I told you that. But you went anyway."

I nodded. "I'm sorry." In truth, I was irritated.

Rachel shook her head and began to pack up her papers. In the corner of my vision, I saw Tracy frown. What did she want of me? What did everyone, finally, want of me?

"I guess it didn't feel important enough to tell me? A phone call or an e-mail if you didn't have the guts to face me?"

And then it all gave way, Virgil. It would be easy enough to play the moment she was looking for, eyes downcast, abject, apologetic. I'd played that part many times before. Instead, I once again felt the same dry crack in my chest that I felt that day in Glendale with my father. This was, quite literally, my moment of truth. I suppose I can report that I did not disappoint.

"*Don't* fucking talk to me that way," I snapped at Rachel. I'm sure she was shocked but it didn't register because I turned to Tracy, my voice even but coiled.

"There's something I need to tell you. Rachel, can we please have a moment?"

I'VE HAD SOMETHING OF A FLASH, Virgil, I've just realized, revisiting it all here tonight, it's not about fathers and sons at all, is it? All this, it's not about the Jews or the war or family history lost and regained. Rachel. Tracy. Rabbi Wolfe. I've been looking in the wrong place.

Don't fuck it up, Matt.

I HAVE NEVER EXPERIENCED as strong a feeling of dislocation as during those weeks I spent at my father's house in New York, erasing his traces, waiting for the decision from Judge Handlebar. Rachel and Tracy had forsaken me. The truth had come out, and neither would return my calls, so I decided to leave town, to use the time to dispose of my father's belongings and clean up his affairs. Better than pottering around my empty house, waiting for the phone to ring.

Tracy had taken the news with a degree of stoicism I hadn't expected. Rachel packed her belongings and left us, and I explained what had happened in Budapest, leaving nothing out. She asked a few questions, all of which I answered, and then she left the conference room, her admirable dignity intact. It was all very adult, no scenes, no tears. They would be shed in private, later, if at all. A week or so afterward, I watched helplessly in our bedroom as she packed her roller bag for a final, one-way trip. I sat there, trying to think of something I might say that could change this outcome but nothing came. The silence dragged on, irritating her.

"You don't have to sit there, you know. In fact, this might be easier if you didn't."

She was right. I collected myself and started to leave, then I paused and turned back.

"That day we spoke on the phone, when I was at the river—"

"Matt, please."

"—you said you didn't know what I believed in—"

"Seriously, there's no point now. It's done."

"—and that I was, what, that I couldn't see past my nose? Is that really what you thought? Think?"

She paused in her packing, long enough to look at me with, it seemed, pity.

"Did you really think I was having an affair with Brian? And that I was somehow plotting against you with your father?"

I shrugged, uncomfortable. Asked in this manner, in this tone, it was obviously a ridiculous notion. She inhaled before speaking.

"I think . . . maybe we were never fully sold on each other, you know? So you had your painting, I had my case, and that got our energy instead. I don't know. I'm sorry, Matt. I really am."

And then she zippered her suitcase and was gone.

She apologized to *me*, Virgil. I cannot seem to fathom the way human beings operate. It's as though, along the way, I picked up all the wrong sorts of knowledge. I can tell you in excruciating detail where Ervin Laszlo Kálmán spent the winter of 1939, but I cannot tell you what that apology meant.

In the days that followed, a deep depression settled over me, a paralyzing gloom. When I climbed out of bed at all, I lumbered from room to room without purpose. Chasing the occasional ray of sunlight beneath which I would lounge, recalling that reclining odalisque Rachel and I saw at the Norton Simon. I stopped eating; the prospect nauseated me. I drank to excess. That's what people do, isn't it? And I flagellated, oh, how I self-flagellated. Played back every moment, remembered every bad decision, tried to imagine following a different path, though I could feel how bound to my fate I had been all along. I did not shower, brush my teeth, groom for days. It was only when I caught a whiff of rotting onions and realized I was the source that I attended to myself.

It was into this wretched soup of malaise that Brian inserted himself, without invitation. The insistent knocking early one Saturday morning roused me from my torpor. I donned some sweats and stomped down the stairs, irritated by the invasion. *What*, I demanded, flinging the front door open, to be brought up short by the unexpected presence of Siegfried on my doorstep. He apologized for disturbing me but he'd been trying to reach Tracy for days and she'd gone off radar. He had news and I could tell from his mien it wasn't good, though I couldn't imagine how Ricky McCabe's saga could get any worse. I invited him in for coffee. He entered respectfully, as though trying to adjust himself to the size of the space, to avoid looming over me. He hung back as I led us to the kitchen, where I prepared coffee. He inquired how my recovery from my incident was progressing, expressed the appropriate level of anger and commiseration over what had befallen me. I was hungover, unhappy, impatient. I drove him to the purpose of his call.

"What's going on, Brian? You look a mess." Hah, coming from me.

He fiddled with an invisible thread on his sleeve. "Where's Tracy? I feel like I should tell her in person."

"She doesn't live here anymore. We split up. But I know where she is. What's up?"

"Oh shit. Man, I'm sorry. I really am." His sorrow seemed genuine, another for the catalog of misjudgments. "That's why she's been so quiet." I nodded and looked at him expectantly. He sighed, then decided to confide in me.

"McCabe confessed."

I gripped the countertop, reeling on Tracy's behalf. No, it couldn't be. Oh, Tracy. She had invested so much purpose, so much heart . . . so much *faith*. And now the story she had believed for so long was about to be taken from her, another narrative unbuckled. I winced as I remembered how I had pressed her about her certainty.

"Jesus. I thought he had a child's IQ? Maybe he's just saying it?"

"I thought so, too. Hoped. But he led the police to where he tossed the gun, which had his prints on it." We stood there staring at each other, sharing a single thought.

TRACY HAD TAKEN UP TEMPORARY RESIDENCE with a friend of hers, another model, Simone, who lived about fifteen minutes away, so I drove Brian over there. We rode in silence even as there were a million things I wanted to ask him. I wanted to know about his marriage, his happy family. To know how he did it. I wanted to know if he ever considered Tracy a prospect. I wanted to know why he did this kind of work, so fraught, so difficult. To know what in him was so configured for justice, for righteousness. To be able to do the right thing seems so mysterious to me, yet it comes so easily to some.

Instead, I asked, "Are you okay?"

Brian stared straight ahead at the road, his classical profile presenting a perfect visage of depth and reflection. He was silent and I worried I'd overstepped, then he spoke in a low voice that I had to strain to hear.

"I'm fucking pissed."

I knew what he meant, and I liked him, Virgil. It was too late, but I liked him.

We pulled up to Simone's house and I indicated her front door. I felt it was best for me to hang back, and Brian agreed. We shook hands and I watched him stride down the path and ring the doorbell. Tracy opened the door and I felt a flood of love, sorrow, and shame overtake me. Surprise registered on her face at the sight of Brian, and as I watched the silent film from afar, her expression crossed into bewilderment. It was clear from her face that she quite literally did not understand what she was being told. It was a terrible sight, and I could only console myself that she had, at least, briefly enjoyed the sustaining power of belief, and I hoped she would believe again. She sagged against the doorframe, and Brian stepped forward to hug her. He closed the front door and I drove off to flee the city, to flee my own self-inflicted wounds.

NOW I WAS BACK IN MY FATHER'S HOUSE, the dutiful son once more. His absence had taken hold, and this emptiness was of a different character than the days after his death. The house was sweltering, having spent the summer months shuttered. It was an angry, accusing heat. Dust had settled in layers and the air was still and thick. The bathroom tap coughed and sputtered before spitting out whiskey-colored water. The place was a mess, a snapshot of the moment I'd left it behind months earlier. There was so much to do. Fortunately, I had some time on my hands. Only the footprints to and from the basement door gave any indication of the activity that had taken place in my absence.

I stood before the door for a long moment, afraid to go downstairs. I knew what awaited me, what I had put in motion, and laughed to think how my unsentimental father would have scorned my discomfort. I pushed the door open and crept down the stairs, as one enters a room that might contain a burglar or a corpse. I felt along the wall at the bottom of the stairs and found the light switch, which I flipped up with a satisfyingly loud, old-fashioned click. The man in the golden helmet scowled at me but that familiar frisson of fear was gone. He looked old and tired, and those eyes that I had once found so forbidding now seemed plaintive and downcast. I swept past him with the sadness one feels beholding senescent, fallen heroes and turned into the main room. I knew what to expect, and still I stopped breathing at the sight.

The basement appeared denuded, like a clear-cut forest. I had found a dealer in model toys who agreed to inventory and pack the collection for a modest sum, providing he could have first refusal on some of the rarest items. He would sell off the pieces for a cut of each transaction. The collection had been boxed up and cataloged, everything was tagged with admirable efficiency. It was too much for me to take in. It was as though I'd been afflicted by a kind of snow blindness, a brightening white light that obscured my field of vision. My nose and lungs began to freeze as though I were in an actual blizzard, and I began to shiver. My father was gone. It was all I could do to turn and stumble down one of the hallways and hurry into the small bathroom at the end of the corridor.

I ran the shower as hot as it would go and filled the tiny room with steam. I inhaled deeply, began to warm, the shivering subsided. My phone rang, its electronic chime a thunderstroke in that small, still space. The glass display still shattered from my beating. I'd left it that way, as a reminder. I grabbed for the phone. Whom did I hope for? Rachel? Tracy? Both?

It was Rabbi Wolfe. I hesitated, nearly missing the call. She was calling, she explained, because she had been meaning to speak to me since my incident in Budapest. This was what people called it now. My incident. I hurried up the stairs as she spoke, careful not to look in the direction of my father's boxed collection. Whatever our circumstance, she went on, this fell outside of those considerations. One of her people had been beaten, she said, and that affected her, affected everyone. She went on to tell me stories, Talmudic tales mixed with historical vignettes, painting a portrait—yes, painting, that's how it felt—of Jewish persecution and Jewish resilience, and I marveled as she spoke, she who had been my adversary, she who was so close to her own creeping, implacable death. Her voice was different now. Not merely weaker, though yes, the exhaustion was inescapable. But I heard, between the words, between syllables and inhalations, something new, something that felt very much like what I felt when Rachel laid her finger upon her mezuzah. In this hidden layer, Rabbi Wolfe now carried with her . . .

Fuck. Why can't I say it? Just say the word, you coward.

God.

She carried God in her voice.

And Rachel carried God and Bernie carried God and the fireplug at the Budapest synagogue carried God and Kálmán carried God and Tracy carried God and even my father, yes, even he carried God, and everyone but me, godless Matt Santos, carried God.

AFTER RABBI WOLFE'S CALL I broke into my father's measly stash of booze. He was never much of a drinker, and the choices were grim: an ancient Chablis, a bottle of Pimm's, a sticky, dusty bottle of Lillet. All the way in the back was a bottle of Jack Daniel's, the seal unbroken. A gift probably, or something kept on hand for visitors. It would do, and it wouldn't take much. I poured three fingers' worth into a coffee mug, collected a pair of empty cardboard cartons, and went into my father's bedroom. I grimaced at my first sip though I found the medicinal bite bracing. There were some clothes laid out at the foot of the bed, a pair of beige corduroy trousers and a purple polyester turtleneck. I wondered if this was the outfit my father had planned for himself the night before his heart attack, set out like a child's school uniform for the morning. I picked up the turtleneck and smelled it—a heady mix of sweat, old man, and aftershave. How soon before my own clothes reeked like that? I gagged slightly and took another sip of the whiskey.

There were so few personal effects to be found. His alarm clock was flashing twelve o'clock. There'd been a power outage since my last visit. On the dresser, a small framed photo of me aged ten or so. More surprising, a single, small black-and-white photo of my mother posed in front of the Funicular Railway on Buda Hill. He never spoke of my mother, but apparently she endured in his memory. I drank down the last finger and pulled open the dresser drawers, hoping to find something more in the way of personal effects, but found only a deck of playing cards containing soft-core photographs of fifty-two sexual positions. I discovered this contraband as a teenager and spent many hours reviewing them.

One by one, I tipped out the drawers onto the bed to begin the business of sorting the clothing and packing it into the cartons for charity. It felt like a violation, handling his clothes in this manner, poring over objects that had been against his body. I was aware of the foot within every sock, the chest beneath each undershirt. And handling his underwear? I needed to refill my coffee cup with another splash of Jack Daniel's to be able to continue. In his closet, the hangers were packed so densely that I could barely pull them out at first. The man kept everything.

I worked for hours. Night slithered in and I was in my cups, sitting amid the piles of my father's old clothes, when I heard my mother knock at the door and enter. Back from her artists' retreat, she had offered to help me with the packing. She appeared in the doorway and regarded me amid the fallen leaves of menswear.

"Ugh. I pleaded with him not to buy that shirt."

I looked down at the shirt I was folding. It was a hideous lilac polo made from some sort of synthetic.

"Not much fashion sense, your father." She walked over and held out her hand. I gave her the shirt, which she examined, smiling.

"He always bought me these blue flowers, blue irises," she said. "I hated them but he always got them for me. They only lived for a day."

The years have been kind to my mother, she has achieved a sort of attractive sturdiness. Prematurely gray in her thirties, she has aged into her mane, which, in the last decade, she has opted to leave loose, as I suppose befits her bohemian identity. It was good to see her.

"You look like hell, son," she said, taking the drink from my hand. "I brought groceries. Let me fix us some dinner."

THERE WAS SOMETHING COMFORTING about the awfulness of my mother's cooking. For the occasion, she'd outdone herself, and the modest meal was inedible. A shriveled pork cutlet, drier than the lid of a shoebox. A gelatinous mass of egg noodles. And a handful of brussels sprouts, burnt crisp in an inch of butter. It made me feel like a child again, and I loved it.

We sat at the dining room table where the three of us ate almost every dinner of my childhood, cheap laminate an unnatural shade of orange, the leaves unevenly jutting up against each other like a fault line. We ate from mismatched plates, using the same tarnished silverware we always used, a dull, gray set with an inset oval of black slate along the shaft. We spoke about all sorts of things, my mother and I, about the case, my trip and beating, her retreat, anything, at first, but my father. I omitted the details about Tracy and Rachel. Only at the end of the meal, when she returned the coffee mug filled with her strong, black brew, did he come up. She asked about the collection, and I told her that the plan to sell it was moving ahead. She frowned at the news.

"What else should I do?" I asked, feeling judged. "I don't want it. I wouldn't know what to do with it. Would you?"

"Of course not. It's the right thing, the only thing to do." She surprised me by brushing aside an errant tear. "It's just, you know. That was him. Everything, really, every admirable trait, every maddening one, he funneled into those goddamned cars."

We sat in silence for a moment. I was unsettled by my mother's sorrow, yet heartened to learn that she hadn't completely rid herself of my father. We held hands from across the table. There were stubborn flecks of aquamarine paint beneath her fingernails.

Eager to change the subject, I said, "Hey. Do you remember the whole thing with the space toy?"

"Of course. Your father was such a softie."

Softie? "What do you mean?"

"The way he replaced your money while you were sleeping. So typical."

"He told me *you* replaced the money."

This surprised my mother. I watched as she reviewed the mental footage. "This was the blue spaceship, right? The fifty dollars."

"It was pink, a car, and it was sixty-five dollars," I said with irritation.

"How odd." This seemed to amuse my mother, and her amusement infuriated me. How could she be so sanguine in the face of such uncertainty? She shrugged. "Well, I suppose it's possible. It was a long time ago, you know."

Why didn't this bother her more? Between the three of us, we couldn't agree on the simple facts of a story we'd all been part of within the last twenty years. How was I expected to place any faith in the outcome of this arbitration, given the span of time, the gaps in the tale, the absence of firsthand witnesses that apparently didn't count for much? Which story are we ever to believe, Virgil? She could see the anger on my face, the helplessness, and she kissed my cheek and said, not without tenderness, "You were always such a silly boy, Matt." She cleared the table, stayed on a few more hours to help me finish packing my father's clothes, and then she was gone into the night with vague promises of a California visit.

I returned to the basement. I had noticed something earlier, out of the corner of my eye, and it had been nagging at me since then, and as I sobered up, I remembered what it was. There was a DVD atop one of the packed boxes. Apparently, my dealer had found it buried on one of the shelves and wanted to make sure I noticed it. It was a documentary on toy car collecting, filmed a few years earlier by a British film crew. I looked at the track listing. One of the DVD's twenty chapters included a brief interview with my father. I'd never seen it, and he had not told me about it.

IN THE VIDEO, my father looks sickly beneath a sallow light as he stands in front of one of his display cases. I'm taken aback at the sight of him alive, talking, briefly restored to me. From his first words, I'm fighting back tears. His eyes look past the camera, addressing an unseen interviewer. He talks slowly, deliberately. He was always aware of his accented English, his tendency to trip up or be misunderstood. He talks about his collection in the broadest terms and at first there's nothing new, I'm mostly just swimming in the stream of his words, this unexpected gift of a last conversation. Then he makes a reference to his own past, to being a young man in Budapest and being an obsessive gambler. This is news, something else he'd never mentioned to me. All at once, the Tower Club makes a new kind of sense and I cannot help but laugh: a DVD has told me more than I was able to learn about him myself. What made me think I could understand this man?

And yet, as I stand amid the boxes containing his collection, his life's work, it seems inarguable that this, here, all this, was where my father's essence was to be found. Not in *Budapest Street Scene*. Not in synagogues across the ocean. Right here, in these neatly wrapped capsules, packed away, waiting to be sold off.

I poke through the boxes until I find the piece I want, the Corvette, and place it under my arm. With a jaunty nod to Rembrandt's man in the golden helmet, I switch the lights off and I'm up and out for the night.

—

WITHIN A WEEK, I erased my father's home. I could not watch as the trucks hauled the collection away, and instead took myself to a movie, some asinine Hollywood thing, all stunts and noise and drunken camera work that gave me a headache. I remembered it vaguely, had auditioned for the part of the computer hacker. Watching the actor who got the role, I had to concede that he played it better than I would have. We crossed paths all the time going out for the same parts. Here, his choices were all interesting and fresh, little flourishes that would never have occurred to me, and he managed to make an unmemorable part linger in memory. I returned from the movies to an empty house, locked it up for the last time with little ceremony, and caught a flight home, to wait on Judge Handlebar's ruling.

I<small>T ALL ENDED</small> with a terse message from Rachel on my voice mail.

"The decision is in. It's yours."

That was all I heard from her. Her paralegal forwarded me a copy of the decision and called to inquire about my plans, whether I wanted to collect the painting or have the firm assist with its disposition. I had no idea what to say. Handle it, I told him.

I thumbed through the fourteen-page decision. I'd expected more complexity, more impenetrable legalese, but in the end, it was all straightforward. It seemed Rabbi Wolfe's claim foundered due to its lack of documentary evidence. Right as always, Rachel. Judge Handlebar had found the photograph of my grandparents' sitting room dispositive. Had the beating I'd received played a role in nudging along his sympathies? I would never know. It was a surreal moment in which, among other things, I was suddenly a millionaire. I know people feel numb at momentous occasions but I wasn't numb. Nor was I elated. I felt forsaken.

I had no one to call with the news. My father. Rachel. Tracy. I wondered whether it was appropriate to contact Rabbi Wolfe, to express my condolences of sorts. Instead, I walked. It seemed a subversive thing to do in this vehicular city, to light out for points unknown and walk as far as your feet will carry you. My phone had begun vibrating. I left it rattling on my dining room table, slipped on a hooded sweatshirt, and set off into the late afternoon's fading light.

EVENTUALLY, I CAME UPON AN OFFICE PARK a few miles from my house and paused before my favorite fountain. It was situated in a fenced circle of green, spires of water leaning in toward one another. I dropped onto a metal bench and gazed into the floodlit waters. I was an incongruous patch of stillness amid office workers streaming from buildings to begin the long commute home. A few passersby seemed to glare at me, offended by my apparent lack of purpose. There was almost nothing preventing me from sitting here, staring at the fountain, for as long as I chose, forever really. The thought disturbed me and I stirred from my perch.

Across the street from the office park was a collective of art galleries, and I decided to wander over and take a look. Most were already closed for the evening, but there were signs of life coming from one. An opening was in progress. Voices and bodies spilled out into the courtyard. I stepped inside to investigate.

The moment I entered, a drink was pressed into my hand. I took a taste: an ordinary red wine that was somehow just what I needed. I gulped it down, set the empty cup on a passing tray, and took a second. Fortified, I began to wander, taking in the art and the audience.

Classical music piped in through overhead speakers to a monochromatic crowd. How much did I stand out, I wondered, the only one not dressed in black? It was an attractive gathering and my eye drifted to women as they passed by, usually deep in conversation with slim, earnest, bearded lads. It took little effort to spot the man of the hour. Muscular, a dark buzz cut, and covered with tattoos—an angry lizard crawled up his neck—he was surrounded by adoring young women and not a few young men. He reminded me of Kálmán, although he was, of course, nothing at all like him. I think at that moment any artist would have brought Kálmán to mind.

I wanted to go over and talk to him. I wanted to ask him how he would feel if seventy years after his death, people were slugging it out in the courts for his paintings. Would he care about the outcome? Would he care about the sort of person who finally took possession? I looked at him more closely. The way he worked the crowd, he seemed a climber, on the make, someone not much concerned with the messy details of posterity. *Slugging it out for me, dude?* I imagined him asking. *Rad*. It would take a few more drinks for me to approach someone like that.

I turned my attention to his work. There were some paintings, some sculpture, a hodgepodge, unified only by the artist's abiding sense of the bizarre. I was struck by a bronze of a human face with massive ram's horns extruding, and topped with white, brittle hairs. On my third glass of wine, I alternated between mirth and fear. My interpretive radar was alcohol-blunted and could not quite differentiate charlatanism from profundity.

A young woman came and stood beside me. She was quite beautiful, dark-haired, festooned with leather wristbands and bracelets, and her arms bore lines of tattooed text. *Don't Give Up the Fight*, her left forearm advised. She spoke to me, resuming midsentence, it seemed, as I regarded the object. She spoke animatedly, never taking her eyes from the art, parsing the work, praising its tension and its surprising depth, given that the artist was such a shallow, womanizing cocksucker.

Then she turned and registered with irritation that I was not who she thought. She stalked away and it occurred to me that I could now buy every last piece of art hanging in this gallery.

I don't know how long I stayed but it was long enough for me to get drunk. The crowd began to disperse and I was swaying before a canvas when I sensed someone at my elbow. I turned to find the artist. He greeted me, said I looked familiar. Did he recognize me? Did he sense my newly minted fortune? Or was he merely being friendly? I told him that I'd just wandered in. A civilian, he said, and asked what I thought of the show. I turned to face him, trying to hold his eye with my own crossing pair, and told him that I didn't really understand it but it scared me a little. He seemed satisfied with the answer. It was a desirable outcome, he said, we placed too high a premium on comfort, spent too little time confronting things that disquieted us, that we didn't understand. That we weren't meant to understand. This confused me. Not meant to understand? What kind of an artist didn't want to be understood?

He smiled without answering. This was the shallow cocksucker? I was so confused I forgot to ask him about posterity. He shook my hand and wandered off to join the young woman of the wristbands, who smiled and kissed him. Arms entwined, they greeted other visitors as I stumbled off into the balmy night, reeling from the cheap cabernet in my veins, and began the long walk home.

RACHEL WAS SITTING ON MY STOOP when I got home. I hadn't seen her since Chicago. I was surprised and not.

"How long have you been sitting here?"

"I don't know. A while."

"Here, come inside."

I moved to unlock the front door but she interposed herself in between. I nearly plunged my key into her belly. She refused to give way. Beneath my mezuzah, she fiddled with the buttons on her coat, agitated, not making eye contact with me.

"I sang to you, Matt."

I didn't understand.

"In your hospital. That night. I sang to you."

So I hadn't imagined it. She said it as though she was confessing to a regretted intimacy.

"I feel like I've been part of something that's all wrong."

I knew she meant the painting but I wondered if she was also referring to that afternoon among the statues. I thought of asking her but I didn't really want to hear the answer. As long as there's an empty space, I can fill it with any version of events that suits me. Once the words are spoken, the cement begins to dry.

"Why do I feel like this? Like there's some deception going on here?"

"I don't know, Rachel. You tell me."

"That thing you did, going to Chicago, not telling me. It was awful."

"I know. And I'm sorry. But this isn't about that. If I hadn't gone, would you feel any different?"

Rachel had no answer for that. She surprised me by pulling out a cigarette and lighting it with a shaky hand. She inhaled deeply, rubbed her eyes.

"I didn't know you smoked."

She ignored me, very much in her own nutshell. "My dad, since his retirement, it's been all Talmud all the time. He's actually become quite the scholar." She paused and looked up. "You do know what the Talmud is?"

I couldn't tell if it was a dig or an honest question. I nodded.

"Not your thing, I know. I guess it's not mine, either, not like with him, anyway. But he read me this bit the other night—he's got a scary sixth sense—from, wait for it, *Ethics of Fathers*, right?" Gallows chuckles. "It says"—she squinted as she recalled the words—"that freedom of choice is granted, and the world is judged with goodness, *but in accordance with the amount of man's good deeds*. So I guess I just wanted to ask you: Does this feel like a good deed to you?"

I stood there aching, my throat constricted.

"It's not rhetorical, Matt. I'm asking you: Does this feel like a good deed?"

Full of desire to speak but without words.

"Rachel . . . I don't fucking know." Too drunk, too tired.

She stamped out the cigarette. "Figure it out, would you? Push yourself."

Pushpushpush. I watched her walk off for what I was certain was the last time. As I watched my father walk away. I am always watching people walking away. Give me the lines and I'll speak them. Spell out the action for me and I'll do it, sometimes with aplomb. But call for volition, agency, and something keeps me rooted in place.

I turned back to my doorframe, to my mezuzah. It appeared to be mocking me, rakishly aslant, and I laughed, a wild and slightly unhinged laugh. I went inside, found my toolbox, extracted a flat screwdriver, and returned to the door. I stood there clutching the weapon, chest heaving under my subsiding laughter, and raised the point toward the mezuzah's edge, which seemed to be giving me the finger, and I began to pound at the butt of the screwdriver with the heel of my palm. It slipped under the body and I twisted and pulled on the screwdriver until, with a crack of protest, the mezuzah leapt from the doorframe and landed somewhere in my bushes, where I left it as I stepped inside and turned off the porch light.

I stood in my darkened dining room and picked up my phone. Eleven messages, mostly from press. I listened to Rabbi Wolfe's voice mail. It was brief, strangely friendly. She congratulated me on the outcome of the arbitration and said she would not try to fight it, that she didn't have the time, and anyway, the evidence had shaken her certainty. She speculated that perhaps this award was in its own way some kind of restitution for what happened to me at the banks of the Danube. *For there is no man who has not his hour*, she said, *and no thing that has not its place.* This long, dark story, so laden with sorrows, where would it end? It was over, yet it felt unfinished. I stepped back out into the night, dropped on all fours, and drunkenly groped around in the darkness until I located the mezuzah. I brushed it clean against my pant leg and slipped it into my pocket.

THIS LONG NIGHT has begun, at last, to lift. I feel the change before I see it, a lightening in the room, a lightening outside the window. The fluorescent glow that has attended me all night has been dimmed by an unseen hand, and I'm reminded of the moment when the house lights come up. Final bows and then it's time to leave the stage. But not before a final twist. Consider it a reward for your patience, Virgil. For your remarkable indulgence this evening.

A month or so had passed since I'd been awarded the painting and I'd settled into a gray and featureless routine of drinking, sleeping late, and occasional auditions. Ricky McCabe had gone obligingly to his death. I spent my time thinking, about Tracy, about my father, and even a little about Rachel. My days were marked by a dullness, an omnipresent regret that weighted me down like a man drowning in a winter coat. I was like a monk who had renounced his worldly self, albeit a drunk, morose, self-pitying monk.

The stillness I'd cultivated was punctured one morning, just days before *Budapest Street Scene* was to ascend to the auction block. I was hungover, as had become my fashion, and at first, in the grips of a nightmare that had me back at the Danube, being kicked and beaten once more. The dream pounding I was receiving blurred with the pounding at my front door and the pounding in my alcohol-addled skull, but eventually

I roused myself and shuffled downstairs. I squinted into the brilliant morning sunshine, which backlit the delivery boy on my stoop like some celestial messenger. He asked for a signature, which I drew with my nail-bitten index finger across the display of his large electronic tablet, and then he turned and departed without further ado, leaving a battered box on my doorstep. I bent over—what a cacophony of trumpets that set off in my poor head—and pulled the carton inside.

The box was large, nearly three feet square, but with little heft. The pitted, sagging cardboard had been battered by a transatlantic journey. My heart was trampolining, its heavy beat further amplifying the misbegotten ache in my head. Why did this box, with all its international transit markings, seem so sinister to me? I backed away from it slowly, and at once felt myself ridiculous. I pulled a pair of scissors from a drawer and attacked the brown paper tape that held the flaps closed. I opened the box and recognized the fusty odor of Klara's Budapest apartment. A small note lay atop the contents. Klara was thanking me again for my kindness, which had so improved her situation. She'd made some repairs to her apartment, had decent food, and would even have heat throughout the winter for the first time in a decade. She'd had some keepsakes from my father—he'd fled Hungary in such a hurry that he left some items with her, always intending to recover them and never getting around to it. She almost handed them over while we were there but held back, reluctant to part with them, with him. But she felt in light of my generosity the only proper thing to do was to send them on to me. She apologized for the delay and hoped I might find them helpful.

I removed the contents, laying them on my coffee table to perform a quick inventory. Mostly junk, useless things, really. A few books and magazines in Hungarian. A child's toy, a battered sailboat. An envelope of photos. These drew my interest first, and I sat down as I flipped through them, no more than two dozen or so. They were mostly black-and-white photos of what I took to be family members I did not recognize. I did a double take when I found a picture of myself as a young boy that turned out, upon closer scrutiny, to be a photo of my father. He was playing in the very courtyard I had visited, and I cannot recall ever seeing him looking so innocent, so like a child. He was always preternaturally old to me but here he was, no less young and joyful than I had been at that age.

There was one last surprising photo of my father as a young boy. He was standing at the front of a temple, was wearing a dark suit and a kippah, reading from what I took to be a Torah. Could this have been a bar mitzvah photo—a bar mitzvah he had never mentioned to me? His father was in the photo, proudly looking on, and there was no anger left in me, Virgil, only sadness.

There were a few other objects Klara had sent along. Some articles of clothing. One of the lace doilies I'd seen in the photo of my father with the Kálmán painting. The last thing in the box was a roll of what appeared to be tattered, musty canvases. I pulled them out and unfurled them on my living room floor.

There were six in all. Four appeared to be preparatory studies for a copy of *Budapest Street Scene*, and two were incomplete attempts, abandoned for reasons unknown to my nontechnical eye, but somehow failing to meet my grandfather's exacting standards. How long I stood there trying to figure it out, Virgil, what a dimwit I must seem to you. Why would my grandfather bother with copies of his own painting? It made no sense to me. My mind returned to my grandfather's storied knack for imitation. And all at once it became clear to me. My father's—and *his* father's—greatest score. It wasn't a copy, it was a forgery. Created to deceive, like my own urgent report cards. It was the only logical explanation: they must have duped Halasz, their Arrow Cross intercessor, and traded him a forgery for their exit papers. Which could only mean the painting about to go on sale wasn't mine, that the painting glimpsed in that creased black-and-white photo that Judge Handlebar had placed such faith in was a copy. However Cassian Yuhaus came into possession of his painting, the genuine article, and whether it really did belong to Rabbi Wolfe or not, it wasn't through my family. *It has nothing to do with you,* my father had said. I sat on the couch, clutching one of the paintings, in awe of the fraud my grandfather had executed. A little bit of talent, or at least skill, had presented itself in the Santos family line, after all. I thought again of those ersatz report cards and smiled. What, after all, is acting, but the skilled copying of another? What, I now wondered, became of the version Halasz took, undoubtedly lost forever? Had he destroyed it when he realized it was a fake?

Fake. The word boomed within me like a thunderclap. I looked over to my father's ashes, still perched atop the fireplace, the toy Corvette resting beside him. You brave, brilliant, sneaky bastard. In that moment, Virgil, I loved him more than I ever had. Something had been restored to me, at last.

THE CEMETERY, perched on a Los Angeles hillside with distant views of the ocean, had none of the wildness, none of the gothic, overgrown atmospherics of its Budapest cousin. Cemeteries and synagogues. How circular my travels have been. The lawns were well tended, the spaces bright and wide-open, bereft of trees, as if to place no obstruction between the mourners and Hashem's heavenly digs. It was a radiant fall morning, crisp and distantly smoky.

"May I?" Tracy asked, pointing at the urn as we walked through the cemetery. It felt strange to relinquish my father's mortal remains, but I handed him over, and she cradled him with tenderness, smiling as though they'd just shared a private joke.

We walked in a silence that was neither rebuking nor punishing but merely acknowledged we had passed into a place beyond words. Only my father's admonition hung as a cloud over the landscape, *Do not fuck this up*. I looked at Tracy with regret, aware of the ruin I'd caused, and felt how totally I had misunderstood my father's final commandment.

The night after Klara's package arrived, I watched McCabe's video myself, in its entirety. I wanted to see what Tracy had seen in it, what had moved her so. What I saw surprised me.

What struck me most was the vacancy in his eyes, a cold,

black emptiness that contrasted with his whispered intensity, as if he were somehow half formed, incomplete. He would respond to each muffled question with a variation on "I didn't do it." There was something almost childlike in his disavowals.

"How did the blood get on your clothes?"

"I don't know." He'd shrug, looking trapped by each question. "I tried to help her up."

"Were you angry at her?"

"No, never. She was nice. Nice old lady."

Please don't let me die.

And on it went like that, McCabe conveying a terrified innocence that I now knew to be a lie. But for his dead eyes, he appeared to have convinced himself of the truth of his narrative—he'd certainly convinced Tracy of it. He'd believed in it wholly, because his life depended on it, but belief isn't enough, and so another unreliable version of history falls. *Documentary evidence*, Rachel had called it. I'm not so sure any such thing exists. Perhaps there is nothing beyond the story.

Tracy had ignored my calls, texts, entreaties, until I mentioned that I was burying my father and thought she might want to join me. After some hesitation, she agreed, and now I wished the walk had taken longer, given us more time in the wordless morning, but we were quickly upon the hulk of rising marble. The inside was quiet and dark and our eyes took a moment to adjust from the sunlight. Every sound, every moment seemed magnified in the polished stillness of the columbarium, where we were met by an attendant. He was tall and stooped, and his dark suit made me think of one of those old Russian chess grandmasters. His gaze was respectfully averted as Tracy handed my father back to me. She brushed a tear aside. I was moved by her sorrow, Virgil. I wanted nothing more than to take her into my arms, to apologize for all my misdeeds, to apologize for underestimating her so thoroughly. My hand trembled as I set my father into his niche, a small padded square in a massive wall of squares, reminding me of photos I'd seen of the Automat. I stepped back and nodded to Spassky, who closed the glass door and locked it, handed me the key, and left us to our business.

As his footsteps receded, Tracy lowered her head and began muttering. At first I thought it was a Catholic prayer, remembered from childhood, but I began to make out the Hebrew words: *Y'hei sh'mei raba m'varach l'alam ul'almei almaya* . . . She continued a moment longer in this vein, ended with a hushed *Amein.* The surprise must have been evident on my face because she blushed a bit and looked away. Mourner's kaddish, she explained. I googled it. She looked at me evenly. You're not the only one who can learn lines, you know. I laughed, a gentle, appreciative laugh, moved by this final kindness.

Teach it to me, I said. I want to say it before we go.

She scrutinized my eyes for a moment, to ensure I was not mocking her, nodded, and led me through the prayer, syllable by syllable. When I looked it up myself soon after, I was struck by the focus on God, the absence of the deceased from the prayer. *Beyond any blessing and song, praise and consolation that are uttered in the world.* I was right. Truly, my Tracy had been touched by God.

Now I must stop calling her that.

She asked if I wanted a moment alone with my father. I nodded and she went to wait outside. We'd come to an end, after so many months, and I pressed my forehead against his niche and my arms wide on either side as if I were holding up the wall. I felt bereft, Virgil. I stood there, my shoulders shaking. So much loss.

As we left, walking in silence, red-eyed, through the cemetery, a memory came to mind, as I suppose they do in cemeteries. My father borrowed the money from his first employer to buy our house. For twenty-five thousand dollars he bought the two-story corner house in Queens across from a lush green park that must have seemed Edenic to him, the house it had now fallen to me to sell. There was no note, no paper. Just a handshake. And for the next twenty years he made his monthly payment religiously—indeed, it was the only thing he was religious about—long past the time when the two men worked together. And after the last payment was made, my father collected us all around the dinner table to celebrate. A modest dream, hard-won. I could see in his eyes how good it felt.

I hadn't called Rachel yet. I was still clinging to my ill-gotten windfall. After all, it might not have been mine, but who's to say it was Rabbi Wolfe's either? So went the rationalizations, each more appalling than the last. I lived in the dim hope that I might work out a different solution to this puzzle that had already been solved. Aware every minute of the indecency of delaying, given the rabbi's condition. Saying goodbye, I have learned, is much harder than it seems, even when goodbye is all that is left to say.

I asked Tracy to sit down on a marble bench that overlooked a man-made rock fountain, painstaking in its attempts at verisimilitude. I told her about the forgery, gave her the last bit of the tale. She was entitled to it, I felt, but I also wanted something from her: I wanted to see my old man for a last moment through her loving eyes, to try to help solve this one last question that evaded me.

At first, I wondered why he refused any discussion of the painting. That, at least, had become clear. He apparently drew his ethical line just short of outright theft. But then why hadn't he waved me off with the truth? It was just the sort of story he loved to crow about—his clever father duping the Nazis! Freedom bought for the price of a cheap canvas and some leftover oil paints. It seemed like a tale he would relish retelling, modifying, altering, reinventing. I couldn't understand it and I turned to Tracy for illumination.

She shook her head. "I don't know, Matt. It could be for a million reasons." She must have sensed my dissatisfaction with her answer, because she took my hand.

"My guess, though, for what it's worth," she continued, "is that it was because of his mother. She didn't get out. That's not a story he wanted to talk about."

She continued talking but I was still hanging on that last part. That's how it was with her, Tracy's Razor, always the most direct and generous interpretation of events. There were, of course, any number of other, equally plausible, less flattering interpretations. It was the final mystery, the last of the things I would never know. I was feeling sorry for myself, for all that had been lost, when something she was saying caught my ear. I turned to her, confused, disoriented.

"What did you just say?"

Obligingly, she repeated herself: "Do not make the mistake of assuming that because you know what someone will do, that you know who they are."

She was talking about my father. She was talking about herself. She was talking about all of us. Which must mean that I have misremembered things, that Rachel did not say this to me in Budapest. Unless. How I hesitate to say this, even now, and yet to not say it is to have learned nothing from all this. So. I say it: Perhaps this was You talking to me, through them both. It seems as good an explanation as any, the most direct and generous. In that moment, I decided what to do about *Budapest Street Scene*.

Tracy let go of my hand, rose from the bench, and began to walk away from me. I sat still for a moment, letting the gap between us widen, and then, surprising us both, I called her name. She paused and turned, and I jogged over to her side and accompanied her back to her car.

VIRGIL'S SHIFT IS OVER and I am inordinately sad to see him go, my friend, my confidante, my comrade in arms. His granite replacement is broad, firm, muscular, as befits the day shift, but he doesn't look to be half the man as my departing shadow. As he shuffles from the room, I catch his eye and nod.

"Thank you," I mumble.

He looks at me with some surprise. "What for?" He trundles onward and I call after him.

"Hey. What's your name?"

"It's Joe."

"Really?"

"Really."

Joe. I should never have asked. What a fucking disappointment.

I STAND BEFORE THE PAINTING as sunlight slants jauntily into the auction house, and now, finally, after all these hours, it truly is nothing more than an object, a thing. Although I can't help but return to him, that figure, my father's restless doppelgänger, and I smile at him as I prepare my own last-minute escape. I have gotten no satisfaction from this brief interlude as a millionaire, and if my agent's cautions are to be believed it may yet be a while before I'm a candidate for that club again, though the work has already begun to pick up ever so slightly. This town, after all, has no memory, the past is perennially washed away, sand castles forever consumed by the surf. Either way, my mind is made up, and despite the weight of sorrow and loss that even now presses against me, I feel lighter, refreshed as I do when I shave after a few days of neglect, and the prickly bristles on my face give way to a smooth lightness.

My instructions to Rachel were clear. She was to withdraw my claim of ownership of *Budapest Street Scene*. I was walking away. Go help Rabbi Wolfe get her painting, I told my surprised attorney before saying goodbye for, I am sure, the last time. I know it is indecent what I have done, allowing the charade to go on so long, right down to this final moment. I feel remorse for this final delay, this last lie in a tale of lies. And yet I grieve to leave this ugly painting, which has become beautiful to me at last. It is the story of my family, or at least as close as I can get to one, so perhaps I will be forgiven this final trespass.

This is a very different place in the light of day, abuzz with people moving with purpose around objects of great value. I step back as the painting is removed from the wall by a pair of white-gloved handlers to begin its final journey to the auction podium. I pause for a moment, staring now at the space left behind by the painting, a faint dust outline on the wall, this empty space my true bequest. Goodbye, dear Kálmán, I hardly knew thee.

I slip my hand into my pocket and pull out the photo of my father at his bar mitzvah. How happy he looked, how safe, how familiar to me yet strange. This is the picture that matters to me now, the one I get to keep. And something Rachel and I talked about comes to mind. "Do not lay a hand on the boy," the angel said, just in time. There's a serenity that's settled in at last, like the stillness after a thunderclap's vibrations have dispersed.

The auction hall has begun to fill with buyers. I wander over to Monsieur Leclos, who stands in the wings, his eyes raking the room, separating the players from the pretenders. He is Armani-clad, bouncing on his toes, electric with anticipation. I suppose I should speak up now, end the charade before it begins, but I've come this far and shall allow myself this final dramatic flourish. After all this, I must stop fighting my nature. I must make do.

Budapest Street Scene is brought to the front of the hall, set in a place of honor, and I feel violated. This lover with whom I have passed all these intimate hours in the privacy of the night is now public property, and there's something almost prurient about the eyes upon it. I feel momentarily protective, jealous, as a man who feels lustful eyes upon his wife.

"Look." Leclos juts his chin ever so slightly in the direction of a man around my age. He's tall and reedy, too thin really, with hair like windblown straw. "Yuhaus's son. I thought he might show up."

The younger Yuhaus looks weary, haggard, as though he's the one who's just spent the whole night on his feet. Perhaps he has. Another son, another mysterious, departed father. Even from this distance I can see that his hazel eyes are cloudy, as though he's oppressed by some intractable problem, a weight he cannot set down. The mystery of his father entangled in a long-forgotten tax settlement. Does he imagine he can reclaim him through this object, as I believed myself? Or do I project? Maybe it's nothing more than idle curiosity and a free morning.

Still, I can't let it go. There's something in his manner that suggests another wayward son, and a peal of sympathy echoes in my heart. I would like to go over to him, to say something, to assure him that . . . that what? That he was a good son? That his father loved him and was proud of him? That the mysteries of our parents will always remain out of reach, no matter how hard we try? That it's not my painting he covets, that mine was a forgery?

He looks up and catches me staring. I nod in acknowledgment and look away.

Budapest Street Scene is announced and Monsieur Leclos takes his place on the stage to commence the bidding. On the block at last. It's time to leave. Any second now, Leclos's phone will ring and the auction will be stopped. I'm sorry, in a way, that Yuhaus will be denied his opportunity to buy the painting back. It seems like it might settle something inside him, though I know now that it wouldn't. Part of me would like him to have the consolation of his illusion, at least for a while. But part of me wants to put my arm around his shoulder, guide him from the room, and tell him . . . *Pay attention.*

ACKNOWLEDGMENTS

I wish to express my gratitude to: Cheryl Arutt, Kathryn Beres, Saffron Burrows, Jennifer Carson, Jack Dettis, David Francis, Yanina Gotsulsky, Eden Jasper, Rabbi Michael Knopf, Jon Marks, Maud Newton, Seth Ribner, Rob Riemen, Eva Sarvas, Scrivener, Marisa Silver, Monika Wolfe, and Rabbi David Wolpe. Also to the students and staff of the UCLA Extension Writers' Program.

At Writers House: Celia Taylor Mobley, and a special thank-you to my agent, friend, and guide, Simon Lipskar.

At Farrar, Straus and Giroux: Jackson Howard, Alex Merto, Rob Sternitzky, Sarita Varma, Stephen Weil; special gratitude to Eric Chinski and Jonathan Galassi; and above all, to my editor and miracle worker, Ileene Smith, who improved not just this novel but all that will follow.

Lastly, thank you, Clara Grace Sarvas. In advance, forgive me.

SELECTED BIBLIOGRAPHY

The following works were invaluable in the writing of this novel:

Barron, Stephanie. *Degenerate Art: The Fate of the Avant-Garde in Nazi Germany*. Los Angeles: Los Angeles County Museum of Art, 1991.

Frojimovics, Kinga, Géza Komoróczy, Viktória Pusztai, and Andrea Strbik. *Jewish Budapest, Monuments, Rites, History*. Budapest: Central European University Press, 1999.

Grisebach, Lucius. *Ernst Ludwig Kirchner*. Taschen, 1999.

Hebborn, Eric. *The Art Forger's Handbook*. New York: Overlook Press, 1997.

————. *Drawn to Trouble: Confessions of a Master Forger*. London: Cassell, 1997.

Ungvary, Kristztian. *The Siege of Budapest, 100 Days in World War II*. New Haven, CT: Yale University Press, 2002.

Wye, Deborah. *Kirchner and the Berlin Street*. New York: The Museum of Modern Art, 2008.

I am deeply indebted to them all. Any inaccuracies, errors, or liberties in *Memento Park* are mine. I also consulted the following additional books:

Barron, Stephanie. *Exiles and Emigres: The Flight of European Artists from Hitler*. Los Angeles: Harry N. Abrams, 1997.

Feliciano, Héctor. *The Lost Museum: The Nazi Conspiracy to Steal the World's Greatest Works of Art*. New York: Basic Books, 1997.

Nicholas, Lynn H. *The Rape of Europa*. New York: Vintage Books, 1995.

O'Connor, Anne-Marie. *The Lady in Gold*. New York: Alfred A. Knopf, 2012.

Shulevitz, Judith. *The Sabbath World*. New York: Random House, 2010.

Soros, Tivadar. *Masquerade*. Translated by Humphrey Tonkin. New York: Arcade, 2001.

Telushkin, Rabbi Joseph. *Jewish Literacy*. New York: William Morrow, 1991.